PUTTING UP ROOTS

Tor Books by Charles Sheffield

Cold as Ice
The Ganymede Club
Georgia on My Mind and Other Places
Godspeed
How to Save the World
One Man's Universe

JUPITER™ NOVELS
Higher Education (with Jerry Pournelle)
The Billion Dollar Boy
Putting Up Roots

PUTTING UP ROOTS

A *JUPITER*™ NOVEL

CHARLES SHEFFIELD

TOR®

A TOM DOHERTY ASSOCIATES BOOK · NEW YORK

This is a work of fiction. All the characters and events
portrayed in this novel are either fictitious or are
used fictitiously.

PUTTING UP ROOTS

Copyright © 1997 by Charles Sheffield

All rights reserved, including the right to reproduce
this book, or portions thereof, in any form.

This book is printed on acid-free paper.

A Tor Book
Published by Tom Doherty Associates, Inc.
175 Fifth Avenue
New York, NY 10010

Tor Books on the World Wide Web:
http://www.tor.com

Tor® is a registered trademark of Tom Doherty
Associates, Inc.

Library of Congress Cataloging-in-Publication Data

Sheffield, Charles.
    Putting up roots : a Jupiter novel / Charles Sheffield.
        p   cm.
    ISBN 0-312-86241-5
    I. Title.
PS3569.H39253P87   1997
813' .54—dc21   97-16926
                                                  CIP

First Edition: September 1997

Printed in the United States of America

0 9 8 7 6 5 4 3 2 1

To Nancy

PUTTING UP ROOTS

CHAPTER ONE

THE apartment was deserted. Josh somehow knew it, the moment that he opened the door. The place also, in a way that he could not describe, felt strangely *empty*. "Mom?"

He did not really expect a reply. His mother was hardly ever home in the afternoon. So why did this feel different from any other day?

He walked into the living room, and knew why. The rented couch was gone. So were the sideboard, and the computer and entertainment centers. The place was practically empty of furniture.

He found the note on a solitary end table, in the tiny kitchen-dinette that formed one corner of the living room.

My dearest Josh,
    This is the hardest letter I have ever had to write. By the time that you read it, I will be gone.
    I have known for a long time that this was no way to raise a child, dragging you from one city to another wherever my job took me. There was always the dream, you see, that the next part would be the big break-through. After that, you and I would have the absolute best of everything.
    Well, it is going to happen—someday. You know me, and I'll never stop trying. But that's not good enough for you. You need to put down some roots.
    In the envelope you will find an air ticket to Port-land and plenty of money to take you the rest of the way to Burnt Willow Farm. Uncle Ryan and Aunt Maria can provide what I cannot, a solid, safe upbringing and schooling. Maybe you wish that your mother had been the steady one, with her life under total control. Some-times I wish it, too. But Maria told me, whenever we used to call each other, that she wished she were like me and had a son of her own.
    It's been a long time since you last met them—nearly eight years, I guess, when I had that summer rep job in Seattle—and Maria and I have been badly out of touch for a while. But I know that you two will get on just fine. And Uncle Ryan, too. And you and Dawn will be really good company for each other.
    Don't worry about the things that are left in the apartment. Just take whatever you want. Someone will come in and handle the rest after you have gone.
                                    Love, Mother

P.S. It's not forever, Josh, and I don't even think it will be for very long. I'm overdue for a change in luck. And my name in lights!

All my love, Mother

Josh felt that first pang of misery again, as the bus jolted and rumbled its way west. He had the letter sitting on his knee, but he didn't need to look at it. In the past four days he had read it a hundred times. He knew it by heart.

"Just take whatever you want. . . ." That was so typical of his mother. It made him want to laugh and cry at the same time. The apartment had been pretty much cleaned out of everything except his clothes and the kitchen table. No wonder it had seemed echoing and empty. ". . . an air ticket to Portland . . ." Sure. The ticket had been in the envelope, exactly as promised. But when he had taken it to the airport, he found that it was no good. It was for an excursion tour that had happened over a year before.

As for "plenty of money to take you the rest of the way to Burnt Willow Farm," that might be true enough—if you first flew to Portland, and had to go only a couple of hundred kilometers east across Oregon. Starting from New York City and heading west was another matter. There had been enough money for the trip—just. You could do it, provided that you slept on buses the entire way, washed and changed clothes at rest stops, and ate the smallest and cheapest meals you could find.

Josh leaned his head on the seat back. In four days and nights he had learned a lot about sleeping sitting upright. He couldn't wait to drop into a proper bed at Burnt Willow Farm.

Another hour or two, and he would be there. He wondered if this whole trip was worthwhile. But what were the alternatives? Come out here, or take your chances on streets already crowded with school dropouts and snapheads—he had seen that at first hand, wandering the city rather than sit alone in the apartment waiting for his mother to come home. He didn't want any part of it. But even that was better than handing yourself over to the crooks and bumbling clowns in the city welfare agency. You'd be better off dead.

He had only the vaguest memories of the place he was going. An old wooden house, smelling of cooking fruit and furniture polish, complicated enough with its two staircases and double loft for a six-year-old to become lost inside. It was different in every way from the cramped apartments that he had lived in. Outside he remembered a big flat yard of hard mud, with animals and farm equipment everywhere, and beyond it the open fields.

His memories of the people were not much better. Aunt Maria was sharp enough in his mind, a little like his mother in looks, but red-faced and fat and cheerful, and always trying to feed him. He had liked her, although she had sometimes embarrassed him by picking him off his feet and swinging him around in a big hug.

None of Mother's friends would dream of doing that. They knew he didn't like to be touched, not by anyone. They were always hugging and kissing each other, but those embraces never seemed genuine. He had seen a few men kissing his mother, too, but that was in private and they did it quite differently.

He remembered Uncle Ryan as a tall, easygoing man, who said little to Josh when the others were around and a lot when they were not. At the end of the first week he took Josh off after dinner to the brightly lit basement, where the works of an old grandfather clock lay strewn on a wooden table. Josh was given the job of cleaning the gears. He did it out of sheer boredom, slowly and methodically and meticulously, making sure that every cog was free of oil and any speck of grime.

"Good job, Joshua Kerrigan," Uncle Ryan said, when Josh laid the last of the gears carefully down on a sheet of wax paper. "I'm surprised. I couldn't have done that better myself. Now where did she ever get one like you?"

It wasn't a question that Josh knew how to answer, though he knew that "she" must be Mother. Apparently no response was required, because Uncle Ryan went on at once, "Come on. You can leave those where they sit for the moment. I'm going to pull the old tractor motor and do a rebore. I think you'll enjoy watching—and maybe helping."

Josh had decided in those first few days that Uncle Ryan knew and could do everything. He had trusted him totally. Now he realized that had just been the way of a six-year-old, before he learned that people did things for their own selfish reasons. Nowadays he didn't trust *anyone* as much as he had trusted Uncle Ryan.

Then there was Dawn. She was Uncle Ryan and Aunt Maria's only child, and here Josh's memories were most confusing of all. She had been as tall as he was, and he guessed that she was the same age. But he couldn't, to save his life, remember any conversation between them. What he did recall, very clearly, was Dawn following him around everywhere that he went. She didn't actually look at him, she looked *through* him, with round, unwinking brown eyes that made him think of the cows in the neatly fenced fields around the farm.

Would she still be living there? Let's hope that if she did, she wouldn't still trail along behind him.

Josh opened his eyes and stared out of the bus window. *Fenced fields.* That was why his old memories of Burnt Willow seemed so artificial. He was only an hour or so away from the farm, but the countryside through which he was traveling was all wrong. If there were fields, they had to be enormous ones. He could see across rolling hills to the far horizon, and there was not one fence or field boundary in sight. It was one gigantic spread of green, with a continuous silver network of irrigation pipes above it and machines dotted here and there below them, apparently at random. Those machines were on the same giant scale, nothing like the little multipurpose tractors used on Burnt Willow Farm.

The bus had no driver. It took its overall control from a satellite navigation receiver located on the roof, while an onboard radar told the computer where other cars and trucks were and how fast they were going. But Josh felt that he had to ask *somebody* what was going on.

He stood up, on legs stiff with lack of use, and walked back a few seats to where another passenger was drowsing, eyes closed and mouth open, in the morning sunshine.

"Excuse me."

Josh was half expecting a scowl or a curse, as you'd get from a stranger in the city, but the man just squinted up at him.

"Eh?"

"I'm wondering if I'm going the right way. I'm trying to get to Burnt Willow Farm. It's supposed to be between Payette and Baker."

"Mm. Never heard of it. Did you enter the farm as your destination in Boise?"

"Sure."

"And the system accepted it?"

"It seemed to."

"Then you're in good shape. You'll be dropped off at the nearest point on the route, guaranteed within five kilometers. To the door, if you paid extra."

"I couldn't afford to."

"Me neither." The man shrugged. "No matter. Nice day for a walk, 'less you've got a ton of luggage."

He closed his eyes again to show that the conversation was over. Josh went back to his seat.

A ton of luggage.

If he had learned one thing in his fourteen years with his mother, it was to travel light. She hauled twelve trunks of clothing around with her, costumes to audition for any part in any play— and what an endless nuisance that had been. Josh had resentfully carried them up and down a hundred flights of stairs. Sometimes it seemed that costumes were the only thing they had in their apartment, every closet stuffed with them, no space for food or furniture or toys.

He had brought with him from New York two small cases, and that was all. All he needed. All *anyone* needed.

The sadness and pain came again. Mother said that she loved him, said she always did what was best for him. But why hadn't she *asked* him what he wanted? Why didn't she let him have a say in what happened to them? He was pretty much of an adult. He didn't mind traveling, didn't mind living in crummy places. He could have traveled with her forever.

He knew the answer. She even said it now and again, when she was in one of her moods. "You're a big load on me, you know. When I ought to be thinking about my career I'm worrying about you—your education, your friends, your clothing, your meals . . ."

Josh laid his head again on the seat back. Maybe it would work out better this way, getting away. It sure couldn't be much worse. And it would let her concentrate on the acting break that she had talked about for as long as he could remember.

"It's not just talent, Josh, or good looks." She would run her hand through her great lush waves of blond hair, and cock her head to show off to him what she always said was her best angle. "I have those. But you need *luck*, too. Up to now I've not had luck."

She was right about that. Maybe his move to Burnt Willow Farm would bring her luck. It might even bring some for him. He felt his wallet, now close to empty. He could sure use a little luck—or if not that, a little money.

The farm had changed.

Josh had been dropped off the bus on a final rise, where the road turned to follow the dried-out watercourse that had been Burnt Willow Creek.

From high above it, the farm stood out against the rest of the landscape as a square-mile patch of drab brown in a sea of greenery. He didn't need to see the fences to know where the lands of Burnt Willow Farm ended. Outside, the silver pipes of an irrigation network provided a fine spray of water that left everything green and vigorous. Within the farm's boundaries, the crops grew less densely. Some patches of land in the middle of fields actually stood bare, devoid even of weeds. Josh imagined the farmlands as an old fortress, one that had withstood a long siege but was now barely surviving.

At least the farmhouse and the outbuildings seemed the same. He hadn't remembered the layout, but when he saw it again everything came back to him. The main house was three-storied, painted a uniform white but with the lumpy, asymmetrical shape of a building that has been added to for generation after generation. The farmyard in front of the house was a hollow square of hard-baked earth. On its left stood a barn with brown walls and red-painted curved roof. On the right was the machine shed, where Uncle Ryan housed the tractors, plows, harrows, seeders, threshers, and combine harvesters. Closest to Josh was the dilapidated old barn, a crumbling ruin where chickens had wandered freely. The pump, once worked by hand but on his last visit to Burnt Willow run by electricity, was in the middle of the farmyard. The dry earth and empty troughs around it suggested that it had not been used for a long time.

Josh continued down the path, noting that it had a well-used look. Someone was making frequent trips up to the brow of the hill. But apparently they did not go beyond, to the road traveled by the bus. The track became almost invisible past the hilltop. It was as though someone climbed all the way up from Burnt Willow Farm, then went right back down again without doing anything.

Close up, he could see other differences. In his mind, the big farmyard was packed with animals, cows and pigs and chickens and dogs and cats, in one glorious mix-up. All he saw now was one brown-and-black cocker spaniel, wagging its tail at his approach but too lazy or overweight to stand up and come to greet him.

He *remembered* that dog! In the old days it had been all over the farmhouse, on beds and sofas and under tables. It had been thin and energetic. Now it looked too fat to walk.

The whole farm seemed very quiet. As Josh approached the main building, he suddenly felt nervous. Eight years was a long time. He wasn't sure what to expect.

Worse yet, what would *they* be expecting? What did Uncle Ryan and Aunt Maria and Dawn remember of him? What had Mother told them, when they all discussed the idea of him coming out here to live? He had better be on his best behavior, at least until he learned what he could get away with.

He stood before the main door of the farmhouse and hesitated. There was no electronic monitor and entry system, as you would find in every apartment building that he remembered. There was not even a bell or a knocker.

Finally he raised his right fist and rapped on the wooden door panel, hesitantly at first and then harder.

The door swung open at once, as though someone had been watching his approach from behind the thick net curtains at the front window.

A girl was standing there. He knew her at once. She had grown taller and her knee-length sleeveless dress showed she was getting an adult figure, but her features hadn't changed a bit. Even if they had, he would never forget those round, brown eyes.

"Hello, Dawn. I'm Josh." And, when she stared through him without speaking, "You know. Joshua Kerrigan."

The brown eyes did not blink. She looked him up and down, from the top of his head—they were almost the same height—to his dusty shoes. Then she did the same thing all over again. He could not say that she looked *at* him. It was as though he was quite transparent, and she could see right through him.

Finally she turned around, still without saying a word, and went off through the left-hand door that he remembered as leading through from the hall to the dining room, with its black Franklin stove.

He did not know what to do next. Should he follow her? Stand here and wait? Or should he head through the far door, which led to the kitchen where Aunt Maria was to be found for much of every day?

He did not have to make a decision. Another woman appeared from the door that Dawn had entered. She was not Aunt Maria. She was, so far as Josh could tell, a total stranger, with pale, severe features and a glory of golden-yellow hair that put even Mother's shining locks to shame.

She came to stand in front of Josh and placed her hands on her slim hips. Her lips, bright with fresh lipstick, pursed. Like Dawn, she gave him a detailed head-to-toe inspection, though in her case she was very much looking at him.

"Well," she said at last. She was frowning. "I didn't believe Ryan, but he was right. She's dumped you on us. I suppose you'd better come on in."

CHAPTER TWO

LIKE the outside of Burnt Willow Farm, the inside seemed to Josh's eye both changed and unchanged. The sitting room that the woman led him to was the old familiar shape, but it had somehow become smaller. The furniture and drapes were surely new. He never noticed colors much, but it seemed to him that the room was both lighter and brighter.

"Sit down there." Acting like she owned the place, the golden-haired woman pointed to an uncomfortable-looking chair with a cane seat and straight cane back. "I'll go and get Ryan."

She was heading out, but Josh couldn't wait any longer. He blurted out, "Where's Aunt Maria?"

For the first time, the woman's frowning expression was replaced by something like surprise. "You don't know?" she said. "I guess Lucy Kerrigan didn't bother to tell you much, any more than she told us. Or maybe she didn't know herself. Ryan hadn't heard a word from her until a week ago. She certainly wasn't one to call or write, judging from the past year and a half. Her sister—your aunt—died near that long back. You didn't know?" She had picked up on Josh's look of sudden astonishment. "Maria is dead. I'm your Aunt Stacy, Uncle Ryan's wife. We were married two months ago. I'm still trying to get this place in shape. Believe me, it isn't easy."

As she went out toward the back of the farmhouse, Dawn peered in from the other door. She nodded her head and said, "Josh—u—a."

"I'm really sorry," he blurted out. "I mean, about your mother—I didn't know. I'm sure Mother didn't know about Aunt Maria, either, or she would have told me."

Dawn came forward and perched on the chair opposite Josh. It had a transparent plastic cover that squeaked as she leaned back on it. He noticed for the first time that Dawn was barefoot. She looked through him again as though he was not there. He waited, but after that single statement of his name, she said nothing.

"If Mother had known, I don't think she'd have sent me here to Burnt Willow Farm." With Dawn silent, Josh felt forced to fill the gap. "It may have been hard for Uncle Ryan and—and—" He could not think of what to call the woman he had just met. Not Aunt Stacy, not yet, even if she was Uncle Ryan's wife. What did Dawn call her? Mother? Dawn was just sitting there, wiggling her bare toes. "It must have been hard for you to reach us," he went on. "You see, with Mother having the job she did, we were on the move a lot. We were all over the place, from New York to Atlanta to Boston. Sometimes we'd have to leave a place in a real hurry, and Mother wouldn't leave a forwarding address."

"Ryan will be here in a minute." Stacy had come back in while Josh was floundering along with his explanations. "He was out back and he has to wash up. You're wasting your time with her, you know. Dawn doesn't understand more than two words in a row. I thought you'd been to the farm and you'd met her before."

Wondering if he had missed something, Josh glanced from Aunt Stacy to Dawn. His cousin was not looking at her stepmother. Her eyes remained fixed on something far away, with an intense, unwinking stare that he remembered from when he was six years old. She was smiling.

"I was here eight years ago," he said at last.

"Then you must know that she doesn't talk, not that anybody can understand." Aunt Stacy spoke as though the girl were not in the room with them. "Dawn is retarded. Badly retarded. She's fourteen, but witless. Quite hopeless around the house, too, though Lord knows I've tried. There's no more sense to her than to a fence post."

Josh, looking again at his cousin, was not so sure. She had stopped smiling. There was a strange expression of misery in those distant brown eyes. And then, before he could say or do anything, she had moved off her chair and was on her knees in front of him. She lifted his left foot and gently removed his shoe.

"Well, there's a first!" Aunt Stacy said. "Maybe with you here she'll learn a bit of sense. She has it right, nobody wears outside shoes in my house. It's slippers, or clean bare feet. I won't have people traipsing dirt in all over my polished floors. 'Specially her, always round the animals. It took forever to drum that into her thick head, but it looks like she's finally learned."

Dawn had taken off Josh's other shoe. She gazed up for a moment, then suddenly she was on her feet and turning toward the back door in a single fluid movement. Someone was coming into the room.

Josh knew that it must be Uncle Ryan, but he could hardly believe what he saw. If Dawn hadn't changed at all, Uncle Ryan had changed enormously. Josh remembered a big-framed, pudgily fat man, tall enough that he had to stoop when he came into a room. He had always been casually dressed, jeans and tartan shirt or leather jacket, and he had clumped around in huge black studded boots that told you by their sound exactly where he was in the house at any time.

Now the stoop seemed permanent. Uncle Ryan had lost sixty or seventy pounds, which made his face careworn and a lot older. The clothes were more formal, a well-fitting dark blue shirt with black string tie and dark-gray pants of pleated corduroy. No boots. He was in his stockinged feet, padding softly—it seemed to Josh, apologetically—over the polished hardwood floor.

"Now, here's the man," he said. "Hello, Joshua my boy, how are you?" But instead of approaching where Josh was sitting, he went across to Aunt Stacy and leaned over to give her a hug. "Now," he continued to Josh, "isn't she just the most beautiful thing you've ever seen in your whole life?"

The sincerity in his voice was obvious. Josh thought that her nose was big and she was too thin, but he wasn't about to say that. He was relieved when Dawn went over to her father's side. Ryan put his other arm around her. "You've grown a lot, Josh," he said. "It's nice to see you again."

"Didn't Mother call you, and talk about my coming here?" Josh had to ask it. He felt totally unwelcome. The problem wasn't Uncle Ryan or the silent Dawn, it was Aunt Stacy, staring at him with a cool and evaluating eye. He might not have recognized the look, except that he had seen Mother rehearsing for a thousand parts and portraying a hundred different emotions. She would say, "Here we are: Betrayed! By the very man who promised me everything!" And she would put on a certain forlorn expression and stance. Or it was, "Guilty secret," and she showed by the downcast gaze and the swiveling of one foot on the floor that she had something to hide.

The look on Aunt Stacy's face was in Lucy Kerrigan's lexicon on expressions. It said, "I don't like this, but maybe if I play my cards right it can become an opportunity."

An opportunity for *what?*

Well, Josh could play that game, too. He would lie low, be nice to everyone, and wait and see.

His aunt was standing up and brushing off Uncle Ryan's embrace. "Another mouth to feed, so I'd best get to it," she said tartly. "It's not going to be easy, Ryan, I'll tell you that. I'll leave you to explain why."

She nodded to Josh as she headed for the kitchen. Dawn was ignored.

"Isn't she the most beautiful thing you ever saw in your whole life?" Uncle Ryan said again. He was not talking about the daughter at his side. He stared raptly after Stacy until she was out of sight.

"I've never seen anyone with hair like that," Josh said. "It's like gold." That at least was true enough. He cleared his throat. "Uncle Ryan, didn't my mother call and discuss my coming here to stay with you?"

"In a manner of speaking." Ryan's eyes strayed now and again after the vanished Stacy, but he actually seemed a little more relaxed when she was gone. "Lucy sent an electronic message to the farm's facsimile and recording center. She just said you would be arriving sometime in the next week or two."

"You didn't talk to each other about it—to plan for my being here?"

"We couldn't. There was no return address. No way to know how to reach you." Uncle Ryan smiled, ruefully, trying to set up a bond between the two of them. "Just like your mom, eh?"

It was, all too like her. Fly by night, and vanish, as they had vanished from the people they owed money to; and now she had flown from him. Suddenly Josh had a new worry. He remembered Burnt Willow Farm as a place of infinite food, food that appeared at every hour of the day or night whether you wanted it or not, more than you could ever eat—soups and roasts and stews, pies and puddings and sorbets, fruitcake and brandied plums, cheese and biscuits and candied fruit. Aunt Maria said a body could never have too much food, provided it was nourishing and well cooked.

"What did *Aunt* Stacy"—he forced himself to say the hard word—"mean, that it won't be easy to feed another person? Am I going to be a problem for you?"

"No, no, no." But Uncle Ryan's tone said, yes, yes, yes. "Look, dinner won't be ready for another hour. Let's me and you go on up the hill. And you'll see for yourself." And, as an after-thought, "Don't put your shoes on 'til we're at the door."

When they came to the farmhouse entrance Josh had new proof that Dawn understood more than Aunt Stacy gave her credit for. His cousin was putting on her own shoes, before he and Uncle Ryan started to put on theirs.

"Will Dawn come with us?"

"Sure she will." Uncle Ryan sounded uncomfortable as he fastened his boots, still liberally coated with yellow powdery dust from the farm's dry soil. "Better if we all go. Stacy doesn't like Dawn around the kitchen. She says she spooks her and gets in the way."

He led them up the hill, along the same path that Josh had followed to reach the farm. Dawn stayed at Joshua's side, always looking at and through him but hardly saying a word. It made him feel really uncomfortable. Whenever he glanced across at her, she smiled and said, "Joshua."

"She remembers you," Uncle Ryan said. "And it's been eight years. I've tried to explain to Stacy, there's some things that Dawn remembers perfectly. Don't you, love? For some things she's a per-fect walking recorder, better at exact remembering than anyone.

But for most things . . ." He shrugged. "I don't know. *Autistic,* that's what the doctors say."

"Artistic?"

"No. *Aut*istic. Dawn is autistic. It's not the same as being retarded. I don't think people know quite what it is. Seems like it's one of them words they use for something they don't really understand. They *say* they understand, but they can't do anything about it. Maybe that will change. You know how scientists are. They tell you something is impossible, like space travel. Then they discover the node network, and suddenly it's not impossible at all. I just wish they'd do something like that here on Earth. I wish they'd find a way to help Dawn." Uncle Ryan peered up at the cloudless sky. "At the very least, I wish they'd find a way to make it *rain* where it's needed."

On his earlier walk downhill, Josh had been too interested in the farmhouse and farmyard below to take much notice of the land on either side of the path. Now, walking back the same way, the parched, water-starved quality of the slope jumped out at him more strongly. The wheat was stunted, no more than half a meter tall, with yellow-brown and brittle stems. The leaves of the root crops were wan and wilted, all the way up the hill. Only off to the right and left, in the irrigated fields beyond Burnt Willow Farm, could he see healthy green plants. They extended as far as the horizon.

"Why don't you irrigate your fields, the way that the others do?" he said, as they came to the brow of the hill.

"The wells ran dry." Uncle Ryan halted, breathing heavily. "You say, 'others,' but there are no 'others.' There's just one *other,* singular. Every independent farm in this area, except for Burnt Willow, went out of business. What you see is all Foodlines. One big conglomerate farm all the way from here to the Pacific. Foodlines owns everything—including the rights to tap into the aquifers around Burnt Willow."

"But weren't you here before them?" Josh remembered his

mother saying that Uncle Ryan's family had farmed in eastern Oregon "forever."

"We were here first, true enough. But that turns out to mean nothing. What matters is who you know, and the arrangements you've made in the state capitol. It's all politics, every bit of it." Uncle Ryan pointed to the west. "Take a big enough wad of cash with you to Salem, and water rights are for sale along with everything else. I learned that, but I learned it too late. The past couple of years, with Maria sick and all, I guess I wasn't watching things close enough. By the time I woke up, the water supply was all locked up. Did you notice, coming in, that Burnt Willow Creek is dry? That never happened when I was young. I've done what I can, with drought-resistant and salt-tolerant plants. They help some. But when all's said and done, you still need water."

"What about rain?" Josh remembered many rainy days, too many, when he had been confined to the farmhouse and chafed to get out into the yard. "If you have rain, you don't need irrigation."

"Quite right." Uncle Ryan pointed to the well-worn track that they had come up. "See that? Dawn and I made it, walking up and down. I've stood here 'bout every day this whole season, looking north for rain clouds."

Josh's formal education had been spotty and random, with all the jumping around from town to town wherever Mother's jobs took them. But he had always had a terminal, and he had learned early to tap the public databases. Eight years had produced a big change in him and in Uncle Ryan, but he knew that it wasn't nearly long enough to make the climate change around Burnt Willow Farm.

"True enough," Uncle Ryan said when Josh made that point. "But Dawn and I haven't seen a rain cloud in two months. See, the moisture is carried this way mostly from the north. Foodlines finagled the rights to seed the southbound clouds north of here, and make the rain fall twenty or thirty miles away. By the time the air reaches us it's pretty well dried out. All we need is one good soaking from a southerly wind and we'd be fine. But we haven't managed that."

While they were talking Dawn had taken off her shoes. She was carrying them under her arm, wandering barefoot along the brow of the hill toward a patch of wild filbert bushes that seemed to thrive on the dry yellow clay. An hour ago, Josh would have sworn that he didn't know those bushes existed. Seeing them now, he realized that they had gathered nuts in that very place on his previous visit to Burnt Willow Farm.

The bushes looked the same, but most other things had changed. The long ridge of the hill was quite bare of even the drought-ridden crops. With no one else around, Josh had a chance to say what had been on his mind since they left the farmhouse. He turned to face Uncle Ryan. "If I'd known things were so bad for you here, with Dawn and the farm and everything, I never would have come. I can leave tomorrow. I can go back east, and find Mother."

He was testing his uncle's feelings rather than looking for agreement, but it was a risky suggestion.

"Do you have money?" Uncle Ryan said. "Do you have any idea where Lucy might have gone?"

"We-ell—"

"I thought not. Don't worry about it. We'll manage somehow." Uncle Ryan nodded along the ridge, to where Dawn was deep in the thicket. "You were too young to notice when you were here. But didn't your mother ever mention Dawn's problems?"

"Not one word. Did she know?"

"Maria told her everything, when the two of you were out here eight years ago, and then later. I can't think why your mother didn't say anything to you. Maybe she was just hoping for the best. Dawn was better for a few years, like when you were here last time. I thought for a while that she was making real headway. But then Maria got sick, and died, and I wasn't much help with anything. I guess I was too messed up myself. It was a godsend that

Stacy came along when she did. Without her, I'd have gone down-hill all the way." Uncle Ryan's face brightened. "Isn't she the most beautiful woman you've ever seen?"

Josh couldn't tell the truth: that he'd give Stacy up anytime for Aunt Maria, fat and cheerful and comforting. He nodded, but he couldn't bring himself to speak.

Uncle Ryan said, "I'd better be getting back down. Stacy likes me to set the table for her. You stay here with Dawn, bring her back with you. No rush." He started down the hill, then turned and added, "Make sure you're home within half an hour, though. Stacy's a great cook, but she gets real riled up when the food is ready and people aren't."

Dawn was still crouched in the middle of the bushes. Josh went along the ridge toward her, wondering what she could be doing. The last time he had been to Burnt Willow Farm it had been fall. It was months too early now for ripe nuts.

As he came closer, he saw that Dawn was not alone. A little wild rabbit sat crouched in front of her. She was gently stroking its gray back with her left hand. At Josh's approach it darted off into the grass and straggly weeds at the base of the bushes.

Dawn stood up. Her knees were marked yellow by the dust. She took his hand, turned it palm up, and poured into it what she was holding in her right hand.

Josh looked at his open palm. The nuts were tiny, green, and immature.

"You can't eat these, Dawn. They're not ready."

She showed no emotion, no sign that she understood what he was saying.

Retarded. Aunt Stacy was right, and Uncle Ryan was kidding himself with his science talk. Dawn must be a real drag on everybody if she was always like this.

"Not ready," he repeated. "You'll have to come back in another couple of months."

She smiled at him. "I had a great time here, Aunt Maria," she said in a child's high-pitched voice. "I wish I didn't have to go, but Mother thinks she has a shot at a part in Philadelphia. Not a big one, but better than the Seattle job. Maybe I can come back next year. I hope I can."

He stared at her. The first real words that she had spoken—and they sounded an echo inside his skull. She was waiting expectantly.

"That was *me*," he said at last. "Wasn't it? When I was little, when I left Burnt Willow Farm last time. I said those things. But that was nearly eight years ago! Were those the very words that I used, when I was saying good-bye?"

Dawn nodded. She reached down for her shoes and put them on. Then she slipped her arm through Josh's and turned down the hill toward the farmhouse.

"Maybe I can come back next year. I hope I can," she said again. Then in a changed voice, deeper and more adult, "Joshua, it's dinnertime."

CHAPTER THREE

JOSH and Dawn arrived at the farmhouse with fifteen minutes to spare. Uncle Ryan used the time to give Josh a quick tour of the changed inside, showing where the data center was located in the old dairy, and where Josh would sleep in a little room near the peak of the sloping roof. Everywhere they went, like ghosts, tantalizing smells of cooking crept up from the kitchen and diffused through the old walls.

Even so, Josh didn't have high hopes when they finally reached the dining room. He was used to carryout meals, or eating on the run in fast-food places, because his mother was always rushing off somewhere or too busy rehearsing or studying parts to do any cooking. Uncle Ryan said that Aunt Stacy was a great cook, but it was obvious that he was totally bowled over by his new wife. He probably thought that everything she did was great, no matter how bad it was. In any case, it didn't seem possible that the reality could live up to the aromas.

As it turned out, Uncle Ryan was right. Aunt Stacy served a superb three-course dinner, soup and an herb-flavored meat pasta, followed by a wonderful chocolate soufflé so light it seemed to float off the plate, all served on the delicate bone china that adorned the dining-room table.

The whole meal was like a trip to paradise. If Josh had a single complaint, it was that he could have eaten more. He remembered Aunt Maria's dinners, loaded dishes arriving in random order and vast quantities until you wondered when they would end. There was no doubt, though, that Stacy was a superior cook. And Josh had as many salad vegetables as he wanted, and as much apple juice as he could drink.

Aunt Stacy even offered a logic for serving smallish portions. "You live longer if you don't overeat, Joshua, and you live healthier. Did you know that animals increase their life spans thirty or forty percent if they are put on a minimal diet? Not that I'm proposing anything as drastic as that!" She smiled at Uncle Ryan, sitting at the head of the table. "But Ryan used to be terribly overweight. I told him he was digging his grave with his knife and fork. Now he eats right. I make sure of that. I want him to live *forever.*"

Josh nodded, barely listening. After four days and nights on the bus, as soon as his hunger was satisfied all he could think about was bed. During dinner he hadn't said much more than Dawn, who ate in complete silence except for "Thank you."

Aunt Stacy and Uncle Ryan more than made up for them. They were having what sounded to Josh like an ongoing discussion.

"You ought to at least *listen* to them, Ryan," Stacy said. "Let them come in here again, and let them make an offer. What do you lose? If you don't like what they have to say, you refuse it."

"My family has owned and farmed Burnt Willow for two hundred years."

"I know that. But every year it becomes more difficult. You've told me so, a hundred times. Seven hundred acres. *Nobody* farms seven hundred acres any more. It's too small to be worth bringing in the big equipment. But Mort Langstrom says that for the price that Foodlines would offer for Burnt Willow, you could retire for life."

"I don't want to retire, Stacy."

"All right. Don't retire. But I bet you could talk Foodlines into giving you a spread on Solferino a hundred times as big as Burnt Willow, as part of the deal. Land is going begging there, and they have that exclusive land development franchise."

"It *should* be cheap. Hey, considering where Solferino is, it should be *free*. It's out on the edge of the Messina Dust Cloud; twenty-seven light-years from anywhere. Three years ago nobody knew it even existed. The only people who've been there so far are the first survey team, and a little Foodlines colony of researchers. Nobody knows what Solferino really has to offer. It's virgin territory. It wouldn't be so much farming, as exploration. That's why land is available, as much as you want of it."

"There's the challenge, then. You always say you like challenges. You could do the experimental work you've always enjoyed. You might discover native plants of real value."

"That's what Foodlines is hoping. It's like a biolab the size of a whole world, where a couple of billion years of evolution has already done the work of sorting out which biological products are most useful. But what about Dawn? She was born here at Burnt Willow. She's not used to living anywhere else."

"That argument again! Of all the irrelevant—" Aunt Stacy checked herself, as though she were used to speaking freely in front of Dawn, but couldn't do it with Josh listening.

It also seemed to Josh that she gave him a strange and speculative look. Was she thinking what he was thinking, that *he* might
be able to go to Solferino, even if Dawn could not?

"Ryan, we'll talk this over later," she continued. "But I'll tell
you now what I didn't want to tell you before: Mort Langstrom of
Foodlines called me while the three of you were up on the ridge.
They really want young people on Solferino. They'd pay all the
costs of equipment, training, and transportation, too. Mort said
he'd like to come out here again tomorrow and talk some more.
And I told him that would be fine."

Josh saw Uncle Ryan sit up straighter, as though he were
bracing for an argument. Then he nodded, leaned forward, and
touched Aunt Stacy's forearm. "What would we do without you,
love, to look after us? I'll talk to him, of course I will. But I'm
telling you, Solferino isn't for me. I can see why they want young
people. There's probably a million opportunities there for a young
man; but I'm getting old."

"Nonsense! You're not old." Aunt Stacy reached out and took
Uncle Ryan's hand in hers. Josh couldn't help noticing that as she
did so she flashed another quick glance at him. Then she looked
away at once.

"But you're right," she said, "it would be a wonderful opportunity for a young person."

Josh didn't remember undressing and going to bed, but he must
have done it, because here he was. The room he slept in was at the
top of the house, with an east-facing window, and the midsummer
sun streamed in soon after dawn.

He lay there for a few minutes, staring at the ceiling. This
room seemed to be a sounding box for the whole house. He could
hear noises coming in from everywhere. He realized that it had
been the sound of voices that woke him, more than the morning
sun. Uncle Ryan had been talking to Aunt Stacy. Their words car-

ried distinctly to Josh's room, but in his semiconscious state he hadn't followed their meaning. Now the voices had ended. He heard running water, a clatter of dishes, the whistle of a boiling kettle, and through the open window a welcoming bark from the old spaniel.

Mister Micklegruber. Josh remembered the dog's name now, from his other visit to the farm. Who had picked that? Aunt Maria, for a guess. The overweight Mister Micklegruber—"Mick," except when he was being told off, when it was *"Mister* Micklegruber!"*—was apparently not included in his new aunt's diet plans. Nor, for a bet, was the dog allowed inside the newly spick-and-span house.

Josh pushed back the covers, and found that he didn't remember undressing because he hadn't. Except for his shoes, which he had removed when he entered the house, he was fully dressed. His two cases sat unopened at the bedside.

He must have been really tired.

The staircase that led to the kitchen was old and creaking. Josh tiptoed down, trying not to make any noise at all. The next level had two doors. One of them was closed, and he remembered it as being Ryan and Stacy's bedroom. The other was ajar. He peered in through the crack and saw Dawn. She was asleep, lying face up with her eyes closed and her mouth open. He realized now why she looked the same as when he had first met her. Her face was absolutely peaceful and unlined, like a baby's.

The kitchen when he came to it bore signs that someone had been and gone. A single mug, washed up, stood neatly in the draining rack.

He was pretty hungry, but he didn't feel that he could just go in and help himself to breakfast—particularly with Aunt Stacy's views on who was in charge of the kitchen.

Instead, he headed for the old dairy at the back of the house. Uncle Ryan had been very specific: Josh was free to use all the computers and communications equipment in the new data center.

He took one quick look at the weather radar displays and satellite precipitation maps on the walls. Burnt Willow Farm stood out as a kind of inverse oasis, an isolated dry spot with plenty of soil moisture all around. He sat down and called for the general database. He didn't know the spelling of the subject that had been on his mind since the previous day, but three tries did it.

Or-tistic. Aw-tistic. Au-tistic.

Autistic—autism. The download began into his headset.

"The terms autism *and* autistic *were first used a century and a half ago, in the 1940s, when two physicians, Leo Kanner of Baltimore and Hans Asperger of Vienna, both described the condition. Curiously, both proposed the same name. Autism takes many forms, but it can be recognized by certain common behavior patterns: a preoccupation with self, a disregard for external events and people, an obsessive repetition of particular acts, and particular, highly focused fixations.*

"Although cases of onset at adolescence or even later are known, autism normally shows itself when a child is very young and persists for life. Autistic people sometimes have strange and singular talents —"

Josh, engrossed in what he was hearing and deaf to normal disturbances, felt a light touch on the back of his neck. He jerked sideways and almost fell off his chair.

He turned. Dawn was standing behind him. He ripped off the headset and gave a command to print the file, so he could look at it later in his room. He glanced guiltily at Dawn, but he didn't have to worry. She showed no interest in knowing what he had been listening to, or in the keywords displayed on the screen.

She was smiling, apparently staring at the wall to the exclusion of everything else. "Breakfast," she said. And then, "Ugh. Not *mushrooms.* You eat mushrooms? I'd just as soon eat worms and slugs."

It was the small-child voice again. Again, Josh was convinced that she was quoting him, directly, from eight years ago. He hated mushrooms nearly as much as he hated olives, and that was saying something.

"Do you remember *everything* like that, word for word? Oh, never mind." He turned off the data unit. "Are you telling me that Aunt Stacy is giving us mushrooms for breakfast?"

It was a waste of time. Dawn pulled her mouth to one side and rolled her eyes, but there was no knowing what she meant, or even if she was responding to his question. Josh followed her to the kitchen.

The food again was great—with one nose-wrinkling exception. Fortunately, Aunt Stacy had prepared each dish separately. The fried mushrooms sat in a neat circle in their own deep bowl. Josh left them untouched but he helped himself to everything else, noting that some of Aunt Maria's breakfast staples had been eliminated. Hot scrapple and bacon glistening with fat, two of Uncle Ryan's favorites, had been replaced by some sort of spiced curd. Liver and steak chops had vanished entirely. On the other hand, the beans and fried tomatoes and wheatcakes were the best that he had ever tasted. And this time there was no problem with quantity.

Josh followed Dawn's lead, loaded a huge oval plate, and ate and ate. As he did so he wondered how he was going to earn his keep. He couldn't expect his uncle and aunt to go on feeding him for nothing. Even if that was what his mother had had in mind when she sent him out here, Aunt Stacy would never stand for it. And although he had been to Burnt Willow Farm before, he really knew nothing about farming. What was he going to do? Would he be able to stay? If not, where would he go?

Aunt Stacy came in while they were still eating. Josh could have asked her his questions, but the previous evening had given him the funny feeling that he did not quite trust her. It was a relief when she said, almost before the "Good morning" was out of her mouth, "Joshua, I have a job for you. Your uncle and I are going to be busy with a visitor, and I don't know how long it will take. I forgot, but Dawn has a doctor's appointment this morning. She can't go alone, of course. I'd like you to take her. Will you do that?"

"Sure." It was a relief to feel useful.

"Then eat up. The doctor's office is in Payette. It's easy to find, once you're in the town." Aunt Stacy glanced at the clock over the stove. "You'll have to hurry, though. I've called for the bus to stop for you, same place as you got off yesterday, in twenty minutes."

He was already stuffed. Just the same, it was a scramble to get washed and changed and ready in ten minutes. And it was a surprise to find Dawn, in a new dress, patiently waiting for him at the door when he thundered back down the old wooden staircase.

She didn't speak, but maybe she understood a lot more than Aunt Stacy gave her credit for. She at once took his hand and began to run them uphill. There was no time today for looking at failing crops, or wandering along the ridge when they got there. Josh had one moment to glance north, at another hazy sky free of rain clouds, and then the PV was in sight. It cruised toward them, slowing as its memory told its sensors that it was expecting new passengers.

Dawn grinned happily at Josh as they boarded and settled into their seats. He wondered again, how much *did* she follow of what was happening? She had the uncanny knack of parroting back exactly what she heard, without adding to it; but the words she quoted always seemed relevant to the question or the situation. That meant she must understand. She merely chose a strange way of answering.

Josh made a decision: if he was allowed to stay at Burnt Willow Farm, he had to be very careful what he said in Dawn's presence. She might be badly retarded, as Aunt Stacy insisted, but her memory and the odd way that her mind worked also made her likely to say things he might not want to hear repeated.

Josh had seen his own role as a kind of chaperon, guarding Dawn to the doctor's office and making sure that she got safely back.

While he waited for Dawn's examination to be completed, he finally had a chance to read the rest of the file that he had printed.

Austistic people sometimes have strange and singular talents, emerging at an early age and developing with amazing speed. These talents can include an intuitive understanding of complex machinery, or great athletic skills. Musical, mathematical, and artistic ability are not uncommon, together with feats of memory that stagger the imagination.

At the same time, the autistic patient appears to lack normal reasoning power. They remember works word for word, but often do not understand them. They recall events but don't interpret them. They may have prodigious powers of computation but no concept of mathematical proof.

Although autistic persons are often retarded in many areas, and cannot function unassisted in the everyday world, "autistic" and "retarded" are not the same and should not be thought of as such. For some autistic people, the words "genius" and "idiot" can be employed with equal logic; hence the term "idiot savant," coined by an early worker in this field, Dr. J. Langdon Downe. It was one of his patients, who, on a single reading, committed to memory Edward Gibbon's multivolume masterwork The Decline and Fall of the Roman Empire *and was ever thereafter able to repeat any part of it. Similar feats have been noted again and again—*

"All right." It was Dr. Ergan, standing at the door. "I'm done with Dawn. Your turn."

"Turn for what?"

"Your examination."

"I'm just here with Dawn. I'm not here for an examination."

"You are, you know. You were scheduled for a complete physical."

"Me? Are you sure?"

"Quite sure. I spoke to Stacy Kelsh less than two hours ago." The doctor was maybe sixty-five years old, but still straight and vigorous, and her bright gray eyes seemed to see right inside Joshua. "She's your aunt, isn't she?"

"Yes." Josh didn't want to get into the fact that she wasn't his *real* aunt. "But I don't need an examination."

"How long since you had one?"

"A physical? I don't remember. Four or five years." Things like physical examinations were low on his mother's scale of priorities.

"Then you ought to have one anyway, whether you think you need one or not." Dr. Ergan smiled at him. "Don't worry, it won't hurt a bit."

Hurt, no. Embarrass, yes.

Josh didn't like the idea of taking his clothes off in front of strangers. He liked even less being poked and prodded and sniffed at, even if the poking and prodding and sniffing was done by spidery little machines, while Dr. Ergan sat behind a bank of monitors and seemed to take no notice of him at all.

After twenty minutes of that she stood up—still without looking at him—and said, "All right. That does it. Clothes on, and come outside."

Dawn was waiting in the office, staring at the same page of the same picture book as when Joshua had left. Dr. Ergan motioned Josh to a chair next to his cousin and sat herself down opposite. For a few seconds she studied both of them in silence.

"Well," she said at last, "I'll be sending the full report to your aunt, of course, but I thought you might like the quick summary. You, Joshua, are in fine physical condition. So is Dawn. I just wish that most of the people I see were in half as good shape. Of course, there are a couple of things. Joshua, how long since you visited a dentist?"

"I don't know."

"I can make a guess. Certainly not since your second permanent molars came in, and probably not for a long time before that. I bet it's five years and more. You ought to be ashamed of yourself. You have half a dozen cavities. Do your teeth ache?"

"No."

"You're lucky. They will, unless you have some work done on them in the near future. But don't worry. Three or four short sessions, and you'll be fine. You can relax about everything else. I don't see anything that would stop you from going—today, if you had to."

Josh wondered what he had missed. "Going *where?*"

"Uh-oh." Dr. Ergan bit her lower lip, and glanced from Joshua to Dawn and back. "I hope I haven't spoiled a surprise. But your aunt didn't say to keep anything a secret. Look." She turned around to her desk, picked up a message sheet, and read from it. "Examine as soon as possible, to make sure that they are medically fit to travel off-Earth, and could stand to make transitions through the node network."

"*Both* of us?"

"That's what it says." She laid the sheet back on her desk. "I'm going to reply to her that you are both medically fit enough, even without the dental work. I see no reason either or both of you shouldn't go up into orbit. Or, if you feel like it, through a node to the Kuiper Belt. Or anywhere else that your uncle and aunt see fit to take you."

CHAPTER FOUR

JOSH had asked Dr. Ergan—twice. On the way back to Burnt Willow Farm he asked Dawn a hundred times more, with no particular hope of getting a sensible answer. What was all this about going into space? Might they be going farther yet, through the node network?

The doctor could provide little information beyond what she had already shown them. She did mention that the medical appointment hadn't been scheduled long ago, as Josh had assumed. Aunt Stacy had made it that very morning, for both of them. She had said it was urgent, without saying why. As for Dawn, whatever she might know about Aunt Stacy's action, she either could not or would not tell it.

All the way home Josh couldn't think of anything else. It must have something to do with yesterday's talk during dinner. Solferino: the planet where Foodlines had biological exploration and exploitation rights, and the place where Uncle Ryan could get as much land as he wanted—if he wanted it, which he didn't seem to. Josh had never heard of Solferino before, but if it was on the edge of the Messina Dust Cloud, as Uncle Ryan said, then the only way that anyone could get there was by transitions through the node network.

It was dark when the PV finally dropped them off and Josh could hurry Dawn along the slope that led to Burnt Willow Farm. Actually, it was much more the other way round. Josh wanted to hurry, but the half-moon was low in the sky and he could see little more than vague shadows. It was Dawn, somehow realizing that he wanted to get home quickly, who took his hand and steered him down a path that she must have known by heart. Had she done this many times before, in the dark? Or was her visual memory so strong that she had a full mental picture of the whole hillside stored away inside her head, like a three-dimensional map?

They reached the farmhouse—at last. Josh rushed in, only remembering when he was at the kitchen door that he had forgotten to take off his shoes. Never mind, he'd take a chewing out gladly to learn what was going on.

He pushed the door wide and burst in. The smell of new-baked bread jumped out at him. The room was empty.

A casserole sat on an electric warming plate on the table. Next to it was a handwritten note:

Eat all you want. Bread in the oven. We got the report from Dr. Ergan, and are glad that you are in great shape. Don't wait up for us—we'll probably be really late. Love, Aunt Stacy.

P.S. Please tell Dawn that her father and I give
her a hug, and she mustn't wait up for us, either.

Joshua was ready to explode with frustration and disappointment.
Don't wait up for us. He knew now how his mother must feel when
a promised acting part didn't come through, and she would pick up
dinner plates and smash them to the ground.

He picked up two dishes from the sideboard. Instead of
throwing them, he set them out with spoons at the table. Then he
went across to open the oven and take out a loaf of bread almost
too hot to hold. While he was juggling it to the table, Dawn finally
came in. She was in her stocking feet. She said not a word, but
came to his side, knelt down, and began to unfasten his shoes.

"Dawn, your father and—er"—What did Dawn call her stepmother?—"Stacy, they've gone out and they are going to be late
home." He cleared his throat. Dawn was still singlemindedly untying his shoes for him, as though she didn't hear one word.
"We're supposed to help ourselves to food. They say, don't wait up
for them. And they send you their love."

To his surprise, she nodded and said, "All right."

A simple sentence. But it was *her* sentence—the first one that
was not a direct quotation from someone else.

And apparently the last, too. All through dinner he could not
get another word out of her. He babbled on about anything that
came into his head, mostly himself. When they were finished he
started for the data center, then wondered if it was safe to leave
Dawn by herself in the kitchen. He went across, took her by the
hand, and led her to the old dairy.

"Sit down. We're going hunting." He placed himself at her
side and called for information about Solferino. There was nothing in the general data banks, other than a reference to an old bat-
tle three hundred years ago, in a country which had not even
existed for more than a century. He didn't follow that to the sec-

ond level, but instead asked for information on the Messina Dust Cloud.

That was better. It was there. But the banks offered so much information, and much of it so technical, that he settled for the shortest and simplest overview that he could find.

Messina Dust Cloud (MDC): Identification, WGC 127,1336A. Mean diameter, 15 light-hours (16 billion km). The MDC is a body of dust and gas about the same size as the solar system, probably of artificial but otherwise unknown origin. It was discovered eighty-eight years ago, by virtue of its anomalous spectral emission lines. The MDC represents the only known source of stable transuranics, Cauthen starfires, and shwarzgeld (consult reference trails for each; attach P-files 1864–1897). Upon the opening of a network node within the MDC, thirty-nine years ago, the MDC became accessible from other nodes, including ones in the solar system Asteroid Belt and in the Kuiper Belt. The MDC was originally mined by independent harvesters and rakehells (P-files 1911–1927). Today, most MDC mining takes place under an exclusive development franchise granted to the Unimine syndicate. Cloud mining calls for special care and special equipment, while the cloud reefs and space sounders (P-file 2113) present their own peculiar dangers. Note: the term Messina Dust Cloud stars is often used to include those stars and their planetary systems close to and associated with the MDC, although not within it. There are eight such systems, five of them brown dwarfs, within four light-years of the MDC. Two of them now have their own network node.

Josh read through to the end and finished more puzzled than when he started. Transuranics and starfires and shwarzgeld? Harvesters and rakehells? He could chase after those references, and maybe he could even find them; but the biggest puzzle was that almost everything in the Messina Dust Cloud seemed to be about *mining.* Uncle Ryan had talked about *farming,* or at least about wildlife exploration, and he said that the development franchise was owned by Foodlines. According to the database, that was wrong. Some other syndicate that Josh had never heard of,

Unimine, had development rights. *Exclusive* development rights. Didn't that mean that no one else could have any?

He set up the search for *Unimine*.

Unimine: Universal Mining Enterprises. Founded a century ago, to mine the more difficult and dangerous regions of the Kuiper Belt, Unimine today conducts operations in the solar system, four node-accessible stellar systems, and the extended region of the Messina Dust Cloud. Specialties: deep body mining (defined for this purpose as forty or more kilometers beneath the surface. Examples: Titan, Caracol. See P-file 9172); ocean bottom mining (Examples: Europa [water,], Jestreen [molten iron]. See P-file 9363); regolith mining (Examples: Cauldron, Styx. See P-file 9461); Messina Dust Cloud trawling and reef harvesting (Examples: various. See P-file 9509); full-planet stripping and refining (Example: Nargol. See P-file 9544). Note: all these operations carry Personnel Hazard Level 6.0 or higher.

Josh leaned back, disheartened. He had missed something fundamental. Not one word about agriculture, or biological product development. And what was a "hazard level"? Presumably, some kind of a measure of great danger. Uncle Ryan could surely have told him what was going on in two seconds—if he were around to ask.

At his side, Dawn stirred and rose to her feet. She had been quiet while Josh was working, though she hadn't seemed to watch the displays at all. Now she said, "Come on," and held out her hand.

"Come on where? Oh, who cares. I'm not getting anywhere here." Josh allowed himself to be dragged out of the data center and up the stairs, higher and higher, until they came to a little room at the end of the loft. He hadn't remembered its existence until he saw it again. Then he remembered that it always used to be locked. Dawn went in and pulled a swing-down ladder into position, which also opened a skylight. She led the way up.

They emerged onto a flat part of the roof. Josh was sure that he had never been here before, and it took a few seconds to orient himself. City kids didn't see open sky very often—too many street-lights and tall buildings—but the rising moon told him which way was east.

The night sky was so clear that you thought you could see a million stars in it, as well as dozens of rapidly moving points of light that had to be ships and stations in low orbit. He thought that Dawn had just brought him up to look at everything, until she took his arm to get his attention and pointed up and to the south-west.

"What is it?" He couldn't see a thing where she was telling him to look.

She giggled. "Belt node."

No wonder he couldn't find anything. No one could possibly see a node in the Asteroid Belt or the Kuiper Belt from here, not if they had the biggest telescope on Earth to look through. He stared anyway, for a long time, and saw nothing.

Then she was pointing farther north. "Messina Dust Cloud."

Again, there was nothing visible. But she certainly seemed to be staring at *something*.

It gave him a definitely creepy feeling. Either she could pick up something that was totally invisible to him, or she couldn't, and she was playing some sort of game of her own. Either way, he didn't like it. For the first time, his feelings about Dawn took a strongly negative turn. With her long silences and her strange re-actions, she really spooked him.

They stayed on the flat roof until the air cooled. At last Josh felt himself shivering. Dawn, in her sleeveless dress, must have been freezing. He said "Come on" and led the way back inside. She followed, and, rather to his relief, continued on to her own room.

He did the same. The house doors were already locked, though that seemed to be of less concern here than in the apart-ments where he and his mother had always lived. This time he undressed and put on night clothes before he lay down on his bed.

He welcomed the chance to be alone for a while. He had a lot to think about. The fact that he had been dropped onto Burnt Willow Farm uninvited; Aunt Stacy and Uncle Ryan and the medical examination; the network nodes and the Messina Dust Cloud; Solferino and Foodlines and Unimine; they all swirled around disturbingly inside his head.

And Dawn. What strange ideas ran around in *her* head, when she lay down to sleep? Did she, like Josh, worry about the next day and her own future? Or did she live all in the present, like Mister Micklegruber, now snoring so loudly outside that Josh could hear him through the open window?

Josh did not know if it was Uncle Ryan and Aunt Stacy's return that woke him up, or the sound of their voices.

He lay flat on his back and wondered what time it was. It felt like the middle of the night. He was ready to turn over and try to go back to sleep when he thought that he heard Uncle Ryan say the word, *Joshua*, with unusual emphasis.

He lay totally still, staring up at the ceiling and listening intently. It was no good—he could hear enough to be sure that they were talking, and sometimes pick out odd words and phrases, but he could not quite make sense of the whole conversation.

He eased out of bed as quietly as he could and moved across to the door. Their bedroom was on the floor below his, but for some reason he could hear even less when he was here at the head of the stairs. In fact, he didn't think they were in their bedroom at all. There was a light on farther down, as though they were still downstairs. He knew how much the old stairs creaked. If he went down, they would surely hear him coming no matter how quietly he tried to walk.

He moved back and put his ear to the wall at the head end of his bed. That was a lot better. Through some trick of the house's construction, sounds below carried here almost perfectly.

He stood motionless and tried not to breathe.

"I'm not saying it isn't." That was Uncle Ryan. "In fact, it's a good deal more than I expected."

"So what's your problem?"

"Well, for one thing it's our existing commitments. I have contracts for crop delivery this harvest."

"Harvest?" Aunt Stacy laughed, but it carried no humor. "If we don't take the Foodlines offer, there'll *be* no harvest. You'll be plowing under dry stalks. But if we take their offer, they'll make water available. And you heard Mort, he'll make sure that our contracts are fulfilled no matter what."

"So he says. You know I don't trust that man as far as I can throw him."

"I don't see why. He's always been straight with me."

"You weren't around when other farms were bought out, Stacy. You haven't heard the stories. Mort Langstrom made promises, but once the deal was signed and people were off their own property, that was the last anybody heard about prior commitments."

"I see." There was a pause, then Aunt Stacy spoke again in a different voice. "Suppose that we could talk Foodlines into signing a deal now, but they agree we can stay on at Burnt Willow Farm until this harvest is in. Would that make a difference?"

"Of course it would. But you know they won't go for that. They were quite clear about the situation on Solferino. If we want to get that early-in working interest that they talked about, we have to have a physical presence there within sixty days. I must say, I've never heard of a contract clause like that in my life. I wonder who put it in."

"I wonder, too." There was a certain tone in Aunt Stacy's voice. Josh recalled his mother's acting-out of parts. *See this now. Wide-open eyes. The mouth parted, just a little. Perfect innocence.*

Aunt Stacy was continuing, "But Ryan, it could still work."

"How? We can't be in two places at once."

"We don't have to be. There's Joshua."

Josh, his ear to the wall, felt the goosebumps rise at the sound of his own name.

"What about Joshua?" asked Uncle Ryan.

"He could go on ahead of us, and establish a presence on behalf of the family. He would need special training anyway, to live and work on Solferino. It would be better if he had it there than here."

Josh gasped with excitement and put his hand over his mouth. But Ryan said, more than loudly enough to cover the noise from Josh, "Stacy!"

"What's wrong?"

"Are you crazy? We don't even know how to reach Lucy to discuss it."

"So what? We can hardly be blamed for that. What makes you think she *wants* to discuss this, or anything else to do with Joshua?"

"She'd have to."

"Why? She sent us all the legal records on him; we can take any action we believe to be to his benefit. Ryan, can't you see that Lucy Kerrigan doesn't give a damn what happens to her son? From all I've heard about her, she's a totally selfish bitch who never did one thing for anybody except herself in her whole life. Who was Joshua's father? Can you tell me that?"

"I don't know. Maria didn't know, either. Lucy never told us."

"Wonderful. So Lucy Kerrigan has herself a bastard. And when it becomes inconvenient to have him around, what does she do? She drops him off on strangers."

"Stacy, we're not strangers. I'm his uncle."

"Right. But she hadn't seen you for eight years. And she didn't even realize that Maria had died. And *I'm* certainly a stranger to her. She doesn't know that I exist."

"Well, of course she doesn't." There was the scraping of a chair on a wooden floor and the sound of footsteps, then Uncle

Ryan went on, "Look, I'm not going to start us arguing by defending Lucy Kerrigan. It's Joshua I'm concerned about."

"And it's Joshua that *I'm* concerned about, too. Ryan, I never want to argue with you, about anything. But we don't disagree at all. This is the best thing that could possibly happen to Joshua. There's no future for him here at Burnt Willow—you know that even if you don't want to admit it. Solferino is a whole new world. It will be marvelous for him. For Dawn, too."

"Dawn can't possibly go!"

"Well, if *we* go we can't possibly leave her behind."

"I didn't mean that. I mean, Dawn can't go before we do."

"Oh, sure." There was a pause, then Aunt Stacy went on in a thoughtful voice. "Mind you, Dawn will need special training anyway, because of—well, you know. She has her problems. It might help a lot if Foodlines agreed for her to go a little ahead of us, so they could take longer with her than usual. I'll tell you what, why don't I call Mort Langstrom tomorrow, and talk all this over with him? But I don't want to discuss it any more tonight. It's getting late, and I'm tired." There was another scrape of a moving chair on the board floor, and an audible kiss. "Come on to bed, love. We'll sort all this out in the morning."

Josh heard footsteps, first on the lower level and then ascending the stairs. He tiptoed to his bed and lay down on top of the covers. There was the sound of running water, then the murmur of voices that gradually faded in the next few minutes.

Josh lay in the darkness with his eyes wide open. He felt too excited ever to sleep again. He knew what was going on, even if Uncle Ryan didn't seem to. Aunt Stacy didn't want Josh around, and the best way to do that was to make sure that Josh was twenty-seven light-years away, on Solferino.

Well, Josh wouldn't say no to that. He could hardly wait. No place on Earth had anything to offer him. He would willingly go to Solferino tomorrow, or tonight, or as soon as they would let him.

But there was one other factor. Josh lay totally still, listening. There was not a sound inside the house. He eased himself off his bed and crept down the stairs to the next level. Uncle Ryan's bedroom door was closed, but Dawn's was open a crack.

Josh peeped in. She was asleep, her face pale and expressionless in the moonlight that slanted in through the window. He stared at her, and his earlier uneasiness changed to irritation.

He had a premonition about what was going to happen. Aunt Stacy didn't just want *Joshua* out of the way; she wanted Uncle Ryan all to herself, for as long as she could get him. And that meant Dawn had to be out of the way, too.

By the sound of it, Aunt Stacy had some kind of deal going with Foodlines and Mort Langstrom. She would work them, as she was already working Uncle Ryan. And who would finish up dragging his dumb and retarded cousin after him through the node network, like a big dead weight around his neck?

Josh had his suspicions.

CHAPTER FIVE

JOSH had thought of little else for two weeks. Now, with the reality sitting in front of him, he rather wished that it would go away.

The node. There it was, right outside the ship, bright and threatening. To Josh's eyes it loomed as big and cold as the summer moon on his last night at Burnt Willow Farm.

Dawn sat next to him, a sketch pad on her knee. He wasn't sure that she knew he was there. She was staring out of the observation port and at the same time drawing furiously, totally absorbed. He glanced down at her pad, forcing his attention away from the node. She wasn't sketching what she was seeing. She was, of all things, making a beautifully detailed picture of Burnt Willow Farm, as it had looked from the ridge.

What went on inside that smooth, dark-haired head? Did she even notice that they were in free fall? Did she realize that in another twenty seconds the ship would enter the glowing pearly sphere of a network node?

Other people were not as oblivious as Dawn. The row of seats held five reclining couches, all occupied. Josh looked past Dawn to the three Lasker brothers. He had been introduced to them for the first time at the spaceport, before they took off for orbit, and disliked them on sight. Like the five other trainee passengers on the ship, they had been ticketed by Foodlines for transportation to Solferino. They had been loud most of the time while they waited to board the ship, and when they were not shouting or fighting they were huddled together and whispering. If their sideways glances were anything to go by, they were sneering at the other travelers.

At the moment they were not sneering at anything. They were staring pop-eyed out of the port. Sig Lasker, only a year older than Josh but a head taller and forty pounds heavier, had a face the color of dirty snow. Rick and Hag, the thirteen-year-old twins, were not much better. All three of them had been throwing up off and on since the ship went into free fall. That was rather pleasing to Josh, because he and Dawn had had no trouble at all of that kind (so far, said a warning voice in his head). He wondered how the Karpov sisters were doing in the row behind. They didn't say much, but Josh had the feeling that all four of them, even little Ruby, were pretty tough.

"Twenty seconds to node entry." The prissy voice on the ship's general address system belonged to Bothwell Gage. He was the Foodlines employee responsible for delivering the trainees to their destination. "Return to your assigned seats," he went on. "Node entry can produce peculiar physical and mental effects."

Gage was a company biologist who did not pretend to be thrilled with his present assignment. As he had pointed out, several times, he was headed somewhere else entirely. He had been given responsibility for the trainees only when someone at Foodlines headquarters realized that Gage knew Solferino well, and the planet was on the way to his final destination. Gage had made clear to the group the extent of his duties: He would tell them about Solferino, get them there in one piece, and hand them over to their teachers when they reached the planet. He seemed knowledgeable enough about facts, but when it came to people he was, in Josh's opinion, totally naive. The biologist was small-boned, large-headed, and round-shouldered, and while he might do well on a place like Solferino, he wouldn't have lasted ten minutes on a big-city street after dark.

"If you aren't in your own seats *now*"—Gage's voice turned coy—"in another half-minute I guarantee you'll wish that you had been."

On his final words, another voice chimed in. It was the control computer of the *Cerberus*, reading the record aloud for the benefit of the humans on board.

"Node surface distance two hundred meters. Velocity match twelve meters a second—eleven—ten—zero relative rotation—distance one hundred meters—velocity match eight meters a second—seven—six— separation forty meters—ship fields off, radio blackout commences—two meters a second, we are beyond abort option. Node entry beginning. Radio blackout is total."

In other words, the ship was cut off from all contact with anything in the solar system. The pearly glow had grown until it filled the sky. Close up, it showed streaks and swirls of darkness, and within those, point scintillations of blue-white light.

"Node entry is beginning," Bothwell Gage took over again from the computer. "The more you can relax, the better you will feel. We are doing fine."

Relax, sure—if you could. But Josh was not doing fine at all.

Something was terribly wrong. It was not the nausea that he had briefly experienced when first entering free fall, but something much worse. As the *Cerberus* passed into the node, Josh felt his whole body begin to rotate in one direction, while the inside of his head went in another. It made no difference if his eyes were open or closed. The interior of the node was a rainbow glow, and it seemed to turn in a hundred ways at once. He was riding a giant multicolored whirligig, that every few seconds chose to vanish and reassemble itself, and then turn all the different parts of him in multiple different directions.

Worst of all, his whole body trembled and shook under an internal force that seemed to have nothing to do with anything outside it. He opened his mouth to scream. In that same moment, the ability to scream was lost. A final spin took him off in a direction where there were no directions.

Josh was twisted out of space itself; and in that ultimate nowhere blackness, he felt nothing at all.

Josh awoke, wondering how long he had been unconscious. According to the preflight briefing, if he did black out it should be for no more than a fraction of a second. But it felt like he had been unconscious for ages.

He opened his eyes. The multicolored glimmer of the node interior was gone. In its place a diffuse blue glow filled a third of the sky.

"All right." Bothwell Gage on the address system spoke as though nothing had happened. "I told you that we would be fine, and we are. We have completed the first node transition. The sensors need a couple of minutes to recalibrate, then we will make our jump to Solferino. That will give you a chance to examine the structure of the Messina Dust Cloud. The physicists back Sol-side claim to understand where it came from and what it's all about, but if you ask *me*"—he laughed, but it was more like a giggle—"if you ask me, they're in a cloud themselves. However, you won't see anything like this again for a long time, so I suggest that you look and enjoy."

The great blue and purple haze of the Cloud was shot through with streaks and swirls of brighter colors, greens and yellows and glowing crimsons. Josh could see that those rainbow lines and curves defined currents and whirlpools, which taken together provided the outline for a set of broader patterns. Those had to be the sluggish space rivers of dust and gas described in the online documentation that he had studied back at Burnt Willow Farm. In those broad rivers you'd find invisible pockets of stable transuranic elements, carried around some unseen center.

"Found *only* in the Cloud," Gage answered a question from Amethyst, one of the Karpov sisters. "And enormously valuable. Unimine ships have looked for stable transuranics in a thousand other places, so far without success. Anyone who does find those elements outside the Messina Dust Cloud is assured of a great fortune. Cloud collection is slow, laborious, and expensive."

And elsewhere in the Cloud, Josh hoped not too close, were the cloud reefs. In those regions of intense electric and gravity fields, something very strange happened to space-time. The Unimine rakehells explored them, because that's where you were most likely to find shwarzgeld and starfires. But there you would also find space sounders, about which the documentation said nothing—except that they were dangerous.

No one knew if a sounder should be thought of as living or nonliving. Rakehells had a habit of disappearing near reefs and sounders, without so much as a call for help. And sounders were supposed to be able to pop out of nowhere, at any time.

Josh scanned the Cloud, wondering how you knew when a space sounder was on the way. Suddenly he was quite willing to head back into the gut-wrenching interior of the node.

"*Velocity match six meters a second.*" The voice of the control computer of the *Cerberus* began again. "*Zero relative rotation. Dis-*

*tance thirty meters—ship fields off, radio blackout commences—two me-
ters a second, beyond abort option. Node entry beginning."*

This time the shock was not so great. Josh, as his insides
were knotted into complex shapes that felt as though they could
never be unraveled, had one final thought: life on Solferino would
certainly be hard, it might even be horrible; but you didn't encounter the word *danger*, over and over again, as you did whenever
Unimine activities were mentioned.

Anything would be better than working for Unimine, bur-
rowing kilometers deep into naked rock, plumbing oceans of
molten iron, or chasing space sounders through the dark unfath-
omed reefs of the Messina Dust Cloud. Compared with that,
Solferino was going to be Funland.

The first solar system network node had been established in the Asteroid Belt, hundreds of millions of kilometers from Earth. The official reason had been caution: The nodes and the network were an
unknown quantity, and danger to Earth must be avoided at all costs.

The true reason, according to Bothwell Gage, was very different: Intense lobbying pressure had come from established transportation companies. They feared their business would be eroded
or destroyed by instantaneous travel from node to node.

That worry should have been nonexistent in other stellar
systems, or within the Messina Dust Cloud. But rules were hard to
change, and habits hard to break. The Solferino node could have
been conveniently placed in low orbit about the planet. Instead,
the *Cerberus* was forced to make a boring three-day trip from the
node to Solferino. It seemed forever until the *Cerberus* computer
announced that rendezvous had been achieved, and passenger
transfer would take place to a vehicle able to descend to the surface of Solferino.

That news apparently revived even the Lasker brothers. At
any rate, they were well enough to jostle Dawn and Josh out of the

way as they all entered the single-stage landing orbiter. Josh pushed right back. It didn't take a genius to guess that there was trouble ahead, but he wasn't going to be shoved around by anybody. He was pleased to see Sapphire, the oldest of the Karpov sisters, give Sig Lasker a vicious elbow in the ribs in the doorway.

"Boys and girls, if you *please*, let us have a little decorum." Gage had noticed what was happening. "Let me remind you that you are not in the Pool now. Save your energy for the surprises you may encounter on Solferino."

Boys and girls. Josh could guess how Sig Lasker, with his starting beard and powerful build, must be reacting to that. Bothwell Gage seemed to think he was dealing with seven-year-olds. Unfortunately, all of them had no choice but to deal with him. The man knew what Solferino had in store for them. They did not. Josh was aware of his own ignorance, although he had picked up all he could in the scattered briefings that began the day after Uncle Ryan and Aunt Stacy had signed the papers on his and Dawn's behalf. What had Stacy said or done to persuade her husband that it was all right for Dawn to go with Josh? Josh would like to have been in on that conversation.

As for *surprises*, you could start with the color of the planet. Josh stared out of the window as he and Dawn, last of the trainees to be shepherded out of the *Cerberus* by Bothwell Gage, settled into their padded seats and waited for the lander to ease away from the main ship. Earth from orbit had been a cloudy ball of blues and grays. Solferino had plenty of white clouds, too, but the ground beneath was a mottled mess of pastel pinks, ugly purples, and random yellow smudges.

"Well, look your fill." Bothwell Gage knew they were all gazing out of the ports. "We are on our way. You will be down there in half an hour. Are there any questions?"

"Whyzit look like that?" Hag Lasker said. The twins were fraternal, not identical, with Hag as dark as his brother Rick was fair.

"Like what?"

"Like them funny colors. It's funny colors down there."

"You mean, purple and pink?"

"Yeah. Them."

"Aha! That has to do with the way that plants on Solferino employ the energy of sunlight. You know what chlorophyll is, don't you?"

Hag stared at Gage as though the man had started to talk Chinese. Josh wasn't sure of the word, either, but Amethyst, the fat one of the Karpov sisters and the only one who, so far as Josh could see, had a working brain, piped up, "Chlorophyll makes plants green."

Her sisters scowled at her.

"Indeed it does," Gage said. "But it does much more than that. It allows plants to use sunlight to convert raw materials—carbon dioxide and water—to foods. Chlorophyll on Earth is actually a mixture of two kinds, one green and one yellow. Plants on Solferino employ only the yellow chlorophyll. Its actual name is 'xanthophyll.' But Solferino plants also use another chemical, called 'rhodopsin.' Did you ever hear of it?"

This time, nobody spoke. Josh thought he might have heard that word before, too, but he had no idea what it meant. Dawn, for all that he could tell, was off in another world. The Lasker brothers and the Karpov sisters, except for Amethyst, regarded Gage with their usual combination of dislike, incomprehension, and utter lack of interest.

Gage seemed more resigned than surprised. "Rhodopsin," he went on, "isn't just found on Solferino. You have it in the retinas of your own eyes. It is necessary in seeing. It can also use the energy in sunlight to make carbohydrates for plants, the same way that chlorophyll does. But rhodopsin is not green or yellow. It's *purple*. The plants on Solferino use rhodopsin, and sometimes chlorophyll. Thus, as you'll see when we land, they range in color from purple to a pinkish yellow. You won't see much green. But if you do, don't be tempted to eat something just because it looks familiar. You will vomit more violently than you ever did in free fall. Are there any other questions?"

"Mm." Ruby Karpov, the youngest of the sisters, had shown no interest in listening to Bothwell Gage. She had been staring out of the lander's window. "What's that?"

She pointed a finger—not down, but up. Gage started to say, "Actually, I meant questions about the *planet,*" but he trailed away on the final word. The lander was entering the atmosphere, and the trainees were beginning to feel weight again as air drag slowed the vehicle. Their ship was on the night side of the planet, where the only thing visible ought to have been stars and Solferino's single moon. But in front of and above the lander, accelerating steadily away from it, was the long plume of a ship's exhaust.

"My goodness." Gage was leaning forward and frowning. "That is certainly not the *Cerberus.* And it is not a conventional lander."

Gage continued—not to the trainees, or to himself, but to the lander's computer. "Tell the *Cerberus* that we have an unfamiliar ship in sight. I think it is not one of ours. Request a spectral analysis of the exhaust, plus anything else that they can tell us."

There was a five-second pause, while wild thoughts ran riot through Josh's head. He had seen this often enough on the tube. A star system far from Earth. Approach to a new planet. An unfamiliar and unexpected ship. *Aliens!*

Before he could go any farther, the computer's quiet voice was returning a message. *"Identification is complete. The ship visible ahead of the lander is a Unimine M-class vessel, the* Charles Lyell."

"Unimine!" Gage snorted in disbelief or disapproval. "Their ships should not be anywhere near Solferino. Don't we have exclusive rights to development here?"

There was a brief pause—time enough for a lengthy exchange of data between the lander's computer and that on the *Cerberus.*

"That is correct," the computer said. *"Foodlines has exclusive*

rights to the development of Solferino for twenty years, unless the com-
pany chooses to give them up. However, that does not prohibit the
Unimine conglomerate access to the space around the planet, or prohibit
travel anywhere within this stellar system. In fact, Unimine has explo-
ration rights for Cauldron, one of the lesser and lifeless worlds of this sys-
tem. The Charles Lyell *is recorded as a prospecting ship, but it is capable*
of planetary landing."

"Doesn't our franchise prohibit other landings on
Solferino?"

"It does."

"Then what's their ship doing here?"

"We do not know."

"So ask them!" Bothwell Gage's voice rose to a squeak.

"We did ask them." A computer could not sound apologetic or
puzzled, but its choice of words was significant. *"The* Charles Lyell
*is under no obligation to answer our inquiries. Regrettably, it declined to
do so. The most logical reason for its presence is that the Unimine ship is
employing Solferino in a gravity-assisted swing-by maneuver on its way
to the outer system and the planet Cauldron."*

"You think that's it?"

*"It is certainly possible. Unfortunately, our analysis assigns that as-
sumption a probability of only one in ten."*

"So what are you suggesting that we do?" The G forces were
affecting everyone on board, and Bothwell Gage's voice was in-
creasingly distorted.

The computer made a minor adjustment to the lander's angle
of attack, and the deceleration forces lessened. *"We have already
taken the appropriate action,"* it replied. *"The presence of a Unimine
vessel close to Solferino has been assigned to the general file of unanswered questions."*

Josh was a newcomer to space, and he knew next to nothing
about either Foodlines or Unimine operations, but even he could
tell that the computer's answer was hardly one that Bothwell Gage
found satisfactory.

CHAPTER SIX

THE lander drifted in and came to rest in the middle of a cleared circle about two hundred yards across. The perimeter was surrounded by a seven-foot silver fence of flat posts. Five orange-yellow buildings with small round windows, like the viewing ports on the *Cerberus*, stood in a cluster well inside the fence.

"Breathing masks on," Bothwell Gage said. And, when Josh and the others stared at him because he wore no mask himself, "I don't need one. I've been here before, and I'm long since acclimatized. The injections that you had when you left Earth take a few days before they're completely effective. You could probably breathe the air of Solferino right now with your modified lung alveoli, but I'd rather confirm that when we're inside a building and have medical equipment handy. Think yourselves lucky. It's full body suits on Merryman's Woe."

He opened the door of the lander and led the way outside. Josh, a light mask in place over his nose and mouth, stepped gingerly onto a surface that felt and looked like a dense purple rug. It was plants, or perhaps all one plant, with springy two-inch stems that flattened under his weight and bounced back upright as soon as he lifted his foot.

He stared around him, noting that the others were all doing the same. The air seemed unnaturally clear. Grisel, the star whose gravity field held Solferino, Cauldron, and the four other planets of the system in orbit, was high in the sky. It was bigger and redder than Sol. Josh had only seen Earth's sun dull and swollen like that at Burnt Willow Farm, when it was down on the horizon and close to setting. In the city he had never seen a sun like that. The high buildings blocked out sunsets.

Thin fingers of purple and yellow vegetation reached up over the silver fence. Beyond them, far off in the distance, the ground ascended steadily to three rounded peaks. On top of those hills sat clusters of gigantic purple and yellow balloons, looking like markers for some colossal birthday celebration.

"You'll have plenty of time to examine everything in the next few days," Gage said. Even the Lasker brothers were staring around in fascination. "Right now I want you all inside. I'm very surprised they haven't come out to meet us. I'll just say this about Solferino: This place is the most Earth-like world we know—except, of course, for Earth itself. But that doesn't tell you half the story."

He began to walk the group toward the buildings at the edge of the clearing.

"The fact is, Solferino is the most Earth-like extrasolar planet that humans have ever encountered, by *every* measure that you care to choose. Grisel is a little bigger and cooler than the Sun, but the temperature range over much of Solferino is something you can tolerate. Gravity is only slightly different from Earth, and the day just one hour longer. The planet has one big moon—a very significant fact in shaping the development of life, if the archaeo-biologists are to be believed.

"Most other planets that humans have visited haven't developed life of any kind. They are of value only for mining and minerals. And if they do have life, it's single-celled organisms. This is the only place we know, other than Earth, where complex, multi-celled life has developed. With minor lung modifications to accommodate differences in oxygen, carbon dioxide, and water vapor, you can breathe the air. This is also the only place where living things exist that we can clearly recognize as plants and animals. My next stop, for example, will be Merryman's Woe. On that planet, all we have found so far are cyanobacteria and things similar to slime molds—very valuable, maybe, but not remotely like multi-cellular plants and animals. But Solferino life is amazingly Earth-like. Many of the animals have internal skeletons and back-bones, the same as we do. The plants have discovered the use of cellulose, which makes large organisms possible, like the ones over there." He pointed to the huge balloons on the distant hills. "Those really are plants, though you might not think so when you first see them. So when you walk around on Solferino, don't think about how *different* it is. Think how like Earth it is, and be amazed."

"Well, isn't that truly, truly wondrous." That was Sig Lasker on Josh's left, speaking too softly for Bothwell Gage to hear and mimicking the instructor's high-pitched and nasal voice. "Hey, guy, you don't have to do a sales job on me. We *wanted* to come here—though I'm not sure we'd have been any worse off if we'd stayed in the Pool."

Josh was inclined to agree. Listening to Uncle Ryan and Aunt Stacy, you'd think that Solferino must be some sort of heaven. The real thing was strange, and definitely scary. What about that tall, silvery fence? It surely hadn't been built to keep anything *in*. What was it keeping out?

"Animals with internal skeletons and backbones," he said aloud.

Dawn was walking at his side. She didn't look at him, but she added, "Lions and tigers and bears."

Everyone turned in unison to stare at the silver fence.

"Not quite," Gage said. "The most advanced—or at least, the most intelligent—animal on Solferino, so far as we know, more resembles another of Earth's larger species, the panda. Solferino life forms need their own classification system, but in our terms the nearest thing would be the *Procyonidae* family—which includes pandas, and also our friend the raccoon, whom you all know well."

The whole group, with the exception of Dawn and Bothwell Gage, exchanged looks that said, *We've got a real bunghead here.* Josh couldn't speak for the others, but he knew that he had never seen a raccoon. He wasn't sure they weren't extinct outside zoos and private collections. Who did Gage think he was dealing with? Rich kids who lived out in the country and took walks on closed game reserves?

"They term that animal *Procyon solferino pseudolotor*," Gage continued, unaware of the trainees' reaction. "A bit of a mouthful, so it's more commonly called a 'rupert.' One reason for the fence, apart from holding back the taller vegetation, is to keep animals like the ruperts out. Some of them like to lie in the open, and they get in the way. They used to be flattened by the landers, because they wouldn't move. I suppose that smartness is relative. The rupert is reputed to be quite intelligent, but extremely shy. However, I'm not sure that I believe either of those statements. No Solferino animal has a great need for cunning and wariness, nor is there a logical reason for it to be shy. Maybe they mean that it is nocturnal, and only comes out at night. The larger native beasts are also, so far as we know, all vegetarians."

So far as we know—there it was again. It was another way of saying, *we don't know*. Josh, walking along last in line, wondered. What did people actually *know* about Solferino?

"And of course, there are some major differences that you might not notice unless you look for them." Gage waved his hand upward. "For example, no Solferino animal has ever mastered the air. You will seek in vain for birds, bats, and flying insects. Plants, however, are another matter."

They had reached the buildings, which put an end to Gage's well-meaning tutorial and mystifying final remark. He had been striding ahead at an increasing speed that suggested uneasiness on his part. He hurried straight into the central building, and the trainees followed. They found themselves in three connected rooms, two dormitories with a combined kitchen and living area between them. As Josh closed the door—a broad flexible skirt on its edge provided a perfect air seal—he heard a mutter of equipment coming to life in the ceiling. A current of cooler air blew from wall vents.

Bothwell was emerging from one of the dormitories. He shook his head in bewilderment.

"Where can they be? There's not a sign of them. Stay here while I check the other buildings. But surely they would have come out when they heard the lander? You can take your masks off now, by the way. You are in a closed environment designed to match Earth's atmosphere in composition."

"No sign of *who?*"

It was the obvious question, but only Sapphire Karpov was bold enough to ask it.

"The other people." Gage realized that was not enough explanation. "We weren't supposed to find this place deserted. Our arrival was *expected*. I am supposed to depart at once in the *Cerberus* for another node transition, and begin my work on Merryman's Woe. There should be Foodlines teachers and scientists waiting for you, as well as someone in charge of the kitchen and general maintenance."

"You mean we won't be able to eat?" Rick Lasker made it clear where his worries lay.

"Oh, certainly you will. There are ample supplies." Gage waved at a line of storage cabinets along the kitchen wall. "And the autochefs are good ones, they can handle most things you are likely to ask for. My worries are more general. A failure of organization like this is quite unusual."

"Why don't you call Foodlines headquarters and ask them?" Amethyst said. "They must know. Or see what the other Foodlines groups here can tell you."

That produced a strange expression on Bothwell Gage's face. "You don't seem to understand, my dear. We are twenty-seven light-years away from Foodlines headquarters. A radio signal would take that many years to travel there. The only way to get a message to headquarters in a reasonable time is by taking it back through the network nodes we used to come here. That would be hugely expensive, but it suggests another thought. If the others are already here and for some reason beyond the fence, messages may have been left in the camp's communications center. I must check."

He headed for the door and pulled it open. As he went out he turned and added, "Stay here until I come back. Don't go any-where."

The door closed behind him and he was gone, leaving an awkward silence. The group stared at each other.

"Don't go anywhere." Sapphire Karpov scowled. "Sure. Where we likely to go?"

Rick Lasker said, "How long's he gonna be away? I'm starv-ing."

There was a murmur of agreement.

"If those are standard autochef designs," said Sapphire, "we'll be all right."

"You know how to program one?" Josh asked.

"I do. And Topaz can make an autochef stand on its head."

The group converged on the supply cabinets and began to raid them for food.

"You know what?" Sig Lasker said. He had not joined the others, and he was standing alone in the middle of the kitchen.

"Nothing you like here?" Hag had his arms full of bottles and food packets.

"I'm not thinking about food. I'm still thinking of *him*." Sig jerked his thumb in the direction of the outside door.

"What about him?" Amethyst asked.

"Gage only answered half your question. He said he couldn't reach Foodlines headquarters easily. But he never said why he couldn't talk to other Foodlines groups here on Solferino, to see if they knew what had gone wrong."

"What do you think that means?" Josh was wondering if he had read Sig wrongly. The biggest Lasker brother looked and sounded like a thug, but he might be a smart thug.

"I think there are no other groups. This settlement is *it*. I don't know what you were told when you signed up, but everything turned pretty vague in our briefings when it came to the number of people already on Solferino. I got other ideas, too. I have to think." Sig headed for the longest of the tables and sat down. After a few moments the others drifted over to join him, all except Topaz Karpov and Rick Lasker, who were studying an autochef, and Dawn, who stood in a corner of the room staring at a blank wall.

The group at the table exchanged speculative glances. Without Bothwell Gage to tell them what to do or how to organize their interactions, they were not sure how to behave. Tomorrow they might fight like their old selves, but the day's experiences had made them drop their guards for a while.

"Other ideas, like what?" Sapphire Karpov asked after a few seconds.

"Ideas, like weird." Sig stared down at his closed fists. "Let me ask you a question. Are your parents on their way to Solferino?"

Amethyst laughed, but Sapphire shook her head. "He's not joking, Amy."

She turned to Sig. "What you ask only sounds funny if you know my parents. They're a little, well, let's say *strange*. How many other people d'you know who named their kids after gemstones?"

Hag grunted, in what might have been a suppressed laugh, but Sig shook his head at him.

"So they're not here," he said, "and you don't think that they'll be coming?"

"I'll bet on it. You'd never get them to Solferino as long as there's a bar or a casino open on Earth."

"So how come you four are here? Never mind, that's none of my business." Sig turned to Josh. "How about you?" He jerked his head to include Dawn, still standing up, but he wasn't addressing the question to her. "Are your parents here on Solferino?"

"We're not brother and sister." Josh cleared his throat. "She's my cousin."

He knew that wasn't Sig's real question, and he went on, "My mother won't be coming. She's . . . busy, back on Earth. But my aunt and uncle—Dawn's father and stepmother—they're supposed to come out in a few months, when they've tied up their other business."

Supposed to. Except that Josh was suddenly sure that Aunt Stacy didn't want to. She wanted to stay and live in the farmhouse at Burnt Willow, even if Uncle Ryan wouldn't be working the farm himself any more. Josh didn't want to tell any of that to Sig and the others. And what he had said just might be true.

Sig put his hands palm up on the table and shrugged his big shoulders. "All right. They're coming to join you. That blows my idea. Let's eat."

Topaz Karpov and Rick Lasker had arrived at the table with loaded plates of food.

"What was your idea?" asked Sapphire.

"Nothing that matters. Forget it." Sig turned to Hag. "And you forget the other thing, too, all right."

"Me? Forget what?"

"You know." Sig picked up a fork and began to eat. "Not another word," he said with his mouth full, " 'less you want a thick ear."

Hag's dark-complexioned face showed injured innocence. But he too picked up a fork and started to eat.

Josh went across to where Dawn was staring at the wall, turned her round, and brought her to the table. He sat her down and took a seat next to her.

Topaz Karpov was on his immediate right. She pushed two plates of food toward Josh and Dawn, and smiled at him shyly.

"She's not really like, brain-dead, is she? I though she was, at first."

It occurred to Josh that those were the first words that Topaz had ever spoken to him, except in answer to a direct question. "No," he said. "She's not brain-dead."

He felt almost guilty, talking about Dawn as though she wasn't there. That's what Aunt Stacy did.

"Dawn is autistic," he went on. All the others were listening closely.

"What's that mean?"

"It means she's different. She doesn't speak much, but she hears everything, and I think she remembers everything. What made you change your mind about her?"

"She said, 'Lions and tigers and bears,' after you said 'Animals with internal skeletons and backbones.' " Topaz craned around Josh, to look more closely at Dawn. "She's beautiful, you know. Can Dawn read and write?"

Josh felt like a fool. He had taken Aunt Stacy's assessment, without bothering to check for himself. "I don't know."

"Can you read, Dawn?" Topaz asked.

She might as well have been talking to herself. Dawn went on eating and took absolutely no notice.

"Total retard," Rick Lasker muttered, after a few silent seconds.

Josh heard that comment with oddly mixed feelings. Somehow it seemed all right for *him* to resent Dawn—after all, he was saddled with her, and he was the one who had to drag her around with him like a baby. But that didn't give strangers the right to insult her. He was saved from having to react to Rick, because Amethyst Karpov suddenly sat up straight and said, "Shut up, all of you."

"Amy!" Sapphire said. "You don't—"

"Shut up, and *listen*. Can't any of you hear it?"

They could. It was the whine of engines from outside.

"He's leaving us!" Rick cried. "He can't."

There was a rush for the door, halted briefly by Sapphire's urgent shout to her sisters: "Face masks!"

Sig, leading the way, jerked the door open with one hand while he was still fiddling with his mask with the other. He halted on the threshold, until the others crowded behind him and shoved him out of the way.

Josh came last in the group. He had paused to bring Dawn along, decided to leave her at the table, and hurried after the others. They had all stopped close to the doorway. He pushed his way through them, and was enormously relieved to see that the lander stood exactly where they had left it, in the middle of the cleared circle.

Bothwell Gage certainly hadn't left Solferino. He had emerged from the building to the right, and he was waving his arms excitedly in the air. The sound of engines was louder. It came from a cargo aircar, settling down fifty yards behind the orbital lander.

While they all watched, the bigger vehicle rolled steadily forward and came to a halt. The engine whine ceased. The carpet of dense purple vegetation beneath, flattened by powerful downward jets of air, sprang back upright.

A strange and profound stillness fell on the clearing.

The contrast between two people could not have been greater. Josh knew that if Bothwell Gage had been left in charge on Solferino, Sig and Sapphire between them would have eaten the helpless biologist alive.

With the new arrival, though, it was obvious in the first two minutes that nothing like that would happen. They later learned that Solomon Brewster was employed as a scientist and settlement manager, but with his height, deep chest, and huge arms, he looked more like a street bruiser. His hair and eyebrows were pale blond, contrasting with dark and penetrating eyes. Josh saw Sig Lasker make a quick evaluation and come to attention. Sig was going to take the man very seriously.

The new arrival glared at the group as though they had no right to exist. His first words were, "What the devil are you doing here? I wasn't expecting anyone for another week."

"A fortunate accident of timing." Bothwell Gage tried a smile, which was not returned. "I was on Solferino two years ago, with the first exploration party. Now I happen to be on my way to Merryman's Woe, and the Foodlines staff coordinators decided that it would be economical and convenient if I accompanied this group as far as Solferino."

"Convenient to whom?" Brewster scowled. "Not to me, that's for sure. Come on. You and I need a minute or two of private talk."

The two men disappeared into one of the buildings. Josh and the others had no idea what was said there, but when they emerged again, after much more than a couple of minutes, Bothwell Gage seemed to vanish into the background. Josh didn't even notice him leave, although later in the day he saw that the small lander was gone.

"I'm going to be responsible for training all of you in addition to my other duties," Brewster said, as soon as the group was settled inside the building. "Let's start with names. Mine is Solomon Brewster. My friends call me 'Sol.' You can call me 'Sir.' What's your name." He pointed a thick finger at Sig.

"Sig Lasker."

"Sig Lasker, *sir*. Is that your full name?"

Sig hesitated. "No."

"No, *sir*."

"No, sir."

"Better. What is your full name?"

"It's Siegfried Lasker."

"All right. You." The finger jabbed at Hag.

Hag swallowed. "Hagen Lasker. Sir."

"And you, the next one?"

Rick looked miserably at his twin brother. "Alberich Lasker. Sir, I'd rather be called Rick."

"I don't blame you. Siegfried, Hagen, Alberich." Brewster glanced from one Lasker brother to the next. "Three characters from a Wagner opera. What is it, your parents are opera freaks? People who give their kids weird names ought to be shot."

The three brothers nodded in vigorous agreement.

"All right." Brewster moved on to Ruby. "How about you?"

"Ruby Karpov, sir."

"Nice and normal. Very good. That's the way to answer." He pointed to Amethyst. "And you?"

While the Karpov sisters squirmed and looked for ways to avoid sounding like a jewelry catalog, Josh breathed a sigh of relief. Whatever his mother's sins, she had not cursed him with an eccentric name. Given her interests and the names from plays that he had heard thrown about since he was old enough to remember anything, he might easily have finished up as Willy Loman Kerrigan, or Hamlet Kerrigan. When his turn came he was able to speak his own name with confidence. "Joshua Kerrigan, sir."

"Very good," said Brewster. He went straight on from Josh to Dawn. "And your name?"

She took no notice of him at all.

"She's called Dawn," Josh said. "I don't think she'll talk to you."

"Talk to you, *sir*. Anyway, you weren't being asked. What do you think you are, her keeper?" But Sol Brewster's question was almost absentminded. He was much more interested in examining Dawn. "So this is the autistic one."

That statement told Josh several things at once. Since Brewster knew that Dawn was autistic, he probably knew plenty more about the group. That was to be expected, if he was going to be in charge of them.

More important, Brewster had *pretended* not to know anything. He had deliberately embarrassed the others by making them state their full names when they obviously didn't want them talked about. Even the "very normal" comment when Ruby Karpov gave her name lost its innocence, if Brewster knew what was coming with the other sisters.

Why would anyone do things like that? Presumably, to show who was the boss. But it also suggested a big mean streak.

Josh wondered if Sig Lasker had read that on his first sight of Sol Brewster. It was a wise decision to be careful how you dealt with the man.

Brewster had apparently had enough fun with names. His attention was now moving elsewhere. "We'll stay here for a few days," he said, "to get you used to Solferino air and gravity. Then we'll travel farther afield. I'll outline the program for each of you tomorrow, but there's some things that can't wait. Like, who made that mess in the kitchen and didn't bother to clean it up? The place looks like it's been struck by lightning."

Josh caught Topaz's eye. Everyone had been eating when the cargo aircar arrived with Brewster on board, and there had been no time to think of clearing dishes. Topaz opened her mouth, but when Josh shook his head she had enough sense not to say anything.

"I don't care who did it," Brewster went on. "All of you can fix it—and soon." He stared at the group again and seemed to come to some decision. "Before you get to clearing up, though, I want to say a few more words. You are probably wondering just what's been going on here in the settlement. I'm sure you could tell that Professor Gage was having a fit when he found this place empty, with nobody to hand you over to.

"That was my doing. I'm in charge here, and a few days ago I made a decision. I took everyone at this installation to orbit, then sent them on to the main Grisel system medical center for detailed evaluation. That's why I wasn't here to greet you. Before you begin to panic, let me assure you that there was nothing wrong with anyone. Quite the reverse, in fact. During the past seven months of operations of this facility, there has been not a single case of sickness. Not even minor ailments. You may not realize how strange that is, with a total of forty-five people present. The on-site medical computers claim it's a one-in-a-billion chance.

"But it goes beyond that. People on Solferino found their old problems disappearing. I'm not just talking about things that might be easily explained, like allergic reactions. Cures like that might be caused by a change in plant and animal allergens. We had half a dozen far more peculiar events. A man with a long-term digestive problem found that he could eat anything with no aftereffects. A woman who had been told she could never have children, married to a man who three times had been declared completely infertile, became pregnant—you can imagine what sort of a shock that was for everybody. I noticed that scars on my own face that I'd had since a skating accident when I was fourteen were fading and vanishing. Other people told me the same thing, the signs of old injuries were disappearing. I finally decided that it was time for people to visit a more advanced medical center when the teeth of the oldest person here started to fall out—and a new set began to grow in."

Josh thought at once of his own teeth. In the general excitement of leaving Burnt Willow Farm, dental treatment had been forgotten.

"So." Brewster stirred in his seat. They had been listening to him in total fascination, and now he looked them over, one by one, as though assessing any medical problems they might each have. "What is it? Something in the water, something in the soil, something in the air, something in the radiation from Grisel? We don't know.

"But I'll tell you this: If you do exactly what I tell you to do while you're on Solferino, you won't come to any harm. And maybe there's more than that. After a few months here, maybe you'll be fixed up to live forever."

CHAPTER SEVEN

MORNING on Solferino.

It was like the first day at Burnt Willow Farm, when Josh had been so tired and had slept so heavily that when he woke he didn't know where he was.

This was even more confusing. He had that early-morning feeling, but the light through the little porthole-like window carried the ruddy glow of late Earth evening.

Josh climbed out of his narrow bunk. Before they went to bed, thin walls had extruded from the floor to divide the single big room of the dormitory into half a dozen separate cubicles. Those dividers must have been soundproof because he could hear nothing, not even the sound of the Laskers' breathing in neighboring cubicles.

He slipped on his shoes, went to the window, and stared out. He was facing the rising sun—was that direction still called "east" on Solferino? Grisel, peeping over the horizon, showed as a thin crescent of a gigantic red disk. He watched the bloated sun creep higher, thinking of what Brewster had told them. Maybe he ought to be outside, breathing the planet's health-improving air deep into his lungs.

Was it safe to do that yet, without a breathing mask? Gage had said it might need a few more days.

As Josh had that thought, he saw a movement on his left. Someone—was it a girl?—had appeared briefly before heading beyond his field of view.

If that was Dawn, and she had gone outside without her mask—

Josh hurried from the cubicle and ran to the building's main door. He reached in for a mask from the dispenser, but the machine apparently knew more than he did. It wouldn't release one.

"*A mask is unnecessary,*" said an impersonal voice. "*Your biological parameters are within the acceptable range. Do you need a mask for some other individual?*"

Josh didn't bother to answer. He continued out through the door. The machine was smart enough to figure out that no answer was equivalent to a negative.

Everything, buildings and fence and cargo aircar, had a drenched, soggy look to it. The stalks of the low-growing plants were bent over and heavy with moisture. Either it had rained in the night, or dew here was heavier than anything Josh had encountered at Burnt Willow Farm. The air was breathless, without the slightest hint of a breeze.

He began to hurry to the left, where he had caught that fleeting glimpse of a girl's figure. Before he had taken half a dozen steps, a sweet and familiar aroma filled his nostrils.

He stopped, rigid with astonishment. *Triple-snap.* He had last encountered that on the grubby back streets of an Earth city. Of all the smells that he might have expected on Solferino, it seemed the least probable. He saw Sapphire Karpov, leaning against the wall of the building. She was staring blank-eyed at the rising sun, the little twisted cylinder dangling loosely from between her lips. What was going into her lungs was anything but health-giving.

Josh made a rough, throat-clearing sound to announce his presence.

She turned slowly, the cylinder drooping from the corner of her mouth. Her scowling glance told Josh that whatever truce might have been in operation the previous evening was now over. Close up, he could see a faint scar that he had never noticed before, running from the left side of her mouth across her cheek and toward her ear.

"Yeah?" Sapphire peered at him through slitted eyes.

"Where did you get that snap?"

"None of your damned business." She took a long, luxurious draw, inhaling to the bottom of her lungs. "But as a matter of fact, I brought it with me. It wasn't easy. I've got to be careful with these, 'cause I'm down to my last dozen."

"What happens afterward?"

"I don't want to think about that." Sapphire removed the tube from her mouth and stared at it. "Maybe the last hit will kill me. That's what you hear all the time, snap is a killer and triple-snap is worse. Maybe I'll kill myself. Withdrawal symptoms are supposed to be a bitch. Maybe I'll kill you, just for the hell of it. And that big hairy creep Brewster, too. Him and his asking all our names. He was rattling our cage on purpose last night. I'd like to kill him—just like I ought to kill my goddamn father." She took another deep draw and shuddered from head to toe as it hit. "Oh, hell. I don't know and I don't care. Bug off, Joshua Kerrigan. I've not got a thing to say to you. Or maybe I do—just one. Keep your dirty paws off Topaz. If you don't, you'll find out if Solferino will cure crushed nuts."

"Topaz?" The switch in subject bewildered Josh. "I've not said one single word to her."

"You think I didn't see you two sniffing round each other last night? You think I didn't notice her bringing you food? If you believe I'm gonna let you mess with my little sister, you'd better think again."

"She didn't talk to me."

"I saw her doing it."

"What I mean is, it wasn't me she wanted to talk to. She was interested in *Dawn*, not in me. Oh, jeeks." Josh remembered the original reason he had come outside. "Have you seen Dawn—this morning?"

"Sure." Sapphire again sagged back on the wall, her eyes closed. "She went out the gate."

"The door of the building?"

"Nah. Not the door, you dummy. The *gate*. The gate in the *fence.*"

Josh hadn't even noticed a gate. But there it was, slightly ajar. When he went toward it, he saw the sign, KEEP CLOSED. But that wouldn't have meant a thing to Dawn.

Or would it? He remembered Topaz's unanswered question, "Can you read, Dawn?"

He opened the gate and went through, nervous about what might be on the other side. He found himself in a dark world of red gloom and purple shadows. It was as though the two-inch stems of the clearing, released from human constraints, grew here to giant size. They were as thick as his wrist and reached up above his head to form a canopy about eight feet high. The top layer was translucent, ribbed and continuous, like open paper-thin umbrellas. The plants competed for light, filling in every square inch of space except in places where a rounded balloon shape somehow cleared everything within three feet of it. There, shafts of sunlight speared down to illuminate an ankle-deep ground cover of succulent sickly-yellow stalks. They reminded Josh of fat, slow-writhing worms. He flinched as he stepped on a bunch, but they proved to be crisp and brittle. When he moved to peer at the exposed side of one of the balloons, fat stalks snapped beneath his feet. He felt a spurt of juice wet the calf of his leg and smelled a pungent, peppery odor.

If touching wild plants on Solferino was dangerous, then he was in trouble. Josh stared upward, and found that the balloon was not as smooth and featureless as it seemed from a distance. Its upper part had vertical corrugations on the surface. He could see tubes, like veins, ascending. Waves of contraction swept rhythmically up them, one after another at regular intervals, as though the tubes were throats and the plant was swallowing *upward*.

A light patter of raindrops above his head strengthened the feeling that he was crouched in a forest of mauve umbrellas. Did they furl when high winds came, or close at night when there was no sunlight?

The umbrella forest seemed so peaceful that Josh hadn't given a thought to animal life. A rustle of brittle stalks behind him changed that in a moment. He spun around, sure that no matter what Bothwell Gage might say, he might be attacked.

It was Dawn. She seemed at ease in the purple gloom, slipping toward him like a graceful ghost through the tangle of thick stems.

He reached out to the side of the balloon plant to steady himself, and was astonished to find that it was warm. He jerked his hand away as if the rough surface might burn him.

A warm-blooded plant? Well, why not? On Solferino, anything seemed possible. He felt as out of touch with things here as Dawn had been on Earth.

"What have you been doing?"

She didn't answer—he hardly expected her to—but she was cuddling something close to her chest. It was a stuffed toy, a pudgy, misshapen little elephant covered with tiny silver beads. Josh wondered how she had managed to smuggle it all the way from the farm without anyone finding it in a baggage check. Sapphire had done the same thing with her triple-snap. Maybe he was the dumb one. Maybe all the other trainees had found a way to bring with them something they specially liked or needed.

Then he noticed that the little stuffed toy was moving. A blind head turned toward him. The trunk waved, and membranes like delicate, iridescent ears spread wide on each side. He heard a series of clicks and chirps. The silver beads expanded like opening flower buds, turning the outer layer to bright orange feathers. The creature was suddenly twice as big and nothing like an elephant.

"Dawn—put it down." But as soon as he said that, he changed his mind. "*No!* I mean, don't put it down. Don't let it go. Come with me."

They had to hang on to the animal, take it back, and make sure that it hadn't hurt Dawn to hold it. Suppose the scaly beads or the orange feathers were poisonous?

He reached out his hand. She took it in one of hers, still holding the thing—elephant, dragon, lizard, whatever—to her breast with the other. But she offered no resistance when he towed her toward the gate.

If only Brewster were up and about, and somewhere that they could talk to him. . . .

Josh pushed Dawn into the clearing ahead of him. As soon as they were through the gate he realized that finding Sol Brewster would be no problem. The man was standing outside, staring up. So was Sapphire, without a triple-snap tube in her mouth. So was Sig, so was Topaz—they were all there. They had noticed what Josh, in his worry about Dawn, had been deaf to.

He could certainly hear it now, and he could see it, too. Another lander, smaller than any that Josh had encountered before, was approaching. While the whole group watched, the little vessel drifted in. It settled lightly, rolled forward, and came to a stop no more than twenty yards from where they stood.

* * *

Compared with Sol Brewster's arrival the previous day, what followed was an anticlimax. The woman who emerged had nothing of Brewster's overpowering presence. She was short and fat, with vague blobby features and mousy fair hair. You wouldn't look at her twice in a crowd. The yellowish tinge to her complexion suggested that free fall agreed with her even less than it had with the Lasker brothers. Her approach to the group was not so much a walk as an uncertain waddle.

Even so, Sol Brewster seemed disconcerted. He stared at the approaching woman, his jaw slack and his mouth open.

"What the devil," he said.

The new arrival glanced at the rest of the group but walked at once to Brewster. She made an obvious effort and stood up straight. "Mr. Brewster? My name is Winnie Carlson. I am reporting for service."

"What the devil!" Brewster said again. He paused, took a deep breath, and went on, "What's happening here? What are you doing on Solferino?"

"Huh? Sir, are you Solomon Brewster?"

"I am."

"Good." The woman smiled. "Then I'm in the right place."

"You are in the *wrong* place. I wasn't expecting any new people."

It was the woman's turn to look bewildered. "You weren't? I'm sorry, sir, but the information should have been provided to you. I was sent here by Foodlines HQ. They told me Solferino has been a maintenance technician short for nearly five months." She patted half a dozen different suit pockets, and at last brought out a small card. "Here. Take this, if you don't believe me, and have a computer read it. It spells out my qualifications, work experience, assignment dates, duties on Solferino, everything."

Brewster took the input card but he didn't look at it. Instead he said, "You'll work for me, and do exactly what I tell you?"

"Yes, sir. Those are my instructions."

"And you were never on Solferino before?"

"No, sir. All I know about this planet I got from reading about it. I did a lot of reading while I was waiting to be transferred out." Winnie Carlson glanced nervously around her, as though comparing what she had read with everything from the distant purple hills to the tall fence and the cluster of orange-yellow buildings. "I have a list of the original equipment that was shipped here, and I know the maintenance schedules. Some of your machines are long overdue for service."

"True."

"I can take care of that, sir. Also, I was told that you have trainees here." She nodded toward Josh and the others. "They should be taught how to look after equipment. I can set up service rosters to include them. Subject, of course, to your review and approval."

Brewster hesitated. "We'll discuss that later. But just now I want to talk to you in private. I agree that the trainees ought to be working, but I'm not sure I trust some of this crowd to blow their own noses. Come on." He started toward one of the buildings.

"Sir!" Josh's cry was urgent. He was afraid that his chance to ask about the animal was disappearing.

"What do you want?" Brewster turned his head but did not break stride.

"That, sir." Josh pointed. The silver beads had closed tight, and the delicate ears were furled. The creature again looked more like an midget elephant than a lizard. "Is it dangerous?"

Brewster offered one quick look. "Of course not. Perfectly safe. Everything around here is safe, didn't Gage tell you? That's only a spangle." As he vanished through the door he added, "Don't eat it, though. Your internal flora and fauna may not be quite right yet."

As Brewster and Winnie Carlson vanished inside, the others moved to crowd around Dawn. Even if she had reacted normally to questions, they came too fast to answer.

"A spangle. What's a spangle?"

"Where did you find it?"

"*Eat* it. Yuck. Were you *going* to eat it?"

"What are 'internal flora and fauna'?"

"Are there any more where you got it?"

"Look at the little trunk."

"It's opening its wings!"

And finally, overriding everyone else, "*Don't touch it!*"

That came from Sapphire. Ruby was reaching her hand out to stroke the silvery beaded back. Ruby ignored her sister and touched the spangle anyway.

"It's *gorgeous,*" she said. "I want one just like it. He told us it isn't dangerous."

"You can't have one," Sapphire said automatically. But then she looked at Josh. "Where *did* you find it?"

"I didn't." Josh gestured to Dawn. "She did. In the woods outside the gate."

"Mm. Fat lot of use that will be to the rest of us." Sapphire turned to Dawn as though she was going to pose a question, then scowled and shook her head. "I won't waste my time," she said, and took Ruby by the hand. "It's all right, Rube. We'll go together, see what we can find. Anyone want to come with us?"

"I'll come," Amethyst said. "Who else?"

Josh and the Lasker brothers shook their heads. "Don't want no dumb animal," Rick grumbled.

"Yeah," Hag agreed. "Bet it stinks."

Sig said nothing, but when Rick and Hag wandered off toward the far side of the clearing he went with them. Josh noticed another closed gate in the fence. He watched the brothers open it and go through. What they would like, and what they were willing to admit they liked, might be two different things.

Josh was left with Dawn, Topaz, and the little native creature. After what Sapphire had said he wasn't sure he wanted to talk to Topaz, but she took care of the problem for him.

"Can I?" She spoke to Dawn in a completely normal way, as though she expected the other girl to understand her and respond. Without waiting for an answer, she reached out and gently lifted the spangle from Dawn's grasp.

The trunk waved and the orange flowers began to open, just for a second, then the animal settled down into Topaz's cupped hands. "What do you think it eats?" she asked Josh.

"I've no idea." That seemed to him a pretty weird question. Who cared what it ate, provided it didn't take a bite out of you? But Topaz, studying his reaction, said, "Have you ever had a pet of your own?"

"No." His mother regarded all pets as dirty and a nuisance, but that was none of Topaz's business.

"Well, if you had, you'd realize that the first thing you have to know is how to look after it properly." Topaz did something that gave Josh the shudders. She put the finger and thumb of each hand on the spangle's head and gently opened its jaws so she could peer inside. "Mm. No help there. Just sort of flat plates. Maybe we ought to bring different things from outside the fence, see if the spangle will eat any of them."

Josh was not keen on the idea of another visit to the purple gloom beyond the fence. Bothwell Gage and Sol Brewster might say that everything was safe, but how did they *know?* Solferino was a whole planet. There was no way that Foodlines staff or machines could have explored every part of it.

Dawn banished his worries. "No," she said. While the others stood and stared, she took the spangle away from Topaz and headed for the gate.

"What's she doing?" Topaz asked.

"I don't know." But Josh was suddenly convinced that Dawn had listened to what Topaz was saying, and *understood* it. She was opening the gate and walking through it. She disappeared.

"I'd better go make sure she's all right." But before Josh could move, Dawn was coming back. She was no longer holding the spangle. She came to where Josh and Topaz were standing and looked right through them as though they were not there.

"Want to go," she said as she passed. "Breakfast." She moved on into the building.

"What did she mean?" Topaz asked. "That the spangle wanted to go free, or that *she* wanted it to go?"

"Or does she mean that the spangle wants breakfast, or that *she* wants breakfast?" It occurred to Josh that he was falling into the same trap as Topaz—the delusion that what Dawn said meant anything at all. Aunt Stacy, who ought to know her stepdaughter better than either of them, had other ideas. Dawn's statements were just the mumblings of a badly retarded person.

But suppose that Aunt Stacy had her own reasons for thinking that way? Suppose that Topaz was right? She seemed to have a real understanding of Dawn. Being autistic wasn't the same as being retarded; everything Josh had read made that clear. The brain might function as well as normal, or even better; it just worked *differently*.

That led straight to something that was really none of Josh's business. But he blurted it out anyway.

"Did you know that your sister is on triple-snap?"

"Sapphire?" Topaz was perfectly calm—or pretended to be. "Yes, I know that. Ruby doesn't, and I don't think Amethyst does, either. I'd like to keep it that way, if you don't mind."

"Snap really screws up your brain. And triple-snap is worse."

"A lot worse. I don't think it has hurt Sapphire permanently—not yet, at any rate." Topaz frowned at him, thick dark eyebrows above clear hazel eyes. "I'm surprised that you know anything about snap. Surely you don't get exposure to it out on a farm."

"I was raised in the city—a lot of cities. Dawn is the one who grew up on Burnt Willow Farm. I've seen a lot of druggies in the Pool, no jobs, no prospects, nothing to do but hang out and look for the next hit. Sapphire has to get off it. It will kill her."

"You think I don't know that? That's why I was so glad to come here. I thought there'd be no pushers, no way for her to get any."

"I don't think there is. She said she's down to her last twelve tubes. After that she doesn't know what will happen."

"It's going to be really tough for her. She insisted on coming here, you know. She didn't do it for herself. She did it for me and Ruby and Amy. Saph acts like she's our mother."

Josh thought of the earlier conversation, Sapphire accusing him of messing around with Topaz. He asked hurriedly, "What about your real mother? You have one, don't you?"

"We have a mother, sure, and a father, too."

"So why does Sapphire think that she—"

"Or maybe I mean we *had* a real mother and a real father. I remember what it used to be like. We had our own house, and we had a cat, and we were going to get a dog. We even had a name for him."

"Was there an accident?"

"You might call it that." Topaz sounded bitterly thoughtful, as if she had been over this in her head a thousand times. "They were both teachers, really smart. Everybody says Amy got their brains—she's the brightest one of us, if you hadn't already figured that out. She's our walking data bank, she'll tell you anything you want to know and a good deal that you don't. Anyway, four years ago our parents entered a contest to name a new food product. You ever hear of Scooners?"

"I've eaten them. They're not very good."

"I know. But they won a trip together for naming them. It was to a place with gambling casinos. When they got back, they didn't talk about anything else. My father said he had a way of beating the odds of the system, and when he explained it to my mother she got really excited, too. They went back and tried it."

"Their system was a failure?"

"No. I wish it had been. Unfortunately, it worked very well.

They bought us all sorts of goodies. Next weekend, they went again. It worked again. They had all sorts of plans, a bigger house away from the city, lots of land, a flower garden, horses for each of us. But that time they lost. And after that they kept on losing. I don't think they ever won again. They couldn't stop, though. It was like they had gone crazy—they both got hooked on gambling as bad as if it was triple-snap. Within six months they lost their jobs, they lost the house, and long before that they'd started to tear into each other. And us. Last year, Dad broke Saph's jaw when she tried to stop him hitting Ruby. He said he was sorry, and he took her for treatment, right away. But if you look close you can still see the scar. Right after that Saph started using snap."

Topaz paused. "I shouldn't be telling you this. I'm gabbing at you. Sorry. Saph tells me I do it all the time."

"That's all right. I don't mind."

"Tell me about your parents. What are they like?"

"I don't have a father. But my mother." Josh took a deep breath. "My mother is just great. I'm really lucky."

"Will she be coming to Solferino?"

Topaz had been busy cooking the previous night; she must not have heard what Josh had told the others.

"I guess so," Josh said slowly. "Yes, I guess she will."

"When?"

"Well . . ."

Josh didn't know how to answer that. While he was still hesitating, Rick Lasker came rushing through the gate at the other side of the clearing. He shouted excitedly the moment that he saw Topaz and Josh.

"Hey! Come over here, both of you. You'll never guess what we found! Hurry up!"

Josh had never thought that he would be happy to have a personal conversation with Topaz interrupted by one of the Lasker twins. But he was.

CHAPTER EIGHT

IT COULDN'T be just another spangle. If Rick and his brothers had found one, they would be carrying it with them.

Josh and Topaz ran side by side across the clearing. She was first through the open gate. Josh knew what to expect, but it was Topaz's first time beyond the fence. She slowed at the sight of the thicket of umbrella plants, until Josh pushed her from behind.

"Go on. You can look at them later."

They could still see Rick, bobbing his way through the stems but turning now and again to make sure that they were following. He waved to them, ducked his head, and disappeared.

Following him, Topaz and Josh found themselves on a set of steps cut into a steep incline. The lush stalks had been removed, to reveal bare red soil. At the bottom, on a lower level, was an area cleared of the tall plants. Sig Lasker was on his knees there, while Hag and Rick stood by his side.

"What is it?" Josh called. But before anyone answered, he could see what had them so excited.

A rough lean-to had been made in the middle of the clearing, using the stalks and huge leaves of umbrella plants. One plant had been left standing like a tent pole, and a rope was tied around its thick stem. The other end of the rope stretched to the edge of the clearing where Sig was kneeling. It was attached to a harness around the chest and back of a huge gray animal. Sig was struggling to undo the rope. The creature lay as though it were dead.

Josh realized that there were no ground-cover plants here, either. Every one had been nibbled down to the roots. He stared at the animal sprawled on the ground. It was like a massive cousin of the spangle, with the same eyeless head and a beaded skin that was gray rather than silver. The iridescent winglike ears were unfurled, but they sagged limp along the sides of the head.

Sig was cursing and making no progress untying the thick knot. The animal had pulled it tight in its efforts to reach plants outside the circle that the rope allowed it to reach.

"Here," Topaz said. "Let me."

She pulled a wicked-looking knife out of a hidden sheath under her armpit. As she bent beside the animal she flashed a glance at Josh and the others. "Sapphire's idea, not mine. Self-protection, she says. But for once it might come in useful."

She sawed steadily, not at the twisted knot but at the rope a few inches away from it. Strand by strand gave way, until she could lift the knife and sever the last thread with a single vicious slash. The animal stirred feebly as the rope slackened. The great ears lifted a few inches and turned toward Topaz.

She looked up at Sig. "Now what?"

It was clear from the expression on his face that he had not gone any further in his thinking. Nor had anyone else. Josh realized that the freed animal must weigh several hundred pounds. There was no way that they could carry that great bulk anywhere, even though it was alive and needed attention.

"Food!" Sig said suddenly. "I bet it's starving. Come on."

His two brothers were ahead of him. The first word had been enough to stir them to action. They left the clearing. When they returned they carried handfuls of wormlike yellow stalks. They dropped them in front of the immobile animal.

Nothing happened.

"No good," Sig said at last. "Let's find something else."

"No, wait." Josh had seen a ripple of movement in the flaccid trunk. While they watched it slowly extended, wrapped around a bunch of stalks, and lifted them to a wide slit that opened where the eyes should have been in the blind head. They all cheered. The delicate ears turned toward them and spread all the way.

"Not sick," Sig said triumphantly. "*Hungry*. Get some more—a lot more. I bet a superspangle needs a ton of food."

They scattered to forage. Josh found a patch where the ground was wet and the plants seemed thicker and juicier than usual. He gathered a great armload. When he came back, the superspangle was balanced on four thick legs and a heavy tail. It ignored the stalks that were being dropped in front of it, turned, and headed ponderously across the clearing and down the slope on the far side. It managed about one pace every two seconds.

"Don't let it go," Hag cried. "We found it, it's ours. Stop it!"

"Yeah, sure." Sig put down the plants that he was holding. "Just tell us how."

The superspangle was continuing in a leisurely but determined straight line, its tail making a furrow in the ground plants.

"It's all right," Josh had seen a gleam of water ahead. "It needs a drink. There's juice in the plants, but I bet it's even thirstier than it is hungry."

It seemed at first sight that he was wrong. When the animal came to the little stagnant pool it did not stop, but went on walking. Only when the water was halfway up its legs did it halt, dip its head, and stick the trunk far below the surface. After a few seconds there was a sound like an enormous belch. Bubbles appeared alongside the spread ears. As they burst an awful rotting smell filled the air and the dark surface of the pool rippled.

"Needs a breath mint," Hag said. "Big time."

"It's only swamp gas, you idiot," said Rick. "And it doesn't smell any worse than you." The insult came from pure force of habit. Rick's attention, like everyone else's, was all on the half-submerged animal.

After another minute the superspangle came up for air. It lifted its head, snorted, and blew a trunkfull of spray high over everything. Rather than turning, it trundled backward out of the water. Then it did swing around, desperately slowly, and wandered toward the nearest clump of plants. It ate for a while, wheezed, and finally lay down.

"I think it's gone as far as it intends to go," Topaz said. "At least until it gets its strength back."

"But we wanted to take it with us," Rick objected. He went around behind the superspangle to push it, then changed his mind. It was too enormous to dream of moving it without a forklift.

"I think it's earned a rest." Sig stared back toward the clearing and the lean-to shelter. "What I want to know is, who tied it up and left it there? If we hadn't found it, it would have died."

"One of the people who went off to the medical center, I guess." Josh started back on the path that led to the gate. "I wonder if Brewster knows about it."

"You're not going to leave it here, are you?" Hag asked.

"No, dummy." Sig was following Josh and Topaz. "We're going to let you bring it with you. It can sleep in your bed."

"I'm staying with it."

"Fine. Have fun outside when it gets dark."

That was enough to bring Hag after the rest of them, but he grumbled all the way to the main building.

They wanted Brewster. Usually there was too much of him around, but this time he was nowhere to be seen. The only person in the main building was Winnie Carlson, and the only part of her that was visible was her ample rear end. The front of her was deep inside an autochef. She was sneezing when she came out.

"He went over to check the message center in the other building," she said. "I'll show you, I need a break anyway. You've been cooking with this thing? I'm giving it a first look and it's disgusting. You're not supposed to get allergies when you are on a different planet, but with anything this filthy, all bets are off."

Her nose was red, and she had transferred great smudges of grease to both cheeks. Josh saw Topaz's expression. It said, *Are we supposed to learn equipment maintenance so we can all look like that?*

Brewster wasn't working at the message center itself when they entered the building. He was prowling around the room, which in addition to the communications equipment was filled with computers and peripherals. He was peering inside and underneath everything. Half a dozen of the computers had been turned on and were showing a variety of data-bank displays.

"I haven't got 'round to the equipment in this room yet," Winnie said. She sounded nervous and uncertain. "There's so much to do. I'll take a look at it later today."

"No!" Brewster glared at her. "I don't want any place even *touched* until I tell you to do it. There's no messages for you."

"Very well, sir. I'll stay out of here."

"And why have you dragged the trainees in with you?"

Winnie gaped at him. It was left to Sig, oldest of the others, to say reluctantly, "We found an animal tied up outside the fence, sir. It seemed to be starving. We let it go, but we wonder how it got there and if we did the right thing."

Not, Josh decided, if Brewster's reaction was anything to go by. He glowered and muttered "Damnation" under his breath. Then, louder, "Where is this beast?"

"We'll show you." Rick and Hag jumped forward like dogs let off a leash. The rest followed more slowly, picking up Dawn on the way, who emerged from between two buildings and drifted after them.

By the time they reached the clearing Brewster had calmed down. He took one look at the animal, lying where they had left it and now snoring, and nodded.

"What you have there is a Bode-Jarman chimera, usually known as a bodger. It doesn't eat anything except leaves and roots, and the only way that it will do you any harm is if you let it sit on you."

"But who tied it up?" Topaz asked.

"I can't tell you that, not specifically." Brewster paused for a moment. "Of course, when I told the group that we were going to the medical center for a more thorough check on everyone's condition, matters became hurried and confused." He paused again. "Somebody must have overlooked the bodger in all the excitement. That was regrettable, but fortunately it is not a tragedy. The animal can fend for itself very well, as you see. It will be fine here." He managed to smile at Topaz. "All right?"

"Yes, sir."

All right perhaps with Topaz, but not with Josh. He waited, until Brewster gave a final nod and headed back up the slope toward the gate with Winnie Carlson trailing obediently at his heels. The Lasker brothers began to fuss over the bodger, arguing about how they might lure it to the compound with water and suitable plants. While they were doing that, Dawn went across and sat down right in front of the big animal. She grabbed the beaded trunk, placed it on her lap, and began to stroke it. Josh was ready to run over and pull her away when the animal gave a great sigh, stretched forward, and rubbed its head along her side.

Topaz nodded, as though something had just been confirmed. "The bodger loves that. But he wasn't telling the truth."

"Brewster? I know."

"How can you?" Topaz frowned at him, as though Josh wasn't telling the truth, either.

"My mother. She's an actress."

"She is? That must be really neat for you."

"Yeah." Josh wasn't so sure. "I guess so. Anyway, she showed me how she acted different things. If a person is saying something they already know or really believe, they talk and they look at you a certain way. If they're improvising—making it up as they go along—the pauses and the look are different. Brewster was improvising."

"And he was *lying*." Topaz seemed very sure of herself.

"But how do *you* know?"

"You said you never had a pet, Josh. I did. That bodger was somebody's pet—you only have to look at how it's basking in the attention it's getting from Dawn. There's no way in a million years that anyone who had a pet like that would 'overlook' it and leave it to starve if they had to go away. At the very least, they would release it. If they didn't have time to do that before they had to leave, the Solferino message center would be flooded right now with urgent requests for somebody to go out and let the animal go. Brewster said he had checked the message center. Obviously, no one sent anything about the bodger from the medical facility."

Josh and Topaz stood and stared at each other. "So we agree," Josh said. "He was definitely lying. But why?"

"I have no idea."

Any other comments were lost in new excited cries from Rick and Hag Lasker. Dawn was on her feet. So was the bodger. When she started to walk, very slowly, back up the slope, the beast lumbered after her.

"Hey. He's ours, not yours," Hag complained. "We found him."

Dawn took no notice. Nor did the animal. It just followed her, slowly and single-mindedly.

"I think bodgers must be like cats," Topaz said. "You don't decide who they belong to. They do."

They started uphill after the Lasker twins. Sig was left standing alone, staring first at the bodger's vanishing rear end, then at the uneaten heap of vegetation. When he finally followed the rest, he stayed at the back and spoke to no one.

At the gate to the compound the bodger halted, turned around twice, and settled on the ground. Dawn paused and made a mewing sound. The animal snorted, but did not move.

"I think you'll have to leave it here, Dawn," Topaz said. "It's pretty smart. It knows it's not welcome inside. And in any case, there's nothing for it to eat there."

Dawn did not look at Topaz, or register in any way that she had heard. But she went on through the gate.

The others, following her, found Winnie Carlson on the way to meet them. She appeared more flustered than ever.

"You have to come, right now," she said. "Mr. Brewster told me to get everybody in the dining room for a meeting."

"What does he want now?" Sig asked.

"I have no idea. But if I were you I would say as little as possible when you get there."

Josh could see why as soon as he entered the dining room. Ruby, Sapphire, and Amethyst were already seated. Brewster was pacing up and down in front of them, his big hands clenched behind his back.

"At last," he said, as Josh and the others filed in with Winnie Carlson bringing up the rear. Brewster looked them over, checking that everyone was present, and nodded.

"Listen closely. The medical results indicate that you are now adapted well enough to local conditions to go anywhere on Solferino. So it's time you learned more about the planet. Reading isn't the best way—even though some of you seem to think that it's

sufficient." He favored Winnie Carlson with a glare of disapproval. "You need to experience things firsthand. We are all going to make a field trip to the Barbican Hills. Those are the three peaks that you see to the south of here. That is where, according to our surveys, the most advanced life forms on this planet are probably located. The site for this settlement was chosen with that in mind. You can expect to be gone for two or three days. Any questions?"

Josh felt that he had about a hundred. But it was Amethyst Karpov who was first off the mark.

"When will we be going, sir?"

Brewster glanced at his watch. "Shall we say, we will leave one hour from now? That will give you ample time to pack whatever you feel you need, and provide us enough daylight when we get there to establish our camp. I will, of course, review what each of you proposes to take. Carlson and I will decide on the general equipment and food supplies."

"Me?" Winnie Carlson stared at Brewster as though she had heard him wrong. "I won't be going, will I?"

"You certainly will. I will need your help."

"But I was sent to service the equipment, and most of that is right here in these buildings." Winnie ignored her own advice to say as little as possible. She went on, "I haven't so much as looked in three of the buildings yet, and I've done no service work at all in the others. I suppose I could check the vehicles that we use, and the field trip equipment, but if I were away that would be all I could do and I know from what I've seen already that much of what's installed here is badly overdue for inspection and maintenance and really cries out for my attention."

She paused for breath, while Brewster glared at her. He had been listening with icy attention.

"Have you finished, Ms. Carlson? Are you quite, quite sure? Good. Now let me make myself perfectly clear, since you do not appear to have understood what I said the first time. We are *all* going to make the field trip. Did you hear that, Ms. Carlson? *All*.

As for your other concerns, I thought that we had agreed on something earlier today: You work for me, and you do exactly what I tell you to do. Agreed?"

"Yes, sir."

"Then I want you ready to leave with the rest of us in one hour. And before that you and I need to assemble adequate supplies of food for eleven people, plus such equipment as we will need. We will do that in my quarters."

"Very good, sir."

"Right now."

Winnie swallowed audibly. "Yes sir."

Sol Brewster headed for the door, with Winnie Carlson trailing submissively after him. No one spoke until the two were safely out of the building. Then Sapphire said, "What an absolute *wimp.*"

"Winnie?" Sig Lasker nodded. "Dead right. A total wimp, working for a total jerk. What did we do to deserve them?"

"They deserve each other," Topaz said. "They ought to get married."

"Maybe they will." Amethyst was lolling back in her chair, a faraway look in her innocent blue eyes. "But don't you think we are missing a basic point?"

"That we're all as big wimps as Carlson?" Topaz suggested. "When Brewster tells us to do something, we salute and run."

"There's certainly that. But I was thinking of something else. Do you remember what Brewster told us yesterday? He was very specific. He said that we'd be staying here *for a few days* to get used to the air and gravity. After that, we'd begin to travel. I don't know about you, but I don't think twenty-four hours is the same thing as a few days."

"So he changed his mind," Sapphire said.

"He did. But I want to know why. And why do we have to leave in so much of a hurry? We could have waited until morning. What happened, in the last day, to *make* him change his mind?"

"She found a spangle." Ruby pointed at Dawn. "And I didn't."

"We found a bodger," Hag and Rick said in unison. They had to explain that whole incident to Sapphire, Amethyst, and Ruby, before Topaz could offer another suggestion: "Bothwell Gage left."

"And Winnie Carlson arrived," Josh added.

"All very true." Amethyst nodded slowly. "But I don't see how any of those things are relevant. So what do we do?"

"I can answer that." Sapphire stood up. "Unless you want to get skinned, you go and pack whatever you need to take with you. Then we all head off on this crazy field trip with Sol Brewster. And then we hang loose, and see what happens next."

CHAPTER NINE

THE cargo aircar, heavy with passengers and supplies, was in the air and on its way. It was flying low in a strong and gusty wind, and the journey had been a bumpy one.

Josh had a window seat in the back row. He was staring out and down. It was easy enough for Brewster to tell them to compare the aerial views of Earth and Solferino, but that made certain assumptions. Josh didn't know about the others, but his own experience of flying was limited.

There had been the trip west, when his mother had the summer job in Seattle. That was eight years ago and he didn't remember much about it. He and Mother had made plenty of other trips from town to town, but they had mostly been by bus and car and train. There had been one flight from Boston to Atlanta, but with clouds and turbulence all the way he hardly saw the ground, and anyway it was hard to think about scenery when people were throwing up all around you. And, of course, there was the recent ascent to orbit, when he had been too scared to notice anything at all.

Josh was convinced that when they landed there would be some sort of test on what they had seen and learned, and he would look like an idiot compared with the others. He turned his head and glanced along the row of seats. Dawn was next to him, staring raptly at nothing. Next to her sat Rick and Hag. They were absolutely rigid, eyes straight ahead and hands gripping the armrests. It was clear that they were trying to keep the vehicle in the air by sheer willpower. They were what his mother used to call "white-knuckle fliers," people who hated to be aloft and wouldn't be able to think straight until they were back on solid ground.

Feeling a good deal better, Josh turned again to look out of the window.

From the compound, the country all the way to the triple peaks of the Barbican Hills had been one smooth floor of purple and pale yellow. Seen from above there was far more variety. At the moment the aircar was passing over a river that meandered and wandered all over the place. Josh could see in the middle of the broad stream a group of islands shaped like teardrops. The plants on the island formed a mauve cover that looked as flat as a pancake, but Josh knew that was not the case. He could see little round circles all over the place. They had to be the tops of balloon plants, and he had learned from experience that they stuck up well above everything else. When Grisel was lower in the sky the balloons would throw their shadows on the rest of the vegetation, and the flat look would disappear.

Sol Brewster had been dead accurate about one thing: You learned better by seeing for yourself, and you took a lot more notice of what you were being told if the object you were being told *about* was sitting right in front of you.

"As you will see by looking out of the window, Solferino is a somewhat smaller planet than Earth. You can tell this, because the horizon is much nearer. You are traveling at a height of one thousand meters, and on a clear day you will be able to see a distance to the horizon of about one hundred kilometers. From this, can you estimate the radius of Solferino?"

Josh stared at the landscape and listened to the voice in his ear—not that he had much choice, since the signal came from multiple sources and reached a focus at his ears alone. No matter how he moved his head, the loudness of the voice did not change. If he asked a question, he alone would hear the reply. The others also had individual information services, designed to take account of differences in age and intelligence. Josh had decided in the first minute that his service thought he was either older or smarter than he was.

The voice was continuing: *"The radius of Solferino is five thousand kilometers, rather less than four-fifths the size of the Earth. The surface gravity of this planet is almost exactly the same as Earth's, but that is merely a lucky coincidence. It occurs because the average density of Solferino is twenty-six percent higher. The smaller size and higher density compensate for each other, which is convenient for human settlers."*

Josh switched channels. You couldn't escape the flow of information, but you could change what you got. The same voice spoke again: *"On the far horizon you can see the dark slopes of the Rayleigh Range, built of volcanic basalt. The high heavy-metal content of the range is strange by Earth standards, but it reflects the fact that the whole of Solferino is unusually rich in these substances. The Barbican Hills, in the foreground, are very different in base materials. Like the chalk hills of Earth, they were created by the deposit on the bed of the sea, over many tens of millions of years, of the shells of countless tiny sea creatures. About four million years ago, a general uplifting of the region brought the hills above sea level. Further buckling created the triple peaks."*

Josh had about as much interest in the Rayleigh Range and the Barbican Hills as they had in him. He tried another switch, but the system had its mind set on the approaching Barbicans and was not about to change.

"The Barbican Hills are a major habitat for Solferino's most intelligent life form. Commonly known as a 'rupert,' this animal stands upright and is about four feet high. Its intelligence has been estimated as somewhere between a dog and a chimpanzee." (Great. Except that Josh had never had a dog, and he had never even *seen* a chimpanzee.) *"Like other Solferino animals, the rupert lacks eyes sensitive to ordinary light. Instead it sees as Earth bats see, by sending out and receiving echoes from intense, brief, high-pitched pulses of sound. The behavior of the rupert is the best support for the claim—"*

Another voice, this one from the aircar's navigation and control system, overrode the first one. *"WE ARE WITHIN TWO MINUTES OF OUR DESTINATION. PREPARE FOR LANDING."*

The channel abruptly went silent.

Just when it was getting to the interesting part! Josh had tried the same channel earlier, and it had been yakking on about the basic genetic similarities between Solferino and Earth life forms, and what it meant that they were both based on the DNA molecule.

Behind him, he heard Winnie Carlson talking to Ruby. That figured. Ruby was so young, stuff for her had to be specially dumbed down. With nothing else to do, Josh found he was listening anyway.

"No, what Mr. Gage told you was quite right," Winnie Carlson was saying. "When you were back on Earth, you couldn't have eaten plants and animals from this world without getting very sick. They may look like Earth plants, but inside they are very different. They have DNA, but they don't use it to produce proteins like the ones in Earth plants and animals. Before you came here, tiny specially designed machines—almost like little animals themselves—were put inside you."

"Are those the same nanocritters that make us so we can breathe the air here?"

"Not quite. They're small, like them, but these live inside your stomach, not your lungs. They make lots of copies of themselves when you eat Solferino plants and animals. Those copies all digest what you swallow, and what they give out you can digest. So it's all right to eat the plants that you find here, or at least most of them. Do you understand?"

"I think so. Ugh!"

"What's wrong?"

"You're saying that I've got lots of these little animals inside me. *They* eat the plants, and all I get to eat is their poop. That's disgusting, isn't it?"

"No. I mean, you shouldn't think of it that way. You ought to think—"

The rest of Winnie Carlson's explanation was lost as the aircar's voice again overrode normal conversation.

"WE ARE ENCOUNTERING STRONG SHEAR WINDS. BE PREPARED FOR A POSSIBLE ROUGH TOUCHDOWN."

The vehicle was cruising along the center line of a long, narrow valley, seeking a wide, clear area suitable for landing. Josh held tight to his own armrests and braced his feet against the seat in front. He checked that Dawn's belt system, like his, had come into automatic operation. Farther along the row, Rick and Hag had their eyes closed and seemed resigned to die at any moment.

The landing, when it came, was so soft and feathery that if Josh hadn't been looking out of the window he wouldn't have known when the ship made contact with the brick-red earth of the Barbican Hills.

On a random impulse, he gave a low, horrified moan and said, "Crashing! We're crashing."

He knew it was a dumb idea the moment he did it, even before he heard the wails of fear from his right. It was a little while before Rick and Hag opened their eyes and learned that they were safely on the ground. Then the vengeful glares that they gave Josh and the laughs of the others made him wonder if his joke had been all that bright a move.

Brewster saved Josh from immediate reprisals. As soon as the car landed he was on his feet. "Outside, everyone. We only have an hour or two to set up camp and stow everything inside."

Josh decided that he agreed with Amethyst. It made no sense to rush out here to fumble around in Grisel's red twilight, when fixing up the camp would be a lot easier in full daylight.

In practice, it turned out not to matter. Setting up camp required just three actions:

First, someone had to decide where the structures ought to go. Brewster did that, insofar as there was any choice. A stream occupied the middle of the valley, and most of the other ground was not flat enough, or was covered with chest-high plants. Brewster picked the one sizable area of level, dry ground, about forty paces from the stream and uphill from it.

Second, the cargo aircar had to release the crated building modules from its hold. Winnie Carlson gave the command for that.

And third, the buildings had to unfold from their crates, establish foundations, and transform themselves into bedrooms, bathrooms, and a kitchen. The buildings were smart enough to do that without instructions from anyone. The camp shaped itself in just a few minutes, while everyone looked on.

In the final stages Brewster returned to the cargo aircar. He said he had to talk with the communications center back at the compound. Topaz and the Lasker twins took over the newly formed kitchen. The rest were free to examine their surroundings, or as much of them as they could see in the deepening gloom.

Josh looked around seeking the giant and colorful balloon trees. The amazing thing was that from far away they dominated the skyline. Here, in the valley, they were nowhere to be seen. They must be on the other side of one of the ridges, shielded from view by the valley walls.

What he could see was odd enough. The vegetation at the water's edge, and all the way to and around the newly erected buildings, formed a springy ground cover like the plants in the clearing where they had first landed on Solferino. On the sides of the valley that changed, very suddenly, to a shorter version of the umbrella plants. Josh walked over to where Amethyst was standing. She was alternately rising on tiptoe and then crouching down with bent knees.

"It's like two different places," she said, as he approached. "You'd never know from one that the other existed. Take a look for yourself."

It wasn't clear what she meant until Josh did what she was doing. The tops of the umbrella plants were pale yellow and paper-thin. All the plants were the same height, and when you stood tall enough to look over them you saw a continuous flat surface that appeared smooth enough to skate on. Only when you were very close could you see that the tops of the leaves were actually full of tiny wrinkles. Crouching down and looking underneath that layer, you entered a new world. A knee-high undergrowth formed a floor of dusky red. The ceiling was the underside of the umbrella leaves. They were not pale yellow and smooth, but dark mauve and rough on the bottom. Between floor and ceiling sat an open layer. That space was clear except for scattered umbrella plant stems, but it faded off as far as you could see in a deepening purple gloom.

Amethyst reached out and touched the underside of the nearest umbrella plant leaf. She pulled her hand back with a startled cry. "Ooh! It's hairy!"

"You shouldn't be too surprised at that." Winnie Carlson had walked over to stand behind them. "A lot of plants on Earth are the same, smooth on top of their leaves and hairy underneath. There's even a special word for it. Hairy leaves are called *tomentose.*"

"Tomentose." Amethyst put out her hand again, and this time rubbed her fingers along the underside of the leaf. "It feels like a hairy felt mat."

"And the top sides of the leaves are *glabrous,* which just means they don't have hair on them. They're also *rugose*—which is a fancy botanical word for wrinkled." Winnie added, as though ashamed at possessing special knowledge, "They made me take all these courses about plants and things, though I don't see why. I don't need any of it as a technician. That's not why I came over here, though. I wanted to tell you that dinner is ready. It's pretty simple stuff, but Rick is putting on a couple of special flourishes to it. We're lucky, finding somebody who likes to cook as much as they do."

"Hey, we ought to have a cookout." Amethyst lost interest in the leaves. "I don't mean cooking outside. I mean like a *shoot-out.* A cooking contest. Rick and Hag take on Topaz, and we see who's best."

"Who'll be the judge?" Josh asked, as they followed Winnie to the new kitchen.

"I will." Amethyst seemed thrilled at the prospect. She was quite a bit overweight, and Josh was beginning to understand why.

There were foldout seats around the little kitchen, but no one bothered with them. They took plates of food and hunkered down on the ground. The plants were springy and had leaves rough enough to be a bit uncomfortable, but people were too hungry to change their minds and seek somewhere smoother.

It was almost completely dark. The first and unfamiliar stars were out and Solferino's single satellite was rising. Bothwell Gage had described it as a big moon, but it was easy to disagree with him. To eyes used to Earth's moon, this one seemed shrunken, no more than a third the usual size. It partly made up for that by shining a brighter silver, like a newly minted coin in the deep purple sky. The evening air was pleasant, and people were beginning to relax when a strange new sound began, high up the valley sides.

"It's all right," said Winnie. "No need to be scared. That's insects—or the nearest thing that Solferino has to them. They're supposed to be edible, if you're desperate."

Before anyone's disgust at that idea could be expressed, Sol Brewster reappeared from the aircar. For a few minutes they had almost forgotten he was with them. Everyone went quiet.

"Something's come up." He walked into the middle of the group. He was so tall, above the level of the lights, that they could not see his eyes. "I've had a message from the medical center. It's not bad news, but it means I have to go back to the settlement. I have to go tonight."

The seated group all looked at each other. Just when everything was set up, and everyone was adjusting, they would have to uproot and leave. Winnie stood up and started toward the aircar. "I'd better tell the structures to pack themselves away again, and stow them in the cargo hold."

"No need for that." Brewster placed himself in her way. "You have plenty of supplies. You can stay here, settle in. I'll be back tomorrow. Then we'll carry on with the exploration."

He turned and entered the aircar, without waiting to hear what anyone might have to say. The door closed and interior lights came on. A few seconds later there was a whine of engines and the vehicle rose into the night sky. They followed its path until it was lost against the stars.

"Suppose he doesn't come back?" Ruby asked.

"He will." Sapphire went across to sit by her young sister. "He'll be back tomorrow. We'll be fine."

"But what if he isn't?" Ruby persisted.

"Then we'll pack bags and go back ourselves," Sapphire said cheerfully. "It would be a long walk, but we could do it in two days."

Josh thought of the view out of the cargo aircar window as they had flown here, and was not so sure. It might be a two-day walk if the land were level and clear. But what about the places where the plants grew chest-high, as they did close to the camp? It would not be easy to walk through them if you had to be crouched over all the time. And what about that wide, meandering river? They would have to cross it, and it might be too deep to wade.

"Would it be easy to walk?" Topaz sounded as though she was having the same thoughts as Josh.

"It might not be *easy*," Winnie Carlson said. "We could do it, though. But don't you think you should wait before you worry about being stranded? We could stay a week here if we had to, waiting for Brewster, and still have plenty of supplies left. And we're completely safe."

"What about animals?" Sig asked.

"There are certainly predators on Solferino, animals that prey on other animals, but they're the size of insects. No animal like Earth's big carnivores—lions and wolves and polar bears— ever developed here. So there's nothing on Solferino dangerous to humans."

As she spoke, a long, mournful wail sounded in the distance. It was answered by another, closer to them. And another. Suddenly the night was filled with strange, sobbing cries.

"It's just the night life, calling each other to find out what social activities are going on in the neighborhood," Winnie said. But her tone was not nearly as casual as her words, and she did not object when everyone stood up and moved toward the buildings. The structures were thin-walled and light and offered protection more psychological than real, but everyone wanted to be inside.

Josh lagged a step or two behind the others, his eye on Sig Lasker. Josh had been next to Sig, and he had seen, even if no one else had, the other's reaction when the night cries began. Sig had stood up, and instinctively reached for the right-hand pocket of his pants.

He must have some kind of weapon there. Josh thought of Topaz, calmly pulling that vicious knife from the sheath under her arm to free the bodger. Did Sig have a hidden knife, too? Or a gun, or something even more destructive?

Sig was a thug, but he seemed to have pretty good survival instincts. Maybe that was what you needed, when you camped out on the "safe" world of Solferino.

CHAPTER TEN

A **DAY** could make a tremendous difference. Yesterday morning Josh would have vowed that he'd be happy if he never saw Solomon Brewster again, and he was sure that Topaz, Sig, and the rest felt the same way.

Today, though, everyone was secretly watching the sky to the north. They were keeping an eye—a weary eye—open for Brewster and a cargo aircar that never came.

They had gone to bed early, but the moaning and a mad bubbling laughter had continued for half the night. Sometimes it was far off; sometimes it seemed to be inside the building. The knowledge that it was "just animals" didn't help. When everyone finally rose, later than usual, nobody felt rested. The morning passed in dull, lethargic waiting. Even Rick and Hag didn't have their normal wild energy and curiosity.

It was after midday when Winnie came wandering out of the camp's combined kitchen and control center. She said, without much energy or enthusiasm. "All right, people, gather round. I have a progress report for you."

Her summons did not rouse much enthusiasm, either. Winnie's previous report had been a dull inventory of food, followed by the conclusion that with the use of local plants and animals, the camp could survive for weeks or months. She had not mentioned which plants and animals. Josh had a vision of chewing on a spangleburger, or dividing up a roast leg of bodger.

"It's bad news, but it's good news, too," Winnie went on. "The bad news: Brewster won't be back today. The good news is that he'll definitely be here by tomorrow evening."

"How do you know all that?" Amethyst asked.

"I just talked to him." And, when they stared at her, "I used the camp radio. There's a standard K-band link included in the control center. I didn't know the carrier wave frequency for the compound, but when I did a band sweep I picked it up easily enough."

Sig and Amethyst nodded, as though they understood what she was talking about. Josh noticed for the first time that Sapphire was missing from the group. He said, "Yesterday Brewster told us he'd be back this morning. Did he explain why he had to stay longer?"

"Sure." Winnie became a more confident person when Brewster was away. "He says there's rough weather forecast, with high winds and heavy rain. Don't worry, though, this camp is perfectly safe."

"I thought he went back for something to do with the medical center," said Topaz. "It has some kind of problem."

"I heard him say that, too. But I know no more about it than you do. He did tell me that he'll be at the compound, and won't be going off-planet. I knew that anyway, because unless he took my lander there's no vehicle available to take him up to Solferino orbit. Even the lander can't be used for interplanetary work. He'd need a system-rated ship for that. Meanwhile, he told us to carry on and do some exploration. I'm to help organize. So let's get to it."

"There might be," Amethyst said. "We saw one the day before yesterday."

Her comment stopped Winnie dead.

"One what?"

"A ship, close to Solferino."

"You mean the one that brought me? That was yesterday, not the day before, and it's long gone. But I don't understand how you could have seen a ship—unless you mean the lander that I used for planetary arrival."

"Not your lander," Amethyst said, "or Brewster's aircar. And it wasn't the *Cerberus*, the ship that brought us here through the node."

"It had to be one of those. Foodlines has no other ships anywhere near Solferino."

"It wasn't a Foodlines ship." Amethyst looked to the others for confirmation. "It wasn't, was it? It was a Unimine ship. I'm not sure of the name, but it was the *Charles* somebody-or-other. *Charles Lyon?*"

"The *Charles Lyell*." Winnie frowned. "Then you must have been far out in the Grisel system, near Cauldron. That's the only place around here where Unimine has mineral rights. What were you doing way out there?"

"We weren't out there. We were *here*, in orbit around Solferino, and getting ready to use the lander. That's when we saw it. Their ship was *that* close to us." Amethyst held up her first finger and thumb, half an inch apart. "You could see it without a tele-

scope." She saw Winnie's puzzled expression and took it for disbelief. "I'm telling the truth, really am I."

"That's all right." Winnie nodded. "I believe you. Only, if
that's the case . . ." Her face went blank. It was another half minute
before she returned to normal and said, "Very well. Enough of
that. Let's get ourselves organized. Brewster will want a report on
what you've been doing when he gets back. Who knows? If you're
lucky, one of you will discover a valuable biological product. Then
you'll be Foodlines's heroes and heroines."

Josh could see one problem with Winnie's upbeat speech.
He wouldn't know a valuable biological product if he fell over one.
The whole point of their training program on Solferino was to
teach them that sort of thing; so far the training hadn't even
started.

Maybe Winnie had the same thought, because she was looking the group over one by one, an odd expression in her watery
blue eyes. Her nose was red. She was apparently allergic to something on Solferino, even though that was supposed to be impossible. She went on, "Your first priority is to get a general feel for the
life forms around here. Take some time to wander around in this
area and see what you can find. Don't go too far away, and be back
here in two hours. I'll try to answer questions when you get back—
though as I told Mister Brewster when I first arrived, all I know
about this world is what I've read or heard in briefings."

Josh decided that she was pulling a Sol Brewster on them:
saying she wanted to do one thing, then almost at once doing the
exact opposite. Three minutes ago Winnie had been all set to organize them. Now she was turning them loose to do whatever they
liked. Something or someone had changed her mind.

The group was dispersing. The Karpov sisters, all four of
them, were moving upstream, following the line of the valley.
Dawn was trailing along behind Sapphire and Ruby on the left
bank, while Topaz and Amethyst walked together on the right.

Josh decided that Dawn would be as safe with them as she would be with him. He was ready to explore the downstream direction, until he saw Rick and Hag moving that way. They had been giving him dirty looks ever since he had scared them during the landing. Worse than scaring them, he had made them do the unforgivable: they had acted like cowards in front of everyone—particularly the four girls. They would not forget that for a long time. It was asking for trouble to let them gang up on him away from all the others. Better to avoid them altogether.

He was turning to the steep bank that formed the valley side when Winnie called quietly, "Sig. Josh. I'd like a word with the two of you."

Josh and Sig exchanged puzzled glances. If they were in trouble, neither one knew why.

"What's the problem?" Sig asked, as they came closer to Winnie.

"I hope there won't be one." She wiped her runny nose. "Do you two agree with Amethyst, that you saw a Unimine ship near Solferino, and it was the *Charles Lyell?*"

"We saw a ship," Sig said, and Josh nodded. "It was our ship's computer that said it was the *Charles Lyell*. We didn't."

"That's good enough for me." But Winnie seemed more worried than ever. "Look, nothing has gone wrong, and maybe nothing will. I want you to help to make sure it doesn't. If anything happens to me, you must look after the others. I said this camp is safe in bad weather, because I don't want to scare the younger ones. But I don't know how safe we are. You two are the strongest, physically."

"Sapphire's older than me," Josh said. It was an indirect way of saying, hey, I don't think Sapphire will take orders from me for one second.

"I know she's older," said Winnie. "I just don't think she's right for an emergency."

"You better believe it." Sig sniffed. "She's a snaphead."

"How do you know that?" Josh thought it had been his secret.

"I've seen enough of 'em, back in the Pool. Saph's a classic case."

It was the first time that Sig had hinted at his own background, but Winnie didn't pursue it. She said, "That's going to make things even harder. There's no way she'll get snap on Solferino when her supply runs out."

"It's not just snap, it's triple-snap," Josh said. It was Sig's turn to give him a startled glance.

"Worse yet, then. She'll need lots of help." Winnie nodded. "All right. That's what I wanted to say to you. Keep your eyes open, and be ready to help the others. If anything happens to me, be even more careful."

"What sort of thing?" Josh asked.

"If I knew that, it wouldn't happen. Carry on. Do your exploring."

Dismissed, Josh turned to climb the valley slope that led to the ridge. He wanted time alone to think, but apparently he wasn't going to get it. Sig was heading in the same direction.

"What was all that about?" Sig asked, as they ducked side by side into and under the chest-high canopy of leaves.

"Beats me." Josh wondered how they were going to walk. You could travel crouched over, with the leaves touching the top of your head, but it wouldn't be easy. And something might be clinging to the underside of the leaves—worms, slugs, caterpillars, he didn't know what. He didn't even know if any of those forms existed on Solferino. But the thought was enough for him to bend over and shuffle up the hill sideways like an uncomfortable crab, looking from forest floor to forest canopy alternately with every step.

"Seems like Winnie Carlson is scared," he said. "She knows something we don't know."

"Yeah," Sig grunted. He was bent over too. "Maybe this

planet isn't as safe as Gage and Brewster make out. I don't see how they can know what's here, when no one has explored more than a little bit of the place."

It was even harder work for Sig. Being taller, he had to bend more. After three uncomfortable minutes, with no evidence that the top of the ridge was anywhere near, they paused for a breather.

"How did you know that Saph's on triple-snap?" Sig asked.

"I saw her doing it. She didn't try to hide, didn't act as though she cared. She seemed to be looking for trouble."

"Not the only one, is she?" Sig stretched upright, poking his head up through a gap in the leaves to take a rest from his doubled-over stance. His disembodied voice came back down to Josh. "You might as well know that when Rick and Hag get you on your own, they plan to beat the crap out of you."

"What do they say that I did?"

"They don't. Not to me, at any rate. I haven't asked, and I don't care. But I know how they feel. I'll say to you what I said to them: When you start to mix it, I won't take sides and I won't stop it. I got my own stuff to take care of."

"Right." Josh decided that Sig, in his own twisted way, had just done him a favor. "Thanks."

"For nothing." Sig crabbed on up the hill, and Josh followed. It was easy enough for Winnie to tell them to see what they could find, but it was hard to evaluate what they saw. A fern of virulent green grew a few feet away to the right. It was striking, it was different, and in its own way it was even beautiful. But it probably wasn't valuable, and according to Gage anything that color was likely to be poisonous. Josh moved a little farther to the left, just to be safe. In that direction, away from the direct line up the valley side, he saw a patch of light.

"Hey. There's a clearing. Up this way." He moved faster, looking forward to being able to stand up straight. With luck they would get an overview of the valley and stream, and learn where everyone else was.

He arrived a few steps ahead of Sig, and paused in surprise. He had said it was a clearing, and that was what he had expected. But it wasn't. What he found was odder than that. It was an area on the brow of the ridge, thirty yards across, where the stems of the plants were as numerous and substantial as ever. However, all their huge umbrella leaves had been removed. It was a forest of thick bare sticks, through which Grisel's ruddy light struck to illuminate the cover of ground plants.

Josh looked for the severed leaves. There was no sign of most of them, but off to his right, in the upstream direction, two had been caught between close-growing stems. They hung snagged a couple of feet off the ground. He walked across and picked up the smaller one.

It was dry and thin, but pliable enough that he could easily bend the sheet double. The hairy underside had shrunk as the leaf dried, to form a dense white mat. The colors on both sides of the leaf were much paler when it was dry.

Sig had picked up the other leaf and was turning it around in his hands. "No teeth marks. Nothing's been chewing on this."

"Even if they had, there's supposed to be nothing dangerous on Solferino."

"Yeah, sure. There's nothing dangerous. And I'm your long-lost brother, and tomorrow Winnie Carlson will beat up Sol Brewster. What's 'dangerous' mean? Animals eat each other here, they must. So who are 'they,' who say the place isn't dangerous? And how do 'they' *know?*"

Josh did not try to answer. Sig felt the same as he did, that Solferino was more of a mystery than anyone in charge was willing to admit.

He stared off along the ridge. At last, with the advantage of height and with the top layer of leaves out of the way, he could see the giant balloon plants. He tried to estimate their size, and decided they were at least fifty feet tall and almost as wide. It was hard to believe that they would survive even a moderate breeze, and strong winds were in the forecast. What would happen to them? Already, up here on the ridge, he could feel the first stirring of moving air. Did the balloon plants have some strange and unknown method of remaining in one place? Did they perhaps *deflate*, like real balloons losing air?

Lower down, Josh could make out the line of the stream. He realized now what he would have known earlier, if he had stopped to think before he started to climb. The view from a height offered no great advantage. The long reach of the stream was visible, and a narrow clear strip on each side of it. But beyond that, the jungle of umbrella plants shielded from view everything beneath them.

Downstream, he could see nothing at all of Hag and Rick. Upstream, he thought he caught a glimpse on the edge of the cleared strip of Dawn's pale yellow dress. A figure in blue was about fifty yards beyond her. He did not know who it was, or even which way she was going. All the Karpov sisters had been dressed in the same color, and without some reference object he could not estimate the girl's height.

Grisel was past zenith, and beginning its long afternoon descent. It illuminated long ribbons of high cloud. Josh turned to Sig, who was examining the top of a thick stem from which the leaf was missing.

"I'm going back. Are you coming?"

"In a minute. Something funny about this." Sig, his attention on the extreme upper end of the stem, gave a dismissive gesture. "You go on. I'll follow."

Josh started, but when he came to the place where the leaves had not been cut off he found that he was in real trouble. After a few seconds he realized his problem. On the way up, he had been uncomfortably doubled over, but because the ground ahead was rising there was always more headroom in front of him. Stooping forward helped. On the way down, the situation was reversed. When he leaned forward, his head moved to a place where the top leaves were lower. He simply could not bend far enough to stoop under the leaf layer.

There was only one answer. He had to go down *backward*, doubled over as before but now stopping every couple of steps and turning to make sure that he was not on a collision course with one of the thick stems.

As he approached the cleared area by the stream, he became too eager. He went backward faster, without looking, and an umbrella tree trunk hit him on the side of his rear end. He twisted, lost his balance, and rolled the last few feet.

He had not come down the same route as he and Sig had used to ascend. When he sat up, rubbing a skinned elbow, he found that he was about forty yards upstream from the camp. Dawn was sitting cross-legged on the opposite bank of the stream. She had taken her shoes off and was dabbling her feet in the clear water. Sapphire, by her side, was staring up at the sky.

Josh walked across to them, trying to act as if his final downhill roll had been planned. "Find anything interesting?"

Dawn didn't answer, or even look at him. That was normal enough—for Dawn. What was more surprising was Sapphire's reaction. She frowned at Josh as though she had never seen him before in her life.

"Uh?" she said.

He recognized that dead-eye expression, wide and staring with irises unmoving. Not from Sapphire, but from some of his mother's friends. This was the final stage, the surfacing after a long, hard hit.

"Sapphire!" He waded the stream, ignoring the sudden chill of the water, and snapped his fingers under her nose. "Come on Saph, come out of it. You're back at the camp. Everything is fine."

She did not speak, but her eyes rolled slowly downward from the sky until she was staring right at him. She smiled, as though everything was for the best in the best of all possible worlds.

"Oh, hell." That wasn't Sapphire. The voice came from behind Josh, and without turning he knew it was Topaz.

"Not that." She advanced to his side. "I was hoping she didn't have any more of it left."

"I guess she does. I've been trying to bring her out of it, but she doesn't seem to hear me."

"You can't—I've tried often enough. It just takes time. By the way, I found out that Amy knows, too. Now we're trying to keep it from Ruby." Topaz moved closer and put her thumb below Sapphire's left eye, drawing down the skin there so she could see the exposed white. "She's still zonked, but she is coming out of it. A minute or two more."

"Sig Lasker knows, too." Josh saw Topaz's reproachful look. "No, I didn't tell him. He recognized it for himself—he says she's a classic case."

"Maybe he'll keep it to himself, then. I can imagine how Brewster would react. You didn't let Ruby see any of this, did you?"

Before Josh could respond, Sapphire took a great shuddering breath and brought her hands up to cover her eyes. "I don't feel good. Where am I?"

"You're with us, Saph," said Topaz. "You're fine. Everything is fine. We're all here. See, here comes Amy."

Amethyst was paddling toward them along the stream, carrying her shoes. Sapphire watched her approach. "Good, good," she said vaguely. "All here. Good." She sighed and seemed to shrink in size.

"No." Josh hated to say it, but he had to. "We don't know where Ruby is. I didn't see her when I got here. I haven't seen her since you all went off along the stream."

Topaz clutched at Josh's arm, but when she spoke it was to her sister. "Saph! Where's Ruby. She went with you and Dawn. Remember? *Did she come back with you?*"

Sapphire frowned, as though someone had presented her

with a difficult abstract puzzle. Then her eyes blinked wide. She stared at Topaz and Amethyst. "Where is Ruby?"

"Oh, no." Topaz groaned. She turned to scan the banks of the stream. "If Saph left her behind . . . Ruby's only ten. She's smart, but she won't have any idea how to get back. And it will be dark in a few hours. We have to find her."

Josh nodded. He followed Topaz's gaze along the reach of the stream, empty of all movement. Behind him, an odd mewing sound had begun. Sapphire, falling hard off her snap high, was weeping for her lost sister.

They tried to get direct answers from Dawn. Josh could have told them that was useless; then he decided, good luck to them. Maybe he was wrong, and anyway what they were trying could do no harm. He left Dawn with Amethyst, while Topaz went to tell Winnie Carlson. He headed in the opposite direction, walking Sapphire along the bank of the stream. Where the vegetation grew taller, eight feet high and more, he halted.

"Here?" He thought he could see a trail, faint marks in the undergrowth.

She nodded. The last time she had been on a snap high, he had not seen her when she came down from it. Now he knew why. She was gray-faced and shivering. Normally she must hide away until she felt better. This time she couldn't. Guilt was driving her on.

"Where did you go next?" The trail was ambiguous, splitting into several possible routes. He led the way in about thirty feet, glad to be able to stand upright without bumping his head on the upper leaf canopy.

Sapphire followed. She hesitated, turning from side to side. Under the shade of the leaves it was already darker. A rustling sound above told them that the wind was rising, although under the canopy the air remained calm.

"I don't know." Sapphire's head slumped forward, her chin resting on her chest. "I'm sorry, but I just don't know. Everything looks the same and different at the same time."

It wasn't expressed clearly, but Josh knew what she meant. The jungle *seemed* different, because it was later in the day now and the sunlight sloped in at a different angle; but it also looked the same, because one group of umbrella plants was just like another. To be sure of finding your way out once you had gone deep inside, you would have to leave a trail on the ground or mark the stems of the umbrella plants.

There was no visible trail. The plants were untouched. Josh was turning to move back to the cleared stream bank when the question hit him.

"Sapphire, listen carefully. Did you mark a trail on your way in?"

"No." She wouldn't look at him, but she answered miserably, "I was high. I thought I knew what I was doing. But I didn't really think at all."

"That's all right. But if you didn't mark a trail on the way in, how did you find your way out?"

This time she stared at him. After a few seconds she shook her head. "I don't know. I think we walked a long way in, but I don't remember coming out at all. I guess we just turned around at some point, and went the other way."

"Maybe. But maybe not. Come on."

Josh turned and led the way back. The group on the edge of the stream had increased in size. Rick and Hag Lasker had returned from their explorations. They carried between them what looked like a bunch of purple grapes, except that each fruit was the size of an apple. Sig was there, too, still holding the giant severed leaf of the umbrella plant.

They were all watching Winnie Carlson, who was squatting on the ground next to Dawn and speaking to her softly. Her face was grim. The wind was picking up strength, and the sky to the west was dark. The ribbons of cloud had become fuller and lower.

Winnie stood up as Josh and Sapphire joined the group. "It's no good. I don't think I'm getting through. In fact, I'm sure I'm not." Dawn stared at the woman and through her, with clear, innocent brown eyes, as Winnie went on, "Did you have any luck, Sapphire?"

There was no suggestion of blame in her voice, but Sapphire looked away and shook her head.

"She doesn't remember," Josh said. "Give us space, everybody. Keep quiet, and don't get in the way."

He reached out his hand to Dawn, and when she took it in hers he lifted her to her feet. The others backed away. No one said a word when he started to walk hand in hand with Dawn along the stream bank. They knew that he was her cousin. They believed that he understood her, and how she thought.

He and Dawn were approaching the place where he had seen the faint trail entering the forest. He went in confidently, as though he knew what he was doing. Once under the leaf canopy he kept hold of Dawn's hand, but he let himself lag a half-step behind. She walked on. Topaz and Sig followed, gesturing the rest to stay near the stream. Josh decided that in the next two minutes he would be judged either a genius or a total idiot.

Dawn made a quarter turn and walked through a little clearing, over a patch of umbrella plants, and on past half a dozen lurid green ferns similar to the one that Josh had seen on the ridge. After that Josh saw no landmarks at all, though Dawn went on without hesitation. They walked up a small hill and down the other side. Then over another.

Josh was getting very edgy. He had been doing his best to note every change of direction, but it was easy to become confused. Grisel was hidden behind cloud, and with that and the dense cover of plant leaves, he no longer knew east from west.

What would Sig and Topaz say when they realized that he had no real idea what he was doing? It wasn't something he wanted to hear.

Dawn paused, suddenly enough that Josh bumped into her. He grabbed her to keep their balance, said "Sorry," and at once felt ridiculous. He was barging into Dawn in the middle of nowhere, then apologizing as if the situation were normal. They were lost, lost hopelessly.

And then Josh saw movement. Something gray and sleek and low was scurrying away through the stems ahead.

"Oh, no!" It was Ruby's voice. She was sitting on the jungle floor on a pile of umbrella plant leaves. "Why did you make so much *noise?* You've scared it away!"

CHAPTER ELEVEN

REJOICING at finding Ruby was cut short by the weather. As Sapphire gasped with relief and went forward to put her arms around her sister, the forest lit up in vivid purple and white. It was lightning, up on the ridge—and close. A titanic clap of thunder followed at once.

"Let's go, Dawn," Josh shouted, and hoped that she understood him. Winnie Carlson had said that the camp would be safe in bad weather—but she didn't say that you could sit out a thunderstorm in the middle of the jungle. "You, too, Sapphire. Bring Ruby with you."

"What about my spangle?" Ruby wailed.

Josh didn't answer. If he was sure of anything, it was that what he had seen running away through the wide-spaced stems was no spangle. It was too big, and too fast-moving.

He didn't wait for Dawn, but headed for Sig and Topaz. They hadn't moved, except to jump at the lightning and the violent crash of thunder. Sig turned to lead the way back, but Topaz waited for Josh and grabbed him before he could stop her. She gave him a hard hug and said, "Thanks, Josh. If anything had happened to Ruby, Saph would never have forgiven herself."

He pulled himself free, embarrassed by her show of gratitude, and muttered, "I really didn't do anything." He turned to make sure that the others were following. Dawn was a few feet away. Sapphire and Ruby were coming more slowly, largely because Ruby insisted on dragging with her a leaf three feet across.

Josh waved them on and turned back to make sure that Sig was still in sight. Dawn could probably lead them out again, if and when she chose to, but he didn't want to have to rely on that. It was suddenly very dark under the leaf canopy, except when flashes of lightning lit the gloom.

"Come on!" Sig was waving, too, at everyone. "It could rain any minute. We don't want to be anywhere near the stream when it does—have you ever seen a flash flood?"

Josh hadn't, and he wondered when Sig had. The Lasker brothers looked like perfect city scruffs, tough and rough and streetwise. On the other hand, someone had given them those peculiar and awful names, Siegfried and Hagen and Alberich. That didn't sound like gangster parents, or uneducated yobs from the unemployment Pool. How had the Laskers come to be on Solferino at all?

It was a question that would have to wait. A sudden patter of raindrops sounded on the broad leaves overhead. It stopped in a few seconds, but it felt like a warning. The real thing could start at any moment.

They emerged abruptly into the clear space that bordered the stream. Winnie was waiting for them, leaning into the wind. Its force was far stronger here, and her short hair was blowing wildly about her face.

"We found her," Sig shouted.

She raised her fist in the air, then gestured downstream.

"Go to the camp. The others are there. I'll make sure of everyone else."

Lightning again showed everything in vivid blue-white. Josh looked up, to see if he could follow its track, and found the sky already dark. But another bolt followed almost at once, and what he saw by its light brought him to a halt.

"Look!" He pointed up and along the line of the ridge that he and Sig had climbed.

The clouds were low, a few hundred feet above the ridge. Below the clouds, seeming almost to touch them, giant shapes came scudding along over the top of the hill, a dozen or more of them, all different colors, huge and round and majestically riding the wind.

Winnie stopped urging the others along. As they emerged from the forest they all halted and stared up. Three of the balloons were passing directly overhead, stately as great sailing ships. Another explosion sounded, more muted than the crash of lightning, and suddenly only two balloons were above them. Josh heard a rattle on the ground nearby, not at all like raindrops. Something hit him on top of the head, hard enough to hurt, and bounced to the ground in front of him.

He picked it up. It was brown and rounded, the size of his thumbnail. He stuffed it into his pocket. As he did so, the real rain came.

Josh was soaked instantly, as thoroughly as if he had jumped into the stream. The drops were mixed with hail, stinging his exposed face and hands. Sig was shouting, "Stay away from the stream!" and Winnie cried out, "Back to the camp and inside, all of you. Keep to the high ground!"

Josh started to run, then changed his mind. He turned. Here came Topaz, Ruby—still hanging on to her leaf—and Sapphire. Then Sig. And, last of all, sauntering despite Winnie's attempts to hurry her, Dawn.

Josh ran back, grabbed her hand, and pulled. She laughed, and ran with him. Over the soaked carpet of plants, up the incline, on into the camp's enclosed but cramped kitchen area.

Winnie Carlson came last. Josh waited at the door and slammed it shut behind her.

Outside, fork lightning flashed continuously in the evening sky. The crash of thunder added to the howl of wind and the ferocious rattle of hail on the roof. Inside, everyone was talking at once and no one seemed to be listening.

"Never again, I promise." Sapphire was so pale that she seemed bloodless. She made the sign of a cross on her heart.

"Huh. Sure." That was Amethyst, her voice bitter. "I bet it was your last one, anyway."

Sapphire said nothing, but she reached in her jacket to an inside pocket and pulled out five little tubes. She stared at the triple-snap for a few seconds, then dropped the tubes to the floor and crushed them savagely under her heel. "I'm off it. Even if it kills me, I'll stay off it."

"We'll hold you to that," Topaz said. But she went across and put her arm around her sister.

"But how could she? I mean, she's a *retard.*" That was Hag to Rick in a different conversation, shaking their heads at each other and trying to pull one of the big grapelike things off the stalk. "I mean, how could she know her way in the forest like that, when we don't?"

"Dunno. I think I'll try this, though." Rick had loosened a purple sphere.

"You can if you like." Winnie had been watching them. "Eat one, I mean. But it may not be what you think. I wouldn't be surprised if it's some sort of precursor to a larval stage."

"What's a larval stage?" Rick had the globe up to his mouth.

"The young stage of an animal." Winnie's manner was just a little too casual. "Something like, say, a caterpillar."

"Uurh! A bug!" Rick threw the sphere onto the floor. Amethyst picked it up and sniffed it curiously.

Sig had kept his eyes on Ruby, who was sitting quietly in a corner with the leaf on her lap. He pushed his way across to her. "Can I look?"

"All right. But it's mine, don't forget."

"I know." Sig gently lifted the leaf and carefully inspected the base where it had been severed from the stem. He noticed that Josh was watching, and signaled him over.

"You had the best view of anyone," he said, when Josh was in the corner with them, "except maybe for Dawn. What did you think it was?"

"The animal?"

"Sure."

"Not a spangle, no matter what Ruby says. It was a lot too big. And not a bodger, not even a small young one. This thing was *fast.*"

"A rupert, maybe?"

"That would be my guess. Though I don't know much about ruperts."

"Then somebody has a bit of explaining to do." Sig turned the leaf, so that Josh could see where he was pointing. "Remember what Bothwell Gage told us? A rupert is the smartest life form on Solferino, and it's somewhere in intelligence between a dog and a chimp."

"That's what he said."

"So look at this." Sig touched the place where the leaf had once been attached to its stem. "I noticed the same thing with the plants when we were up on the ridge. That leaf wasn't broken off, and the stems on the ridge weren't chewed through, either. Everything has been *cut,* with something like a sharp metal knife.

That's one hell of a dog or chimp, if it can make and use a knife."

He handed the leaf back to Ruby and turned again to Josh. "I want to have a talk with her, when the storm ends and things calm down a bit. And you might want to see if you can get anything out of Dawn."

Within an hour the thunder and lightning had ended. The rain stopped, the clouds cleared. It seemed not like a true ending, but a brief respite. Wind still muttered menacingly along the line of the ridge. More bad weather was on the way from the west.

While the storm raged, no one could think about eating. Now they could think about little else.

People clustered about the oven of the little kitchen, sniffing and drooling and doing everything but steal raw food. Topaz and Rick weren't really cooking, they were just heating whatever would be ready fastest.

Dawn had to be as hungry as anyone, but she didn't stay in the camp. She walked barefoot down to the stream, swollen by the rains, and stood on its bank. Josh wasn't worried much about her safety, because Dawn had grown up with Burnt Willow Creek and must have learned how to respect it in all seasons and conditions. He followed her for a different reason: he had an idea.

Sig was an insane optimist if he thought Josh might get something out of Dawn by talking to her. Dawn did talk a little, in her own fashion and with her own unknown agenda. What she did far more, though, when the time and means were at hand, was draw. In the past weeks Josh had seen beautiful sketches of everything from Burnt Willow farmhouse to the Messina Dust Cloud. Dawn's drawing wasn't just fast, it was easy and fluent and uncannily accurate. And she would sometimes draw on demand.

He didn't have a sketch pad—anything like that was back at the main compound—but he did have colored pens in his pocket. For the rest, he had to improvise. He took the big flat leaf that Ruby had carried with her from the middle of the jungle.

"Dawn." She turned as he spoke her name, and he held out pens and the broad leaf. "Will you draw for me what you saw when you were with Ruby and Sapphire, in the forest? The animal, the one that ran away."

She took the materials from him without a word. She smiled, and went on smiling for the next few minutes. What she did not do was draw. Josh waited impatiently, glancing up at Solferino's moon. Clouds were racing across its face, and they thickened as he watched. He could count on a few more minutes, no more, before the storm hit again.

And then suddenly, surprisingly, swiftly, Dawn was drawing. She had turned the leaf away from Josh, and the urge for him to tilt it and see what she was doing was almost overwhelming. He forced himself to watch and wait in silence. In a few minutes, she was done. She handed him the leaf, smiled again, and strolled away toward the camp.

He stared down in the wan light of Solferino's moon, and felt huge disappointment. What Dawn had sketched was not the sleek animal that they had caught a glimpse of as it ran away. Her drawing was of a series of leaves, each similar in shape to the one that he was holding but far smaller in size. Each drawn leaf held its own drawing within it. Sometimes it was meaningless sharp-edged marks, darts and kites that sprawled up and down and anywhere. Four of the drawings were more structured, even if they were no more informative. Two showed a sort of hut built of umbrella-plant stems and leaves, rather like the lean-to where they had found the captive bodger. The other two little leaves contained within their frames what were, without a doubt, miniature sketches of spangles. The point was made extra clear by an umbrella plant on each picture, offering a sense of scale.

Well, it had been worth a try. Josh was tempted to drop the leaf into the swollen stream. Instead he hung on to it and lugged it with him back to the camp. By the time that he had taken those forty uphill paces it was raining again. He went into the kitchen–living area, resigned to a disappointing end to a turbulent day.

"What's that you've got?" Topaz was sitting cross-legged near the door. She had been talking to Dawn, heads close together, when Josh entered.

"Not much." Josh held out the big leaf. "I was hoping she'd draw the animal for me that Ruby found in the forest, but no luck."

He eased his way past them toward the far side of the kitchen, where a big tray of food had been set out on a table folded from the wall. From the look of it, everyone else had already eaten. No knives, forks, or plates tonight—it was fingers or nothing.

Josh dug in and gobbled down mouthfuls of something like a greasy and half-cold omelette. He decided it wasn't a good idea to ask what had been used to make it.

As he ate, he surveyed the crowded room. Winnie was in earnest conversation with Sapphire, who looked like she was still on either snap withdrawal or a bad guilt trip. Probably both. Near to them Ruby, egged on by Hag and Rick, was holding a knife and under Amethyst's direction was cutting one of the big purple grapes carefully through the middle.

Ruby finally held one half out in triumph. The inside was a firm, pale-orange fruit with a brown center.

"I *told* you Winnie Carlson was kidding about the bugs," Amethyst said. "She's a lot more laid back when Brewster isn't here. I bet that's just fine to eat." The Lasker twins glared at her for a moment, but soon turned their attention to the fruit.

Rick cut a thin slice and nibbled it. "Pretty good."

Josh decided he might try a piece—once a few others had done the same, and they hadn't rolled around in agony. Rick didn't count, he would eat anything.

Josh looked toward the door. Topaz still held the leaf, and she and Dawn were crouched over it together. He noticed how similar they were in appearance—the same height, the same hair color. The other Karpov sisters were fair-haired and blue-eyed, but

Topaz and Dawn looked like sisters. Odder yet, Sig Lasker, watching Dawn and Topaz but pretending not to, could have been the older brother of either of them.

While Josh was still comparing, Topaz glanced up and gestured to him to come over.

"I've asked Dawn about this," she said as he approached, "but I want to check with you."

"She *spoke* to you? Did you, Dawn?"

"We're getting there." But it was still Topaz speaking. "What I want to know is this. Dawn draws things she has seen, you told me that. Does she also sometimes draw things *from her imagination*—things that she couldn't possibly have seen?"

"She could, if she wanted to." Josh felt an irrational need to defend Dawn. "She's not stupid."

"I know she's not." Topaz bristled back at him. "But you are." She calmed down almost at once, as Dawn laid a hand on her arm. "I'm sorry, Josh. But that's not what I asked you. I didn't say *could* she draw what she hasn't seen. I want to know if Dawn ever *does.*"

"She draws—" But then Josh had to stop and think. Every one of Dawn's drawings was something that he knew Dawn had looked at; or else, like the views of Burnt Willow Farm, it was something that he had every reason to believe she had seen. "I don't think she invents. If she draws it, I think she has actually seen it. There may be little details she leaves out, but she doesn't make things up."

"Good. Now take a look at this." Topaz held out the leaf with the drawings that Dawn had done. She pointed to two of the little sketches. "What would you say these are?"

Josh needed only one glance. "They're spangles. But Topaz, Dawn has *seen* spangles."

"I know. But look at these. Look closely." Topaz lifted the leaf so that it was no more than a few inches from his face. "See them?"

She was pointing at a faint series of lines that crisscrossed Dawn's drawing of the spangles.

"I see them. But I don't know what they are."

"Well, I do. Those are bars. That's a *cage*, Josh. Can't you see it? That's a spangle, sure, but it's a spangle sitting in a cage."

"It can't be. If there had been a spangle sitting in a cage where Dawn went, Sapphire might have been too zonked to see it—but Ruby would surely have noticed."

"That's what's bugging me." Topaz sat back on her heels in frustration. "Dawn draws what she sees, and she saw an invisible spangle in an invisible cage. Did you, Dawn?"

"*No.*" Josh's inspiration came in an overwhelming sweep, so fast and complete that he could not guess what led to it. "She didn't see a spangle in a cage. Did you, Dawn? You saw a *drawing* of a spangle in a cage. Each of these"—he pointed to the set of little drawings of leaves, neatly sketched on the big leaf—"every one of them is a *drawing of a drawing*. The original drawings were much bigger, one to a leaf. Right, Dawn?"

She was smiling benignly, nodding her head very slowly.

"But that can't be right." Topaz looked from one to the other. "You were there when Dawn found Ruby. You saw that animal, whatever it was, running away. You didn't say it was carrying a big stack of leaves."

"It wasn't. It left a stack of leaves *behind.*" In frustration, Josh crumpled the edge of the leaf that he was holding. "Don't you see, Topaz? When we found Ruby, she was *sitting* on them. We never gave the leaves another glance, and I bet Ruby didn't, either—she was interested in the rupert, not in some bunch of drawings."

"We can check easily enough." Topaz stood up. "The leaves should still be there. We'll go out tomorrow morning, and we can—unless—"

She paused and stared outside, to the rain that was falling harder than ever.

"Unless." Josh finished her thought. "Unless the ruperts do their painting with something that *washes off* in water."

CHAPTER TWELVE

THE storm continued for half the night. The animals outside were subdued by the elements, or perhaps they had gone far off to seek shelter. At any rate, they were quiet. Josh slept deeply, and awoke determined to do a more thorough exploration of the forest. Last night's discussions had taken them nowhere. Ruby had hardly noticed the piled umbrella leaves, and he hadn't been able to get a useful word out of Dawn. As for Sapphire, all she did was shake her head and look wretched.

He came outside to a drenched but sunlit world and learned

that he was not the first one up. Topaz was in the kitchen with Dawn, drawing on a pad resting on the tabletop. Sig was by her side, watching. When he saw Josh he scowled and turned away, as though embarrassed by his own interest in what mere girls might be doing.

"Did you go already?" Josh came to Topaz's side and stared down at the pad. It was the letters of the alphabet, upper- and lowercase.

"Go where?" Topaz carefully added another, the letter K. Dawn copied it, easily and accurately.

"Did you go and look for the pile of umbrella leaves that Ruby was sitting on?"

Topaz raised her dark eyebrows. "Give me a chance. It's only been light for half an hour. We didn't even eat yet. If you're so keen, why don't *you* go?"

"I think I will."

Josh was irritated as he headed out of the kitchen. Topaz probably thought she could make Dawn less autistic, but based on the evidence it was working the other way round—Topaz was becoming as inscrutable and impenetrable as Dawn.

He had gone only a couple of paces when he halted. He was facing away from the rising sun, and something had flashed bright silver in the corner of his eye. He turned to stare. It was moving fast across the sky, a stubby little dart that left behind a thin plume of white.

It could not be Sol Brewster and the cargo aircar. The shape was wrong, and the path that the ship was taking would bring it nowhere near the camp.

"Sig! Topaz! Come see this." He turned to make sure they were on the way.

They weren't—they were still staring at Dawn and that stupid pad. "Did you hear me? Hurry!"

Already the speeding ship was halfway to the horizon and shrinking in apparent size every second. Sig had finally begun to move, but with no great haste. Topaz was behind him, staring down at the pad she was holding. Dawn did not move an inch.

"Look at this, Josh." Topaz began to speak before she was fully outside. "I didn't spell it out or anything. She just did it for *herself!*" She lifted the pad and turned it.

Josh glanced at the pad impatiently. The drawing was unmistakable—it was of Topaz, smiling and in half-profile. At the bottom, in the right-hand corner, the word "Dawn" was neatly printed.

"She can write her name!" Topaz wasn't looking at Josh or where he was pointing; she was too busy grinning at the signed picture. "I bet if I keep working with her, she'll be able to read and write anything."

Normally Josh would have been as excited as Topaz, but the speeding ship was on the far horizon and the sun glint from its body was already lost.

"Never mind the picture." He pointed. "Look over there."

It was almost too late. Josh could see the dark dot of the ship, but that was because he knew exactly where to look. The plume of the exhaust was no more than a tiny white feather in the sky.

Sig and Topaz were squinting up into the bright morning glare, but he could tell from their puzzled expressions that they were missing it.

"Look at what?" Sig said. "I don't see anything except clouds."

"It was a ship. A space-rated vehicle, like the one that took us up from Earth. You can still see its exhaust."

But it was obvious that they couldn't. Sig turned from scanning the sky to stare skeptically at Josh.

Topaz seemed even more dubious. "There are no ships around Solferino at the moment," she said. "It's supposed to be another week before the medical center service ship comes back here. Brewster said so. You just imagined you saw something."

It wasn't an argument that you could win. How could you

prove that something now vanished had ever been there? Josh was ready to try anyway, with the indignant statement that he *had* seen a ship, definitely, certainly, undeniably; but a new sound from behind stopped him before he could start. Even before he turned, Josh recognized the familiar whine.

"Oh, that's what it was," Topaz said. "A *cargo aircar.*"

"No, it wasn't!" Josh began, and gave up. No matter what he said, he wouldn't get their attention now.

The aircar feathered down beside the camp. As it touched, blowing a ripple of dew across the wet ground, Ruby, Amethyst, and the Lasker twins came hurrying from the camp dormitories. They had heard the arriving car.

The whole group froze, waiting. When the door of the vehicle opened and Brewster stepped down the three-rung ladder, the tension increased. Yesterday might have been hectic and scary, but at least Brewster had not been there to push people around.

"Where are Winnie Carlson and Sapphire Karpov?" Brewster didn't waste any time on greetings.

No one answered, until Topaz provided a reluctant, "I guess they're in bed."

"Indeed?" From the tone in Brewster's voice, it might have been after midday. "If they are in bed, go and rouse them. The rest of you, get to work. We'll be breaking camp as soon as possible. I don't want to waste another minute here."

Brewster did not wait to see that his order was obeyed. He was striding back toward the aircar when Josh raised his hand and said, "Sir!"

He was surprised by his own boldness, especially when he saw the impatient glare that Brewster gave him.

"Yes? Kerrigan, isn't it? Didn't you understand what I told you? Or do you have a hearing problem?"

"I did understand, sir."

"So what are you standing about for?"

It occurred to Josh that *everyone* was standing about, wondering what Brewster was going to do to him. But he was committed.

"I think something very important happened yesterday, while you were gone."

At least that got Brewster's full attention. The pale eyebrows raised above the dark eyes. "Important in what way?"

"We found a new animal."

"That is hardly a surprise. Humans came to Solferino only three years ago. The planet must have a million species that have not yet been cataloged. What did it look like?"

"It was a rupert."

"Then it is not a new animal at all."

"But this one was different, sir. I mean, it was a different sort of rupert. I mean . . ."

Josh knew what he wanted to say, but his tongue was tripping over itself. He started to explain what had happened, then realized he could not tell Brewster that Ruby got lost because her sister was drugged out of her mind. He tried to edit what he was saying as he spoke, and heard things coming out choppy and illogical. No one else helped him out, and it was a real relief to see Topaz returning with Sapphire and Winnie Carlson in tow. Winnie looked awful, pale-faced but dark under the eyes, and yawning as though she had been awake all night.

Brewster turned on them. "Ah. It is nice of you to favor us with your presence. I hope you are enjoying your Solferino vacation." But then it was at once back to Josh.

"So, Kerrigan, let me get this clear. An animal was discovered in the forest. Not by you, and you did not obtain a clear view of it. But despite the fact that you did not see it, you believe that it is intelligent. Who did see it?"

Josh didn't want to do it, but he had no choice. While Sapphire looked pure murder at him, he pointed to Ruby and Dawn.

Brewster's eyebrows went up farther. "You saw this animal?" he said to Ruby.

She nodded without speaking.

"Describe its appearance." And, when Ruby hesitated, "What did it look like?"

"It was gray, and a bit smaller than me. It looked very cuddly."

"Did it do anything?"

"Yes. It stood there, and it *stared* at me while I stared at it. It had little beady eyes, like black pebbles."

"I don't care what it looked like. Did it act *intelligently?* Did it have tools with it, or wear clothing? Did it try to speak?"

"Oh, no. Nothing like that."

"I see." Brewster turned back to Josh. Everyone else was silent. Hag and Rick were grinning at his misery, while Winnie Carlson, the only one who might have been able to help, stood with her head bowed and her eyes staring at the floor in front of her feet.

"Well, Kerrigan," Brewster went on. "You didn't see the animal, and the only person who did see it detected no signs that it might be intelligent. So how did you reach your own conclusion? By mind reading? By divine inspiration?"

"No, sir." Josh knew this was only going to get worse, but he could think of no way to stop it. "It was the pictures, sir."

"The rupert drew pictures?"

"Yes. Well, I mean, no, not exactly. Dawn drew them. She drew the pictures. Pictures of pictures that the ruperts had made."

"No gibbering, if you please." Brewster turned to Dawn, but she was not looking at either him or Josh. She was staring at the stream, as though no one else were around.

Brewster returned his attention to Josh. "So she *told* you about the pictures. Of course. But naturally, since she talks to no one but you, there is no way of checking what she said, is there?"

"She didn't actually *tell* me. I realized . . ." Josh didn't try to finish the sentence. Under Brewster's questioning, everything that he said sounded ridiculous. He had trouble believing it himself.

But last night, and early this morning, it had seemed obvious that the ruperts must be intelligent.

"I think that's more than enough nonsense for one day." To Josh's relief, Brewster seemed to have done with him. "I'm going to say a couple more things, and then we'll go to work and get out of here. I have a low tolerance for nonsense, as you will learn. And it's nonsense to give me a far-fetched story about an intelligent rupert, when every survey of Solferino shows there's no such thing. It's not just the surveys. It's common sense, too. The smartest animals are all carnivores and omnivores—either they have to develop brains to outthink their prey, or they have to be able to find something edible where other animals can't. That's why a sheep doesn't have one-tenth the intelligence of a wolf, and why humans can live just about anywhere on Earth. But every animal on Solferino big enough to have a thinking brain is a herbivore, and it just eats plants. You don't need to be clever to catch a plant. And don't get confused because an animal shows some of the signs of intelligence. Did any of you ever see a beaver lodge?"

There was a general mutter, which Brewster took for agreement. "So you know that it seems impossible for an animal to build that lodge without being very smart," he went on. "But a beaver isn't *intelligent*, it's still just an animal. Same for a beehive, or a termite colony. Very complex, and you might think whatever made it had to be intelligent. But we don't go around saying bees and termites are intelligent. We know better. Same with ruperts. It's also nonsense to say that you saw a rupert which had eyes, when everyone knows that ruperts navigate using ultrasonic signals, the same as bats.

"I told you when you arrived, if you take your orders from me you'll be all right. But I go away for a day, and what happens? With no one in control, even when there's supposed to be"—he stared hard at Winnie Carlson—"you start doing crazy things and thinking crazy thoughts, before my vehicle is off the ground."

He glanced at his watch. "All right, that's enough wasted

time. I want this camp *clear*, so I wouldn't know we've been here. And I want it done in fifteen minutes or less. If you are still here then, you'll wish you weren't."

Josh wasn't much impressed by Brewster's arguments about the ruperts. All the man had done was say how intelligence had developed *on Earth*. Why couldn't it have developed for quite different reasons on Solferino? And Josh was pretty sure that beavers only ate plants, and they were one of Earth's smartest animals. He also wanted to ask about the ship that he had seen, but only a total fool would mention it now. He had even less evidence for that than for the smart rupert. As they cleaned up the camp and the buildings folded themselves away, he hunted for the great leaf on which Dawn had done her drawings. There was no sign of it.

He gave up after two minutes, when he noticed that Brewster had his eye on him. He joined in the general mad scramble to clear the camp area, and twelve minutes later he was boarding the cargo aircar with the others.

He considered where to sit. He didn't want to be anywhere near Brewster—nobody did, though Winnie Carlson had no choice. Brewster had summoned her to sit next to him, probably to tell her what a fool she was to let the camp get out of control. There would be no words of praise for bringing everyone safely through last night's storm. That wasn't Brewster's style.

Josh was heading for the rear seat, until he noticed that Rick and Hag Lasker were already there. He was sure they were still out to get him, and just biding their time. This wasn't likely to be their chosen time and place, but why take risks?

He settled for the third and middle row. Sig and Sapphire were already there. Josh sat down next to her, and was amazed when she said, "Thanks, Josh. For not telling how Ruby got lost. And I'm sorry for what I said about you and Topaz. That was really dumb, and I wouldn't normally have said it. Topaz is big enough to look after herself."

Josh looked doubtfully at Sig, but Sapphire went on, "It's all

right, Sig knows about my problem. It's hard to keep secrets in a
group like this, even when you're not zonked out of your mind. I
guess everybody knows, except Brewster. I hope he never finds
out."

"If he does, it won't be from me or my brothers." Sig jerked
his head toward the rear of the aircar. "I told those two they're
dead if they ever even hint at it. The one to worry about is Winnie. She's all right when Brewster's not here, but once he shows up
she turns into Jell-O. I bet if he asked her, she'd spill her guts to
him about Ruby and everything. I don't know why she doesn't
stand up to him. I mean, she works for Foodlines headquarters.
She doesn't have to take his crap."

Sapphire shook her head. "It's not that easy. She's scared of
him. So am I."

There was a pause, then Sig said, "Yeah. Me, too. He's so big.
He could probably take on the lot of us, all at once—and beat us."

The aircar was lifting off. Everyone was quiet until they were
safely in the air and a few hundred feet up. Then Sapphire said,
"It's not just size. My dad was a real little guy, smaller and lighter
than me."

"So how come he beat you so bad?" Sig asked. "You're pretty
big, and you look strong. How come you couldn't stop him hurting you?"

Josh stared. Did everybody know every last thing about
everybody else? But the question didn't seem to surprise Sapphire
at all.

"I didn't know the answer to that question then," she said
thoughtfully, "but I guess I do now. He was my dad, you see—I
couldn't hit him hard. When he was hitting Ruby, I pulled him away
from her with everything I had; but when he went for me, I held
back. And *he* didn't hold back at all. You know the worst piece? If
it happened all over again, I still don't think I'd be able to hit hard.
How can you hit somebody you love—even if they don't seem to
love you?" She rubbed her fingers along the left side of her jaw.

"It doesn't show," Sig said gently. "I didn't notice 'til I was told." And then, before she could ask, "It was Topaz. But Amy told me the same thing later. You guys really look out for each other."

"Someone has to do it." Sapphire produced a sound between a laugh and a sniffle. "And you're no different. You watch out for Hag and Rick."

There was a long pause, as though she was waiting and Sig was thinking something over. It occurred to Josh that, despite the people in front and behind, this was the most private moment since leaving Earth. No one else would hear what was being said above the sound of the engines.

"How much do you know about us?" Sig asked at last.

"Not much. I know the three of you ran away, and somehow your parents agreed that you could come out here instead of going back home. Were you beat up, like us? Or did your mother dump you, like Josh?"

The shock of that hit Josh so hard and so quick that he felt his stomach lurch. Was this what everyone thought about him and his mother? Aunt Stacy had said the same thing.

And the worst part—were they right?

"Nothing like that at all." Sig bunched up his right fist and stared at it. "I was the one who wanted to hit somebody, you bet I did, but we weren't treated badly. Just the opposite, most people would say. Do you know who my parents are?"

Josh and Sapphire looked at each other, and shook their heads.

"Well, I'll tell you," said Sig. "My parents are Dietrich Lasker and Emma Mascani."

"That means nothing to me." Sapphire turned to Josh, who shrugged and said, "Me neither."

"Good." But Sig scowled. "They never hit us, but they're the reason, no matter what Brewster makes us do on Solferino, it's better than being back on Earth. No one here has heard of my par-

ents. When I was ten, I thought everybody on the planet knew
them."

"But who are they?" Josh was glad to be in a situation where
ignorance was better than knowing something.

"Dietrich Lasker is the most famous baritone singer in the
world. I've heard people, talking about him, say he is the best for
a century. My mother, Emma Mascani, was a child prodigy as a pi-
anist. She was giving public recitals when she was seven. She still
plays, but nowadays she's better known as a composer. She may be
the world's greatest composer.

"They have six children." From Sig's tone of voice, he might
have been discussing total strangers. "Three boys, three girls. Split
down the middle, you might say. And split down the middle in
more ways than that. My sisters are like my mother and father.
They have perfect pitch, and they can remember a piece of music,
with full harmony, after hearing it once. And me and Rick and
Hag—did you ever hear any of us sing?"

Sapphire and Josh shook their heads.

Sig laughed. "You're lucky. Not one of us can carry a tune—
not even close. It took years and years before my parents would
admit it. They gave us lessons, and they even had medical tests
done on us. They couldn't understand how anyone who was asked
for a C sharp minor chord couldn't just sing the notes, one after another. They gave all of their children names from Wagner operas—
I guess they thought we might sing in them one day, or at the very
least worship the music the way they do.

"When they finally had to admit the truth, they didn't know
what to do with us boys. Their families and friends were all musicians. When my mother said, 'Siegfried is not musical,' I could see
the misery on her face. Or one of Father's friends would say, 'This
looks like a beautiful new piece. Alberich and Hagen, why don't
you sing the soprano and alto parts, and your father and I will sing
tenor and bass?' And Father would shake his head and say, 'Alberich and Hagen do not sight-read,' the way he might have said,

'Alberich and Hagen strangled their baby-sitter when they were four years old.' I think he would rather have been able to say that. "They loved us, in a sad way, but we knew how ashamed they were of us. Nothing that we ever did could change that. We stood it until six months ago. Then one afternoon, when a whole bunch of famous musicians were coming to dinner, we ran for it.

"Of course, we were picked up eventually, but only after we'd had four months living on the streets. Very educational, the streets are. We knew we'd have to go home eventually, so we did our best to learn to act like brainless thugs."

"You certainly succeeded," Sapphire said. But she spoke with a smile in her voice.

"Thanks. And I thought that here on Solferino we were losing the knack. But we had it all right when we went home. Mother and Father took one look at us and that was *it*. When an opportunity came along to send us here, they took it. They said they didn't want to do it. But we wanted it more than anything in the world. Rick and Hag and me, we absolutely jumped at the chance. And here we are."

Sig and Sapphire turned to Josh. He was convinced that they were going to ask him for the horrible details as to how he came to be on Solferino. Instead, Sapphire said, "You know Dawn a lot better than we do. Are you really convinced that she and Ruby saw some kind of intelligent rupert?"

"Yes. But I'll never persuade Brewster."

"Not without an actual animal sitting in front of him," said Sig. "And maybe not even then. Saph, why don't you ask Ruby what she saw?"

"I did. She doesn't know about it being smart, but she swears that it had eyes. And Topaz agrees with Josh, Dawn was drawing what she had seen."

"So you believe in it?"

"Yes. For me, the little black eyes confirm it. Ruby wouldn't make up something like that."

"Good. I believe it, too."

"Then why didn't one of you say something?" Josh burst out. "Instead of leaving me there for Brewster to roast."

"Do you think it would have made any difference to him, if we'd said we agreed with you?" Sapphire asked gently.

"No. But it would have made a difference to *me*. It would be nice to have somebody suggest I'm not a total idiot."

"Maybe. But it would also have dragged the whole thing on a lot longer. And we don't think you are a total idiot."

"But that's not the real issue, is it?" Sig glanced around, to make doubly sure no one could overhear. "That's not why I didn't want to make a big deal of it with Brewster. We all three think there may be intelligent aliens here on Solferino. If we're right, that's the most important discovery in the whole of history. The real question is, what are we going to do about it?"

"Isn't that Brewster's job?" asked Sapphire.

"You might think so. But I've got an idea about that. I believe that all the rules would change if it turned out there was true non-human intelligence here. Foodlines would have to operate completely differently. Brewster wouldn't be king of the castle any more, and he'd probably be kicked out of here."

"I'm not going to weep about that," Sapphire said.

"Nor am I. But it explains why he doesn't want to think about the idea of intelligent ruperts, and why he's behaving so weird."

"But it doesn't." The others stared at him, as Josh went on. "He was being weird long before I mentioned about the animal that Ruby and Dawn found. You said it yourself, Sig. First he tells us we'll be at the compound for days and days. Then before we know where we are, we're on the aircar and dropped off at the camp. He leaves us to ourselves. Then he's back, and now it's the camp that's the wrong place for us, and we have to rush back to the compound."

"Josh is right, you know," Sig said. "Brewster has been peculiar from the start."

"And there's one other thing." Josh decided he might as well go all the way. "The ship. You came too late to see it, Sig, but I saw it very clearly. It was real, and low, and it wasn't an aircar or even a lander. I wouldn't be surprised if Brewster knows all about that ship, but he chooses to deny it."

"But why?" Sapphire asked. "Why any of it?"

"One thing at a time," said Sig. "We haven't answered my first question. What are we going to do with the idea that some of the ruperts may be intelligent?"

"We can't do a thing." Josh looked to Sapphire for confirmation. "We're traveling at four hundred kilometers an hour, and we're going away from the place where we found the ruperts."

"No argument with that." Sig nodded. "So we have only two alternatives: Either we find smart ruperts near the compound, or we have to go back to the place where we found them the first time. That means we have to make two sets of plans."

The way Sig said it, for a moment Josh actually thought it might be possible. Then he decided that Sig was out of his mind.

But it was a fine, attractive madness.

CHAPTER THIRTEEN

BREWSTER had no intention of letting anyone rest. He was giving orders almost before the cargo aircar had touched down. There was no time for planning return trips to the Barbican Hills, or anything else.

Josh was ordered to report to the communications and computer center in five minutes and help Winnie Carlson. That gave him just long enough to drop off his gear in his bedroom cubicle. He was throwing his bag on the floor and shoving it under the bed when he noticed a slight difference in the way his clothes and personal belongings were laid out on the little cabinet at the end of the bed. It wasn't much, and no one else would have seen it, but Josh had become very precise in the years-long wandering with his mother. In their monthly—sometimes weekly—moves from one apartment or hotel to another, the layout of his own possessions was one of the few constants of life.

Not now. The little framed image of his mother in the role of Titania was facing slightly away from the head of the bed. His spare toilet kit lay between his socks and his shirts, instead of behind them. His pants were not folded quite as usual.

But who in his right mind would come in and fiddle with pictures and toothbrushes? He suspected Rick and Hag, but he couldn't see how or why.

Josh rearranged his things as they ought to be and puzzled over them, until he realized that five minutes and more must have passed. He rushed to the building that housed the communication center and hurried inside.

Winnie Carlson was not in the room, but Rick and Hag Lasker were. By the time Josh realized they were the only people present, the twins were moving between him and the door.

They didn't say a word to him or to each other, but they worked together as if by instinct to cut off his retreat.

Josh didn't waste time on speech, either. He had never thought he would be thankful for all those lonely hours on the streets when he could not face a lonely apartment, but that experience might pay off now. He had been a bystander to plenty of gang action, and he knew a threatening move when he saw one.

He didn't turn or take his eyes off them, but retreated as fast as he could until his back was against a blank part of the wall. Maybe they were just out to humiliate him and smack him around a bit to show who was boss. And maybe they wanted to go a lot further than that.

He stood and waited. They would have learned a lot, too, in four months on the streets. Everything could be a weapon, fists and feet and knees and skull and teeth. The best thing Josh had going for him was that he had seen all that, but they didn't know it. In their eyes he was a farm hick.

They came in together, as he had expected. Rick swung a punch at Josh's head, at the same time as Hag tried a kick. They didn't think he'd be able to handle both at once, and they were right. Josh turned, so that Rick's fist just brushed the side of his head; but Hag got in a solid boot high on his left thigh.

It hurt, but that wasn't the worst part. Josh felt his leg muscle stiffen and his knee go wobbly. One more kick like that on either of his legs and he'd be as rigid as a tree. They would chop him down at their leisure.

As Hag kicked again, Josh hopped to one side and grabbed the leg as it swung wide of him. He twisted as hard as he could, but at the same moment Rick put an armlock on his neck. All three were off balance. No one let go and they staggered sideways together, to run into and knock over a tall blue cabinet standing along the wall a few feet away. Still locked together, they all fell squarely onto the overturned unit. There was a sound of breaking plastic and twisting metal.

They let go of each other, scrambled free, and stared at the flattened mess they had left behind.

"*Schütz!* We're in trouble now." Rick turned to Josh. "It's your fault, you brainless turd. You pulled us over onto it."

"*Me!* Get screwed. If you hadn't started on me in the first place we wouldn't have been near it."

"You're as much a retard as your idiot bimbo cousin."

"You leave Dawn out of this. At least she knows how to sing. Give us a tune, *Alberich*—if you can."

"Our m-mother didn't d-dump us." Rick turned white, and he could hardly speak. "She didn't ab-bandon us with s-some whore of an aunt—"

"—who couldn't stand you, either," Hag added. "So she shipped your fat hide out here."

They had been getting louder. Fists were clenched and they were all set to go at it again when Winnie Carlson walked in.

She took one look at the wreckage on the floor. "What the hell do you think you're doing?"

"Nothing." They all spoke in unison.

"Fine. Then you won't mind if I go and get Brewster, to show him what happens when you do nothing."

The three exchanged grimaces, suddenly in agreement. "No need for that," Josh said, and Hag added, "We were just fooling around. We didn't mean to smash anything. You don't have to tell Brewster, do you?"

"We'll see. I must say, I'd rather not bring him in if I don't have to. He'll blame me for getting here late. First things first. Is anyone hurt?"

"No."

"No."

"Oh, no." The denials were prompt and vigorous. Rick stopped rubbing his shoulder, while Josh tried to stand naturally on his bruised leg. Hag muttered, "We can fix the damage."

Winnie moved to examine the squashed case. "Don't bet on it. This unit has had its day. The big question is, what have we lost from the system?"

She went across to the main console and began to call up system components, one after another. The others could only watch her facial expressions and hope that she knew what she was doing.

At first they were encouraged. Winnie said, "You may be lucky. That whole unit was only second-level backup. We haven't lost anything." But then she began to frown. "I don't understand this. Whole segments of memory have been wiped clean, and half the system modules are sending failure messages. Were you fooling around at the console before you started to fight?"

Josh hadn't been present, but Rick and Hag's surprise and instant denial seemed genuine. "We didn't touch anything over here," Hag said.

"Cross our hearts," added Rick.

"Well, someone certainly did." Winnie called up a display. "See these? None of the units shown is working. And it's not just processor failure. Here's another list. These are databases—nothing to do with the ones you damaged, these are supposed to be in primary storage. We should be able to access data from any of them. But we can't. Actually, I'm being told the data themselves don't even *exist.*"

The list didn't mean anything to Josh. It had uninteresting labels, like ROSTER OF SOLFERINO PERSONNEL, PERSONNEL MEDICAL RECORDS, PERSONNEL TRAVEL RECORDS, and SOLFERINO PERSONNEL ASSIGNMENT AND DUTIES. Even less relevant to anything were entries named FOODLINES CHARTER FOR THE EXPLORATION AND DEVELOPMENT OF SOLFERINO: TERMS AND CONDITIONS, and one called LEGAL INTERFACES AND INTERCORPORATE AGREEMENTS CONCERNING CONGLOMERATE RIGHTS AND RESTRICTIONS IN THE GRISEL STELLAR SYSTEM. Attached to every item on the list was a notation: DATA FILE CORRESPONDING TO THIS LABEL DOES NOT EXIST.

Winnie Carlson did not seem to share Josh's view as to what was important. She was making a note of places where data tables were missing.

"It's worse than it looks," she said. "I can't reach the backup files, either. Those data are just plain *vanished.*"

"Did we do that?" Hag asked.

"No, you didn't. Those were different files entirely. And it's impossible to ruin a whole system by smashing a piece of peripheral storage hardware." Winnie was puzzling again over the list that she had made. "But why are there no backup files? Normally, everything has a second copy in case the original is accidentally destroyed. Not this time. It's unbelievably bad luck to lose processor capacity and data files, all at once. In fact, it's such unbelievably bad luck that I don't believe it."

She stood, staring vacantly at the list, until Hag said, "Do you have to tell Brewster?"

"Soon. But not yet." Winnie came out of her trance. She pointed to the ruined data unit. "You get that out of the way. Dump it where Brewster won't see it. I'll reconfigure the system to operate without it, make a backup copy of the data, and see what else is out of action. For the moment, you say nothing to Brewster. All right?"

It was more than all right. Josh felt the same relief as he saw on Rick and Hag's faces, at the same time as a part of his brain asked a question of its own: *Why was Winnie Carlson doing this? Was it just to protect them from Brewster's anger?*

That didn't seem plausible; but he could think of no better answer as he and the Lasker twins packed the broken unit into a big trash bag. While they waited for Winnie to tell them they could take it away—she was still messing around at the computer console—he massaged his sore thigh.

Rick saw him doing it. "We got you good, eh?"

"No, it's nothing. How's your shoulder?"

"What shoulder?"

"That will do." Winnie swung around in her seat. "Whatever it was, the three of you have had it out with each other. If you want me to forget this, you'd better do the same."

"It's forgot already," Hag said. He lifted the bag with the broken storage unit inside it. "We can put this outside the fence, far enough away so nobody's going to find it. But what if Brewster sees us going and asks what we got?"

"He won't." Winnie stood up. "I'll make sure I have his attention while you get out of the way. Give me three minutes, then you can head out of here. Beyond the fence is fine, but make sure you stash it in a place where nobody will find it. I want you back in half an hour. There's real work for you to do here. Smashing things doesn't count."

She left. "I had her wrong," Rick said. "I was sure she's so scared of Brewster, she'd run right off and tell him what we did."

"She doesn't seem as afraid of him as she was." Hag hefted the bag. "Maybe she's changed."

That was Josh's opinion, too. He even thought he knew the exact moment that the change took place. It was at the camp, when Amethyst said they had seen a Unimine ship—not near the far-off mining world of Cauldron, but in low orbit around Solferino.

But what was the big deal about that? Even though Foodlines had exclusive development rights for Solferino, surely other ships were free to orbit the planet.

"Three minutes." Hag interrupted Josh's thoughts. "She said, give her three minutes. Is it that long yet?"

"Must be." Rick moved to the door and looked out, to check that no one would be watching when they ran for the fence. "Come on. Let's go."

No one seemed to be around, but they all felt edgy until they were at the gate and Josh could swing it closed behind them.

"How far?" Hag asked. "She didn't say how far."

"She said put it where nobody will find it," Rick said. "Hey, I know. The unit would sink in water if it wasn't in that bag. Let's put it in the bodger pool."

"Great."

The twins glanced at Josh to see if he agreed.

He nodded. "Perfect place. Only trouble is, it's way over on the other side of the compound."

"Think we should go back through?" asked Hag.

"Are you crazy?" Rick started to walk, following the line of the fence as closely as he could. "Winnie didn't say she could hold Brewster forever. We'll go round."

It sounded easier than it was. The umbrella trees, fighting for sunlight, pushed their stalks to within half a foot of the fence. Something in the soil, or a field projected by the fence itself, prevented them from growing closer. However, as Rick and Josh quickly proved, a human, even one without a trash bag full of equipment, could not squeeze between the fence and the rigid tree stems.

They had to move farther out into the forest and make a much bigger circuit around the compound. There was no chance of getting lost, because the fence was always visible on their right. There was also no danger that they would overshoot, since they must eventually reach the second gate. But Josh, struggling along in purple gloom through the wilderness of trees, realized that without the guiding fence it would be easy to become completely lost within fifty yards of the compound.

With that thought came another. Sig had suggested two alternatives: Either make another trip to the Barbican Hills, or find a smart rupert close to home.

The first idea seemed completely impossible. It meant stealing the aircar, flying it (which none of them knew how to do) back to the campsite, and locating a rupert in a forest where everyone except Dawn seemed to get lost in the first five minutes.

Now he realized that the second idea was just as bad. Not because there was no such thing as an intelligent rupert. He still believed the evidence of what Dawn had drawn, and he was more and more convinced that no matter what Brewster might tell them, humans didn't know one thousandth of what there was to know about Solferino. This was a whole world, and humans had been here for only three years.

And not because there were no smart ruperts in this area. The odds were the other way round. If their party could plop itself down at a random place in the Barbican Hills and meet smart ruperts on their first outing in the forest, they must be in many places. They might be shy, and they might be nocturnal, so they had not been discovered in the planetary surveys. Maybe only a few of them were intelligent. But you had to find a rupert, before you could know any of that.

The difficulty was a practical one. In their spare time—and Brewster had made it clear how little of that there was going to be—they had to explore far from the compound without becoming lost; they had to discover a colony of smart ruperts; and they had to return with a specimen. It all must be done secretly, without Sol Brewster or Winnie Carlson having any idea what was going on.

Josh didn't see how it could happen.

And then, suddenly, he did. But before anything could be done he would have to find Sapphire, and obtain her permission. And to get that—Josh was learning—he would first have to convince Sig Lasker. Saph trusted Sig's judgment. Any way you looked at this, it wasn't going to be easy.

Josh was blundering along, deep in his own thoughts, following Rick and Hag and relying on them to know where they were going. He stopped when they did—suddenly—and stared around him. "Is this the place?"

"You tell us." Hag had dropped the sack. "We passed the gate all right, and it looks like the same cleared area down there, though the plants have started to grow back. But there's no sign of the bodger."

"It must have wandered away," said Josh. "You didn't leave it tied up."

"I know. But where's the lean-to?"

They walked together into the clearing. Josh found an upright tree stalk in the right place, with chafe marks from a rope around it; but the leaves and stems of the tentlike lean-to had been scattered far and wide.

"Do you think animals did it?" asked Rick.

"Nah." Hag was on hands and knees, inspecting the ground. "Not unless they could untie knots. The rope has gone, and it was artificial fiber—not the sort anything could chew through. Look at this, though." He stood up holding a piece of rope about six inches long, frayed at one end but severed cleanly at the other. "Someone did that with a knife."

"Brewster," Rick said. "Has to be. But why would he come down here and take the place apart?"

"Looking for something?" Josh suggested. "I noticed that somebody had been rummaging through my stuff, back in the compound. I thought it might have been one of you."

"Not guilty," said Hag, and they went on down the slope to the stagnant purple pool. Hag hurled the broken data unit into the middle and they watched it sink out of sight.

"Nothing makes sense any more," Rick said morosely. "You know what I think? Winnie Carlson didn't send us out here to get rid of that thing because she wanted to help us. She did it because she wanted us out of the way, so she could do something by herself in the computer center."

"Like what?" asked Josh.

Rick shook his head and they headed back up the slope. "I have no idea. I'm just saying, I don't trust *her* to do us favors, any more than I trust Sol Brewster."

At the gate they paused.

"You worry too much," Hag said to his brother. "So here's one more thing for you to worry about. What do we tell Brewster we've been doing, if we go through—and he's waiting for us on the other side?"

They opened the gate cautiously and slipped through. As soon as they were within the compound they found that they could not see Brewster—but they could hear him. He was angry, and he didn't mind who knew it.

Rick was ready to head right back through the gate, but Josh grabbed his arm. "Not us," he said. "Listen."

"You incompetent, flat-faced halfwit." The roar blew across

the compound at gale force. "You present yourself as a qualified maintenance technician—something I never asked to be sent—and you ruin the first thing you put your fat soft hands on. If you don't know what you're doing, the least you can do is leave things alone."

"He's chewing out Winnie," Josh said softly. "We'd better stay clear."

But they found themselves edging toward the computer center anyway, as though an invisible string was quietly pulling them along. The other members of the training group were already there, listening in fascinated silence. Josh moved to stand next to Topaz.

"What did she do?" he whispered.

"Shhh." She put a finger to her lips. "You'll hear."

"Sir, I was not the cause of the computer problems." Winnie's voice was polite and lifeless. All trace of personality seemed to vanish from her when she faced Sol Brewster. "Also, I cannot understand how such a situation could possibly have occurred."

Rick and Hag stared at each other, but Josh shook his head. "We're all right," he said softly. "She's not going to say anything about us."

"I am simply reporting," Winnie continued woodenly, "on a situation which I feel you need to know about. I have here a complete list of hardware component failures."

"I don't want a damned *list*. I'm no data technician. I want to know the effects of what you've done."

"I did not do it, sir. But I can tell you the consequences of what has happened. We have lost a great deal of data. I believe that copies of most of it will exist back at Sol-side headquarters, but the equipment loss is more worrying. Our long-distance communication modules are out of action."

Josh and the others stirred uneasily, but Brewster simply said, "Rubbish!"

"I'm afraid it's true, sir. We can still send messages to an aircar or an orbiter, but we will not have through-node contact until the next Foodlines vessel arrives at Solferino from Earth. Do you wish to confirm that for yourself?"

The group outside the communications building waited tensely for Brewster's reply. Instead, he was suddenly looming before them in the doorway.

"Are you all enjoying your vacation?" He surveyed them angrily. "I heard you muttering out here. It was my impression that you had been given assignments. If you think differently, stay here and I'll give you more than you bargained for. Otherwise, get the hell out of the way and stop listening to what's none of your business."

It was the tone, even more than the words. They scattered like nervous rabbits.

"What about us?" Hag said as they hurried away. "Our duties are supposed to be in there with Winnie Carlson."

"And it *is* our business, what he's talking about with Winnie," added Rick. "It's *all* our businesses if off-world communications are out."

"Fine," Josh panted. They were moving as fast as anyone could, without actually running. "Go back, then, and tell him that. Be my guest."

It was no surprise that neither Rick nor Hag accepted his invitation.

CHAPTER FOURTEEN

WHEN the flight from Sol Brewster's anger ended, the members of the trainee group returned to the complex of buildings. They acted nonchalant—but no one went near the computer and communications center.

Rick and Hag headed into their dorm. Josh kept going and entered the next building, where the laundry and a little recreation area and gym were located. He had seen Sig go in there and was hoping for a private word, but to his disappointment Topaz was already inside. Sig had moved to sit on a gym bench next to her.

Josh decided he would speak anyway. He pulled a chair across, sat down facing them, and said to Sig, "You remember you agreed that Dawn and Ruby saw a smart rupert, but that Brewster wouldn't believe it unless he saw it for himself?"

Topaz's eyes popped, but Sig nodded casually enough and said, "Yeah, that sounds about right."

"Did you think of any way that it could be done—catch a rupert, I mean?"

Sig shook his head. "Not a chance. If ruperts are as shy as everyone says, it would be impossible."

"Right. For you, and me, and Topaz, that's true. But I think Dawn could do it. You haven't seen her with animals. She's wonderful."

Topaz said, "I thought you were just telling us ruperts are too smart to be thought of as animals."

"You know what I mean. I'd like Dawn to have a chance to find one. But she'd need somebody with her."

"You've heard Brewster's opinion," Sig said. "He'd tell you it was a waste of time, and he'd never let you go."

"I wasn't thinking of me."

"Who, then?"

"The only one who's not going to be given heavy duties, apart from Dawn, because she's too young. I was thinking of Ruby. And I was thinking you might help persuade Sapphire that it would be all right for her to go with Dawn."

Sig didn't have a chance to answer, because Topaz was way ahead of him. "Are you out of your mind? Saph spends her life trying to make sure the rest of us don't get into anything dangerous. Now you want Ruby to go off into the wild woods, on a planet humans know almost nothing about, and try to catch an animal we know even less about."

Josh felt like an idiot, especially when Sig raised his eyebrows and added, "Couldn't have put it better myself. It's the last thing in the world that Saph needs, considering what she's going through at the moment. She feels like shit. Josh, you get the dumb-idea-of-the-week award."

It only helped a little when Topaz reached out, patted Josh's knee, and said, "I'm sorry. I think the ruperts are intelligent, too, and I think it's really important to prove it. But not this way. Could Dawn go by herself? She's a lot smarter than people give her credit for. She's learning her letters, even if it's slow work. If she keeps it up she'll soon be able to read and write."

"She is bright, in her own way." But it was Josh's turn to feel uneasy. "Maybe Dawn would be all right in the woods alone. I'm afraid to let her go, though."

"We're all protecting somebody," Topaz said. "With Sig it's the twins, with Saph and me it's Ruby. With you, it's Dawn."

As Topaz was speaking, Dawn herself came into the room from outside. She smiled at hearing her name, but said nothing. She seated herself on the floor between Sig and Josh, reached up, and handed Josh her sketch pad.

It showed a landscape, a distant view of the Barbican Hills as seen from the departing cargo aircar. He didn't remember all the details that Dawn had included, but he felt sure they were accurate. He was about to offer the pad to Sig when Dawn gestured for him to turn the page. He did so, and found he was looking at a photo-accurate drawing of the ship that he had seen passing overhead early the same morning. But Dawn could not have seen it then— she had been busy with her lettering, inside the kitchen.

"When did you see this, Dawn?" And then, to Sig. "I told you! That's what I saw. It's not a cargo aircar or a lander, it's more like the ship that carried us up from Earth."

"It's a deep-space vessel all right." Sig was head-down over the drawing, studying the fine details. "But if it's the way Dawn drew it, the design is different from the ones we've used. The exhaust isn't the same—see those little side plumes, like feathers? And the hull is shorter and fatter."

Josh should have been as intent on the drawing as Sig. He

wasn't. While Sig was speaking, Topaz's fingers had moved up from Josh's knee and were gently scratching the outside of his left thigh.

It tickled rather than hurt, and it was actually rather pleasant. But he could not understand why she was doing it in public, and certainly not at this particular moment. He turned to face Topaz, not sure how he was going to ask her to stop.

She was leaning forward on the bench, examining Dawn's drawing. Her two hands rested lightly on two knees—her own.

Josh glanced down. Nothing was on the outside of his pants, but something was *inside* them. There was a bulge near the bottom of his left pocket. As he put his hand down toward it, the bulge slid up his leg a couple of inches.

He jumped to his feet. He started to put his hand into his pocket, then hesitated. He knew what it was—or what it had been. That was the pocket where he had dropped, and then forgotten about, the brown seedlike thing that fell on his head as the giant balloon exploded in the stormy sky above them.

But what was it *now?*

No matter what, he couldn't bear to leave it there, crawling invisibly up his leg. He inserted his hand into his pocket. He had to force himself to do it, but he felt his way downward until something soft and warm squirmed against his fingers.

He flinched, and a touch like wet feathers ran across his fingertips.

"What is it?" That was Topaz, alarm in her voice. He did not look up. If he didn't do it now, he never would. He took a breath, reached deeper into his pocket, and closed his hand on a wriggling ball of damp fur. Trying to ignore its attempts to escape, he pulled the object free.

His instinct was to throw it far away without even looking at it. But the others were crowding around, wondering what was happening. He forced himself to reach down to the floor and open his fist.

When you could see it, the imagined horror looked small and harmless, even pathetic. A blunt gray head sat at one end of a multicolored ring of feathered fluff. Free to expand, little plumes of crimson and deep blue were gradually rising, opening into the shape of a badminton birdie. Josh couldn't see any legs, but the creature was edging its way toward him.

He took a pace backward. He couldn't have picked the thing up again to save his life, but he didn't have to. Dawn was bending and lifting it in one smooth movement. She cradled the object to her chest in both hands, lowering her head to examine it more closely. The plumes were fully open, extending three inches from the domed back and gradually changing to lighter colors in the open air.

"What is it?" Topaz asked again.

"I don't know." Josh became less worried when he saw that Dawn was comfortable and relaxed. "I thought it was a plant seed from the balloon trees. Now it seems to be an animal."

"Maybe on Solferino a thing can be both," Sig suggested.

"Bothwell Gage told us differently." But Josh realized that Gage hadn't said that. Solferino, according to the biologist, was the only world other than Earth where living things like plants and animals existed; but it didn't mean that an organism had to be either one or the other.

Meanwhile, Dawn was ignoring all of them. With her nose just a couple of inches away from the creature, she was muttering and crooning to it, or maybe to herself. Five seconds more, and she set off without a word for the building exit. Josh and the others followed in silence.

Dawn paused when she reached the cleared area outside the gym. She went down to one knee on the dense purple carpet of plant cover and scratched a clear patch with her fingers. She put the animal she was holding into the middle of the patch, and waited.

Nothing happened, except that after a few seconds the little creature set a determined path for the edge of the cleared area.

Dawn murmured her disapproval, reached down, and picked the animal up again. The blunt gray head lifted and quested, and the tiny trunk seemed to sniff the air. The body wriggled.

Dawn took no notice. She was off again, holding the animal firmly and heading for the gate that led out of the compound. Once into the forest of umbrella plants she kept going, moving uphill until she found a place where the leaf canopy was less full and Solferino's reddish sun could break through to light the surface. She halted in the sunniest area and again reached down to place her little captive on the ground.

It lay for a few seconds without moving. Then an explosion of fine soil appeared on all sides of it. The body began to sink, surprisingly quickly. In less than thirty seconds it had vanished. All that was left as proof of its presence was a small conical heap of red dirt.

"Plant, or animal?" Topaz was the first to speak. "I guess we still don't know."

"We were told Solferino wasn't *dangerous*," Sig said. "We still don't know if that's true or not, but one thing's for sure. There's plenty here that's strange and mysterious."

Topaz took Dawn's hand in hers and regarded her in a way that Josh found perplexing. "Very true," she said. "The most mysterious thing I've ever met is right here." Her smile at Dawn took any ill feeling away from her words. "And of all the things on Solferino, this is the one that I'd most like to understand."

That was the end of the incident with Dawn and what—for want of a better word—Josh thought of as the balloon-tree seed. But in a curious way it wasn't the end for any of them. Josh realized that later in the day, after Brewster's rage at Winnie Carlson had died down and he felt free to go to the computer room. He had expected to find it empty, and was hoping to learn more about Solferino's native life forms. Instead he saw the unlikely pair of Sig

Lasker and Amethyst Karpov, side by side at one of the consoles. They nodded at Josh, acknowledging his existence, but otherwise they took no notice of him.

"More like *this*, I think," Sig said. He was working with a graphics package, and he had drawn on the display a wispy plume with indistinct sides.

Amethyst shook her head decisively. "Then it's not a Foodlines ship. Before we left Earth I studied everything I could find about the Foodlines fleet. Nothing has an exhaust like that."

"So what is it?"

"It's easier to say what it isn't." Amethyst was fiddling with the keypads. "This is really annoying. The data banks I'd most like to look at have disappeared. There's nothing here about the Unimine line— in fact, I can't find anything about Unimine at all, nothing on the franchises for Cauldron or anything else. Everything involving the Grisel system seems to have been wiped out."

That was bad news for Josh, too. Solferino life forms certainly ought to be part of the Grisel system data banks. But Amethyst was continuing, "I'd like to prove that what we saw when we were in the lander, and what Dawn drew, are both Unimine vessels. But without data, we're guessing."

"How about what you think you saw?" Sig turned to Josh.

"I don't *think* I saw it. I *did* see it." Josh came closer for a better view of the display. "That sure looks like the same ship exhaust to me. What are you two up to?"

"Worrying," Sig replied. "At least, I am."

"What about?" Josh was worrying, too, but mostly concerning Dawn and the ruperts.

"This place. Nothing makes sense. We're shipped off to camp in the Barbican Hills almost as soon as we arrive, before we even know our way around this compound. The whole computer system falls apart as soon as we get back." Sig gestured at the display. "When did you ever hear of hardware failure and data loss that had nothing to do with each other? That's what supposedly happened here. Then there's Brewster. He acts as though we were dumped on him, without warning, and he's just as astonished when Winnie Carlson shows up."

"But he didn't know we were coming."

"Wrong. Not if you believe Sapphire. Right, Amy?" Sig looked to Amethyst for confirmation.

She nodded. "We weren't the only Foodlines trainees, Josh. There were scores more. Saph saw a complete list when we were back on Earth. She says that Brewster not only knew we were coming to Solferino, he *requested* each one of us. We are what Brewster felt he needed."

It was such an improbable idea, Josh had to ask a delicate question. "You say the person who saw all this was Sapphire. Was she—I mean, could she have been . . ."

"Stoned, and out of her mind?" Amethyst provided the words for him. "Some of the time she was, yes. She was when we first got here. But I know Saph. Zonked or not, this isn't the sort of thing she'd make up. I'm willing to believe that Brewster didn't know anything about Winnie Carlson; but us, he picked out. He knew we were supposed to come to Solferino. The only thing is, we arrived a week early because Bothwell Gage was available to drop us off. Brewster would have known that, too, if he'd bothered to check his message center."

"He was away at the medical facility."

"Wherever that is." Amethyst touched the console pads again, and a familiar-looking message appeared on the display. MASTER LIST OF FACILITIES AVAILABLE WITHIN THE GRISEL STELLAR SYSTEM: DATA FILE CORRESPONDING TO THIS LABEL DOES NOT EXIST. "I know my way around most computer systems, but I've been getting nowhere with this one. Everything I want to find out about seems to have vanished."

Josh thought of the ruined storage unit, sitting at the bottom of the bodger pond. Winnie had assured him, along with Rick and

Hag, that the computer problems had nothing to do with what they had done. But why assume that she was right? Brewster certainly wouldn't.

Perhaps the fight and the broken unit that resulted were the source of the computer difficulties. But if so, Josh wasn't going to be the one owning up to it.

He nodded, vaguely agreeing with Amethyst, and backed away. She had ruined his idea that he could learn anything from the computer files about balloon-tree seeds, ruperts, or anything else on the planet. He saw no reason to stay and possibly be questioned by Sig and Amethyst.

It was dusk outside, and the day's experiences had made him supersensitive. When a hand gripped his arm as he left the building, he shied away instinctively.

"Shh! It's only me."

Josh could breathe again. Topaz. She was standing close and spoke in a whisper.

"What do you want?" Josh did not use the same low voice, and she at once put her hand across his mouth.

"Shh. I have to talk to you—but not here. Don't say anything. Just come with me."

Josh followed her around the building. He wondered what was next on the agenda. The day had been full of surprises, but regardless of Sapphire's suspicions about him and her sister, Josh couldn't see this as an evening invitation for a hot date.

Near the back wall of the building, Topaz halted and turned. She moved closer, until her face was only a few inches from his. Off to their right, Grisel was dipping toward the horizon like a great, glowing ember.

"I'm sorry I was rotten to you earlier." Topaz's cheeks were ruddy, and her expression earnest in the half-light. "But what you suggested was really impossible."

"It was?" Josh wondered what she was talking about.

"Yes. Impossible for Ruby, I mean. She's too little, and Saph would never agree. But it's not impossible for *me*. I like Dawn a lot, and I think I get through to her better than anyone. I feel sure that she likes me, too. I'd take really good care of her."

"But what about Sapphire?" Josh had finally caught on to what the conversation was about. "And what about Brewster? You must have as many duties as I do. What will he do if you and Dawn up and vanish?"

"Who cares what he'll do? What *can* he do, worse than what he does all the time? Especially if we come back with a smart rupert. He'll have to admit that you were right. It was your idea, you know, not mine."

"So if anyone goes, it ought to be me." But something inside Josh hesitated at the thought.

"No. I'd be better—and it's not because you're incompetent, or anything like that."

"Then why?"

"Because you're male. I'd be able to help Dawn with female stuff, and you wouldn't. Do you want to hear the details of what I mean?"

"No." On that point at least, Josh was sure.

"So you agree?" Topaz leaned closer. The sun had dipped below the horizon, and her face was a pale blur with no features distinguishable. "If you do agree, I'll start to make plans. It won't work the way you suggested, though. I can't just wander off with Dawn, and then if we don't find anything, come back and do the same thing over again the next day. Brewster would never allow it to happen twice. This has to be a one-shot deal. All right?"

"Go slower. I guess I am dumb, even though you say I'm not. You're right about it being a one-time opportunity, but I still don't understand *why*. Why do *you* want to do this? It can't be just to find a rupert."

"You're not dumb. You're supersmart to realize there must be something more in it for me. If you promise not to tell anyone else—ever—I'll explain what it is."

"I'll never tell." Josh felt oddly flattered. "No matter who asks me."

"Good. Now tell me, I'm one of four sisters. Which one am I?"

"You're Topaz." That was enough of an answer for Josh, but obviously not for her, because she stood waiting. He tried again. "You're the second oldest."

"Right." But it still wasn't the correct answer, because Topaz made an annoyed noise that Josh had heard a thousand times from his mother.

"And—you're the most attractive," he said at last.

Topaz snorted louder this time. "Get lost, Josh Kerrigan. I'm not fishing for half-baked compliments. You had it right before. I'm the second oldest, number-two child. That's all you or anyone else can think of to say about me. Saph is the oldest, she's the boss and acts like she's our mother. Amy is the brain, she remembers everything she reads on the first go while the rest of us struggle. Ruby is the baby. We all look out for her and try to give her whatever she wants. But I'm not anything, I'm just child number two. *That's* why I want to do this. I want to be someone special and different."

It was no reason at all, and that's why Josh couldn't argue with it. He nodded, realized that Topaz probably could not see the movement, and said, "All right. I agree. And I do trust you with Dawn. I always have."

"Thanks, Josh. I appreciate that."

"And I meant what I said about you being the most attractive."

"Now you're trying a come-on." Arms reached out in the darkness, located Josh, and hugged him. "That's all right, I like it anyway. You couldn't have said anything to make me happier."

It was always nice to feel that you were someone special, Josh had to agree with that. It was also all right to be hugged.

There was only one problem. Josh, strolling back around the building with Topaz on his arm, under the alien sky of Solferino, was sure that he had done nothing to deserve either.

CHAPTER FIFTEEN

NEXT morning Josh awoke filled with excitement. The feeling faded as the morning went on, for during that day and the three following it became clear that planning was one thing, but carrying something out was quite a different matter.

The problem was Brewster. He was loud, and bullying, and sometimes strangely ignorant or disorganized; but he was the boss. He kept everyone running from early in the morning to late at night. Even Ruby was not excused, which shot down Josh's idea that she might be able to come and go as she pleased. Winnie

Carlson was the subject of special wrath and scorn. Something on Solferino did not agree with her, and she appeared each day yawning, pale, and blotchy, with dark bags under her eyes. Brewster assumed that she was his personal slave, and ordered her around accordingly; Winnie never uttered one word of protest.

Josh was able to talk to Topaz for only a few minutes a day, and rarely alone. Their plan had to be unsuspected not only by Brewster, but also by everyone else—especially Sapphire. Josh had to be content with a quick nod from Topaz, or her terse, "Getting stuff together. Making a food cache beyond the fence. Pass me anything you can snitch—I can't take too much, and I don't think we dare try to live off the land." He had no idea what Topaz said to Dawn, but his cousin's smile was as Sphinx-like and mysterious as ever.

The compound and buildings began to feel like home. Everyone learned how to use the cleaning facilities, the kitchen, and what was left of the computer systems. After four days it even felt natural to wake to a dawn of reds and orange, or stroll from building to building across a purple sward.

Finally, the evening came when Topaz, standing at Josh's side putting plates into the disposal, muttered: "Tomorrow. Don't look for the two of us after midday."

Before midday, however, other events intruded.

Early in the morning, when everyone was waiting in the dining area to be assigned their daily duties, Sol Brewster threw them another curveball.

"You've all adjusted to Solferino." He was standing at the wall display, and grinning as though something was giving him special pleasure. "That's good. What's not so good is that you haven't done a stroke of work since you came here."

He watched closely for signs of protest. Everyone stoically waited, and finally he went on: "I mean *real* work. Something that will repay Foodlines for the expense of shipping your carcasses out here and training you. Well, the holiday ends today. You begin to earn your keep. Take a look."

The wall behind him came to life. It provided a view of Solferino, taken from space. As they watched, the picture zoomed in on one area of the upper hemisphere.

"We are here." Brewster placed his finger on a point near the center of the display. "To give you an idea of scale, these are the Barbican Hills, near the bottom. But the area that the company is more interested in is this one." He tapped the wall, where a long, dark gash showed in the surface of Solferino. "That is the Avernus Fissure. It's a low-lying area, some of it well below sea level, and it's volcanically active. It was chosen by a space survey as a place which may have new and valuable biological products. However, there has never so far been a systematic *ground* survey. I, with your assistance, will be performing the first. We'll be taking the cargo aircar there later this morning. Each of you will be issued a test kit, designed to detect the presence of certain substances valuable to Foodlines, in the native plant life. I will assign you your territories and monitor your results. All clear? Good. I want you back here and ready to leave in"—he paused, as usual when he was giving out schedules—"five minutes. A personal pack is not to exceed six kilos. Don't try to bring your usual rubbish. Carlson!"

Everyone stared at Winnie. She had been standing with her mouth open and her eyes closed, and she came to attention only when Brewster shouted her name.

"Yes, sir."

"Did you hear what I said, Carlson? You certainly didn't look like you were listening."

"I was, sir. Sir, do you wish me to go with the group?"

"Why, yes, I think that would be nice." Brewster's voice dripped sarcasm. "I certainly had it in mind. Surely you do not imagine that we could get along without your valuable presence? What other plans do you have? To spend the period of our absence loafing in bed?"

"No, sir."

"Then *let's get moving.*" His voice rose to a roar. "Any questions?"

"How long will we be gone, sir?" Josh was breaking the golden rule: With Sol Brewster, you never drew attention to yourself in any way. But he had to ask for Topaz's benefit.

The question didn't receive Brewster's usual dismissal of the questioner as a total moron. It rather seemed to surprise him. "Three days," he said after a moment of frowning uncertainty. "Yes, that's right. You should plan to be away for three days. Any other questions? No? Then go to it."

Topaz walked with Josh to the door. As they went out she muttered from the side of her mouth, "Think he guessed, and did it on purpose? We're screwed. I daren't take the cache on the flier, and by the time we get back most of the food will spoil."

The test kit was so simple, even Ruby would have no trouble using it. Brewster demonstrated it as the flier's automatic pilot took them east.

"Here's the feeder." He pointed to an aperture in the top of the unit, which was a squat upright cylinder about six inches tall and three across. "All you have to do is put in a sample of the plant you've picked. Leaves, stem, or root—but don't assume that because you've tested one part, there's no need to test another. Some plants concentrate materials in one particular place."

"Like hydrogen cyanide in peach kernels, sir? Or vanadium in tunicates."

It was Amethyst again, determined to show off even if it guaranteed a roasting. The comment didn't get praise from Brewster—nothing seemed to—but this time all it led to was a startled glare and a mild, "When I want your inputs I will ask for them."

"Yes, sir."

"You put the sample in here." Brewster took a piece of umbrella plant leaf. For a change, he sounded enthusiastic about what he was doing. "There's only one thing to remember: You put the plant into the unit *where you collect it.* Don't go wandering off with a sample, then decide it's time you processed it. There's a good reason for that. Each kit has its own inertial navigation system, good enough to determine your position on the surface of Solferino to within a meter. But the unit doesn't know where you pick the sample, only where you are when you process it.

"Once the sample is inside, you press this." He touched a button on the side of the cylinder. "Then you wait for five to ten seconds. If there is nothing in the sample to merit more detailed analysis, this light on the side will flash yellow. That will happen most of the time. Any substances that we already know about, but find interesting, will be identified here. The light will flash red. Real anomalies—substances that the test kit has never seen before, and can't explain chemically—make the light on the side flash bright blue. Before you get excited, I'll tell you that an anomaly is a one-in-ten-thousand chance. It's so rare that you shouldn't expect to see it at all in your whole five days of testing."

"Three days," Ruby said promptly. "You said three days."

The others winced in anticipation, but Brewster only frowned and said mildly, "Three days. Yes. That is what I meant. Three days of testing before we return to the compound."

The little light was flashing yellow. The kit had finished its work with the umbrella plant leaf. And the dark scar of the Avernus Fissure was coming into view on the far horizon.

Josh had given up on the idea of the search for ruperts. Topaz hadn't.

After the flier had landed, and while they were watching again the miracle of the self-erecting buildings, she edged over to Josh. "Tonight. Outside, by the fissure. Wait until you're sure everyone else is asleep."

The message seemed clear as could be, but after everyone else was in bed, and Josh was wishing that he was, he found himself alone in the darkness. It was a crescent moon, on a chilly, cloudless night. The camp was on his left. The Avernus Fissure, smoking and ominous, was a red glow and sulfurous smell off to the right. The stars were bright overhead. But of Topaz, there was no sign at all.

It was more than chilly. It was *cold.* Josh shivered, crossed his arms over his chest, and cursed. He was ready to give up and head off to bed when he glimpsed a dark shadow moving away from the camp.

He almost called out, until he realized that the almost-invisible figure was not heading toward him, but angling away to the left. He peered into the darkness, suspecting that maybe he was making up the whole thing from half-seen patterns of light and dark.

Before he could convince himself of that, a second spectral figure appeared from the camp. It flitted across his line of sight, heading the same way as the first one.

Josh had suffered all that he could stand. He stole toward the camp, determined to follow what he had seen and find out for sure what was going on. Halfway there he saw yet another dark shape, creeping along uncertainly toward the edge of the fissure.

By now his eyes were as adjusted to the darkness as they would ever be. He reached out and took Topaz by the arm. It was her turn to jump and utter a near-inaudible squeak.

"Is that you, Josh?" Her hand groped for and took his.

"Yes. Topaz, something really strange is going on here. You're the third person who's come out of the camp. Do you think that Sapphire knows what you're planning to do?"

"I'm sure she doesn't." Topaz was still holding hard to his hand. "When I left her she was asleep with her arms around Ruby. Snap withdrawal is hitting her really hard. If she didn't feel she has to look after the rest of us, I think she'd fall apart."

He could see her eyes now, wide open and glinting reddish-brown in light from the Avernus Fissure's smoking deeps. She was glancing from side to side, imagining people where there were only shadows.

Had he done the same? Or had he really seen people leaving the camp?

"What's going on, Topaz? Why did you want to see me outside here?"

"To tell you that I'm going ahead. If we stop every time Brewster makes us do something we didn't expect, Dawn and I will never get started."

"You're going to do it *here?*"

"Where else can I do it? Here is where we are. And from the point of view of finding ruperts, one place is as good as another."

"But what about supplies?"

"I'm going to steal them. Why shouldn't I? I won't be in any worse trouble with Brewster, just because I helped myself to a bit of food. What's wrong?" She was still holding his hand. "You're all tensed up."

"I sure am. Maybe it's that." He turned his head toward the dim red glow. "I don't care what Brewster says, or Bothwell Gage says, or anyone says, the Avernus Fissure is a dangerous place. What would happen if you fell into it?"

"You'd burn to a crisp. But don't worry, Josh, we won't be going that way. Dawn and I will head in the opposite direction."

"There could be other fissures out there."

"Sure there could. There could be boojums, too."

"What?"

"Ask Amethyst, she'll tell you more than you want to know. Look, Josh, I didn't get you out here to ask for your approval. I came to ask for your help."

"How?"

"Dawn and I are going to sneak away before anyone gets up."

"Do you think she understands that?"

"She does. Trust me. The trouble isn't Dawn, it's my sisters, 'specially Saph. Now she's off triple-snap she doesn't sleep normally. We're in the same expanded dorm room, and Saph wakes up a few times in the night and checks that everything's all right with the rest of us. Provided it is, she goes back to bed."

"I can't do anything about that." Josh had an awful feeling that he knew what was coming.

"Sure you can. Saph won't wake me up, she'll just check that I'm there. I want you to go back right now, get into my bed, and sleep the rest of the night there."

"Topaz!"

"Of course, it won't be nearly as much fun as if I was in there with you. Sometime, maybe, but not tonight. This isn't about fun. Will you do it, Josh? Will you go right now and pretend you're me, in my bed? Say you will."

"Topaz!"

"Say it, Josh. Promise you will and I'll owe you forever."

"I won't—I mean, Topaz, I just can't." Her face was only a few inches from his. He could feel her breath, warm on his cheek. "Oh, all right. I will. I'll do it."

"Great! Let's get back. I don't want Sapphire even suspecting that I might not be there."

As they headed toward the camp, Josh had only one thing on his mind. It wasn't the warm touch of lips on his cheek when he said yes, though that was unexpectedly pleasant. It wasn't the hint of possible things to come, which sounded ever better. It wasn't the mystery of who else had left the camp, and what they were all doing, which at the moment felt abstract and remote.

No. At the top of his head was the thought of what he would say and do when Sapphire found him in Topaz's bunk.

Josh knew that he would not sleep for a single moment. He would lie all night in the darkness, waiting and worrying.

It was a great shock to open his eyes and find he was looking up into Sapphire's perplexed face.

"Where's Topaz?" she said. "This can't be what it looks like, because she's not here with you. What the hell is going on?"

There were times when a person could plead innocence and ignorance. This wasn't one of them. Josh pushed back the covers and sat up.

"I can explain everything."

"You sound just like Sig Lasker." Sapphire glanced down at him. "At least you've got all your clothes on and you aren't bare-ass naked. That's a good start."

"Of course I'm not!" Josh scrambled out of bed. He looked to where Amethyst and Ruby were still peacefully asleep. "Look, I'll tell you everything, but only if you promise not to tell Brewster."

"I wouldn't tell Brewster if his ass was on fire. Talk, Josh Kerrigan. Amy and Ruby usually sleep another hour, both of 'em. I want to know what's going on before they wake up—and keep the noise level down."

Josh's explanation, in the chilly orange light of dawn, sounded worse than stupid. Sapphire simply shook her head.

"She talked you into it, didn't she?"

"No, I don't think so."

"Well, I do. You have to know our Topaz. She'd talk a witch out of her broomstick. The question is, what are we going to do about it? Are you worried about your cousin?"

"I should be. But it's funny, I feel more comfortable than I expected, knowing the two of them are together."

"Funnily enough, so do I. But I guess we'll act as worried and puzzled as everyone else, and we don't tell anybody what happened to Topaz and Dawn. Except maybe Sig."

"Does he have to know?"

"If we don't tell him, he'll probably guess. He's smart."

Josh sensed that there were other reasons for including Sig, but he didn't pursue them. "What about you?" he said. "Do I have to worry about you?"

He didn't want to have to explain that question, but luckily Sapphire was ahead of him.

"No. You would have had to worry, four days ago." She breathed deeply, as though inhaling an invisible something into her lungs. Her eyes, like Winnie's, had black bags underneath them. "I feel like it's killing me, but it's for my own good."

"You don't have any more of it?"

"Not a single sniff." Sapphire smiled, but without a trace of humor, and her eyes wandered around the room as though seeking out hiding places where a small tube might have been mislaid. "Oh, hell. If I did have any, I'd be taking a whack right now. May I make a suggestion?"

"Anything."

"Good. Now you've fooled me for long enough, and told me how and why, get the hell out of here and back to your own bed. You probably think you look like Goldilocks. But I think Amy and Ruby will have a few questions if you're still here when they wake up."

Josh expected to be the one grilled most severely. In fact, it was the Karpov sisters who bore the brunt of Brewster's questions. Apparently Sol Brewster shared Aunt Stacy's view, that Dawn was a total retard, so nothing that she did could be expected to make sense.

Amethyst and Ruby were genuinely worried and puzzled, and only a little reassured by Sapphire's shrug and dismissal with, "Topaz knows how to look after herself. I'm not her keeper."

If Brewster had been more sensitive to relationships, he might have realized that Sapphire saw herself as exactly that. Instead he grumbled and threatened about what he would do when Topaz and Dawn came back.

"But the rest of you are going to work," he said. "You don't get away with anything, just because they think they can. Take your test kits. I'll tell you the areas where each of you will operate. I don't want you straying outside the places I tell you to be. This part of Solferino has natural hazards, but as I told you before: Do as I say, and you'll be in no trouble."

While Brewster was talking, Josh examined the rest of the group. He was no longer sure what he had seen the previous night. But if his eyes had not been deceiving him, who could it have been?

His first choice, from what he had seen recently, was Sig and Sapphire, sneaking off together. Since that wasn't the case, then who?

The twins were game for any sort of wildness, but they would surely have gone together, not one at a time. Ruby and Amethyst had been asleep when he crept into Topaz's bed. That left two people: Sol Brewster and Winnie Carlson. He grinned at the idea of those two going off together. He didn't believe it for a moment.

His pondering ended when he was given one of the test kits and walked by Brewster to the area assigned to him. It was closer to the fissure than he had been before—quite a bit too close, in Josh's opinion.

Brewster then moved him to a point thirty meters closer yet, well past the place where all plant life ended. "This is a little farther than you should go. It's perfectly safe here, but I can't vouch for what happens if you start fooling around here. Take a good look. Then go back up and get to work."

He left. Josh took a look, a very good look, and wished that he were back at the main compound, or Burnt Willow Farm—or anywhere else at all. From his position the ground sloped down, steeper and steeper, to become a vertical wall that dropped to the bottom of the fissure. The opposite side was a couple of kilometers away, and the length of the chasm stretched out of sight in both directions. A thin pall of yellowish smoke sat over the great rift in the surface. It never dispersed, even though Josh could feel a steady warm breeze on his face.

He stared along the steepest line of descent. Nothing grew or moved, except at the very bottom where a dark something churned and smoked. In daylight it was all blacks and grays. He knew from the previous night that when the world was dark, the fissure bottom glowed with its own dull red fire. If it were not hot enough to make the rocks molten, it was close to it. A human who fell to the fissure floor would not survive more than a few seconds.

He heard a sound beside him, and turned in alarm. It was Amethyst, peering down toward the fissure bottom.

"Brewster told me I could," she said defensively. "I'm working just up from you, but this is a lot more interesting. Do you know how hot it is down there?"

"No. But if you look at it at night it glows a sort of dull red."

A mistake—Amethyst might ask him how he knew. Instead she merely said "Interesting" again, craned forward, and added, "For something naturally black, like the rocks there, a dull red heat means it must be at least five hundred Celsius. Fall down there, you'd be burned to a crisp."

A fact that Josh had no wish to hear again—Topaz had said almost exactly the same thing. But Amethyst was apparently marking time on the way to her real subject, because she added, still without looking at Josh, "You know where Topaz went, don't you?"

"No, I don't."

It was literally true, but it didn't work. Amethyst said, "All right, maybe you don't know *where*. But I bet you know *why* she went. And I bet I do, too. She's gone off with your cousin. They're looking to catch a rupert."

"Why would you think a thing like that?"

"I don't hear you denying it. I'm not an idiot, you know. You've been babbling about ruperts ever since that first night at camp. You try to give everybody the impression that you're totally cool and you don't care about anything, but Topaz says that's not true, inside you care an awful lot. You really want to prove you're right about the rupert. Saph says you hide your feelings like this because of the way you were brought up, with your mother and everything. You've learned not to let things show, 'specially when you care a lot."

"Have you finished? How I feel about things is my business, not yours. And what I said was true. I don't know where Topaz is."

"I believe you." Amethyst sighed, heavily and artificially, and oddly it reminded Josh at once of his mother. "Topaz is so lucky, you know. The rest of us really envy her. She can talk anybody into anything." She studied Josh as if she had just discovered a new Solferino life form. "You seem to have your head screwed on the right way, but you went along with it. Do you mind my asking, what did Topaz do to persuade you?"

Josh did mind. He minded this whole conversation. He was saved from having to answer by a bellow of rage from farther up the hill.

"Are you two going to stand there and bullshit all day long? I said a *quick look* at the fissure. Get working."

"Topaz is so lucky. Talks anybody into anything," Amethyst started back toward her assigned territory. "Except maybe for horrible old Frankenstein's monster up there. I'd like to do something to *his* fissure. He's immune to all human feelings. Nobody mentioned *him* when Saph asked us if we'd like to go to Solferino. If she had, we might have stayed home. At least we'd have thought about it twice."

CHAPTER SIXTEEN

THE work with the test kit was interesting at first. You picked a likely looking piece of plant, popped it into the top, and waited. After a while, the yellow light came on. That was the trouble. Yellow, yellow, yellow. No matter how much you willed the red or blue light to appear, it never did. And after a while, what had started out interesting became just boring.

The day was warm. It was easy to imagine that half the heat

came from the hidden fires of the Avernus Fissure, only a few hundred meters away. The red disk of Grisel crept across the sky with terrible slowness. As the hours wore on, Josh found he had plenty of time to think and plenty to think about.

Where were Topaz and Dawn at the moment, and what were they doing? They were probably miles and miles away. He was sure they wouldn't have stayed near the fissure, where the other trainees were working and Brewster might find them. They would surely have gone the other way, up to the heights surrounding Avernus. That's where the shape of the land suggested you might find plants—and animals—more like those in the Barbican Hills.

By now he'd bet that all the other trainees knew what had happened to Topaz and Dawn. He'd as good as told Amethyst, and she wouldn't have kept it from Ruby. And Sig would know, too, because Saph seemed to tell him everything. And Sig would have been bugged by Hag and Rick, and he had no reason not to tell them whatever he knew.

So they all knew—except for Sol Brewster and Winnie Carlson. It was curious that those two had not grilled everyone harder about Topaz and Dawn's disappearance. Maybe they had worries and secrets of their own. Josh still hadn't come up with a plausible explanation for the two dark figures he had seen while he waited in the dark for Topaz.

Brewster was far more focused now that they were at the Avernus Fissure. He had stopped running people off their feet in pointless work, or shipping them off somewhere before they'd even had time to settle in. He was purposeful and organized. And even Winnie Carlson seemed less of a sad sack here, in the scary volcanic region surrounding the fissure.

Were all these things connected? It seemed odd to Josh that they would be testing plants close to the edge of the fissure, and not in the forests where growth was more abundant. That's where you would expect to find more plant types.

Maybe he ought to talk things over with the others, especially Amethyst—old bulge-brain, Topaz called her (but not when she was there). Maybe Amethyst would be able to put everything together and make sense of it.

Josh took a break from his musings and turned to look at the sun. It was lower in the sky. Night was only an hour or two away, and he had long since eaten everything in his food packs. He had been testing for what felt like forever. Maybe Brewster had forgotten all about them. On the other hand, maybe he hadn't. Josh didn't relish the notion of being the first one back at the camp, and alone with Brewster.

He glanced idly at the test kit—and stopped dead. He had been wandering along on autopilot, working without thinking. Suddenly, while he was not looking, the blue light had started to blink.

Blue—anomaly. Only once in ten thousand times, Brewster had said. But there it was, as bright and beautiful as you could ask. There was a temptation to run screaming and shouting up the hill toward the camp. Josh damped that urge. Suppose he had somehow screwed up (though he didn't see any way that he could have). Then the more he shouted and waved, the bigger idiot he would look when he was proved wrong.

He backtracked to the place where he had taken the last sample, pulled another piece from the same plant, a stem this time rather than a saw-edged leaf, and dropped it into the test kit. The wait seemed endless, though it was probably no longer than usual.

It came at last—blue again, unless he had developed a sudden case of color blindness. As casually as he could manage, Josh strolled back up the hill.

Of course, that raised problems of its own. He had to walk right past Rick Lasker.

At first the fair-haired twin took no notice of Josh. He was squatting close to the ground. In one hand was his test kit. In the other, near the test kit's opening, Rick held some kind of fat black worm that wriggled to escape.

As soon as he became aware of Josh's approach, Rick put the worm down and stood up.

"I really wasn't going to." He stared at Josh uneasily. "See, I was just wondering. Wondering what it would feel like."

"That doesn't look like a talking worm. It won't tell you. Stick your finger inside the test kit, if you're that keen on knowing what it feels like."

Rick looked at Josh doubtfully. "You don't mean that, do you? You're joking."

"No, I'm not. In fact, you can stick any part of you in there that you like, and it would suit me fine." Josh started to walk past, up the hill toward the camp, but it was no good. As dusk approached, the flashing light became harder to conceal.

"You've got one!" Rick came to Josh's side and bent to peer at the test kit. "*Blue light.* Didn't Brewster say that's the best kind of all?"

Before Josh could respond, Rick shouted loud enough to carry to the camp and a mile past it, "Over here! He's got one! Josh Kerrigan bagged a blue!"

So much for the idea of a quiet walk back to camp. It had never occurred to Josh that the work was any kind of competition, but apparently Rick and Hag saw it that way. Hag came running over from a spot farther along the fissure. He peered, turned, and shouted, even louder than Rick, "Hey! Josh has one! He found an enorm-ally."

Other people popped up from nowhere, Saph and Sig and Amethyst and Winnie. Most surprising of all, Brewster emerged from the main building of the camp—and he came *running* toward Josh and Rick across the uneven, ill-lit ground. Brewster, who never went anywhere faster than a stately walk! For the first time, Josh had the feeling that he might have discovered something truly important.

"Aha!" Brewster grabbed the test kit out of Josh's hand and held it close to his face. "Yes, yes, yes. So far, so good. Now let's see just what we have."

He turned the test kit around, took something like a blunt screwdriver from his jacket, and poked it into half a dozen small marked pits. The kit beeped, and three of the pits glowed white in the dusk.

"Perfect! The best three." Brewster handed the kit back to Josh and rubbed his hands together. "Show me exactly where you found it. Quickly, before it gets too dark."

Josh knew that he would be able to find the plant just as well in the morning, and anyway the test kit was supposed to have its own accurate locator. However, he wasn't about to get into an argument with Sol Brewster, even when the man was in a good mood. With everyone trailing along behind, Josh led the way to a sparsely covered piece of ground. He pointed to the plant that he had used. Brewster broke off a couple of purple leaves, grabbed a different test kit from Sig Lasker, and dropped them in.

Josh held his breath. If the whole thing was just something wrong with his test kit . . .

After another endless wait, the indicator light on the other unit flashed blue.

"That's it!" Sol Brewster knelt down and peered at the ground. What he could see in the fading light was beyond Josh, but apparently it satisfied the other man because he took the blunt screwdriver again from his jacket and drove it effortlessly into the hard earth to mark the spot. He leaned back on his haunches.

"Excellent. Your work is over for the day, and a good day it's been. You can all head back to camp now. I'll stay here for a few more minutes, I have additional tests to carry out." And, when everyone hesitated, interested to see what he would do next, "Have you gone deaf? I said *move*. This isn't a circus, and I don't need an audience."

They headed reluctantly back up the hill. When they had gone about thirty yards, Josh turned for a last quick look. Brewster was still crouched in the same place. Rather than doing anything to the clump of plants, he seemed to be *digging* in the ground next to them, with another tool that looked from a distance like a curve-bladed trowel.

What was he doing? Josh asked Winnie Carlson, but all she did was shake her head and act vaguely worried. And when Brewster swept back in, half an hour later, no one had the nerve to say anything.

He was in his best mood ever. "I felt sure that something was here," he said exultantly, "and by God I was right. But I thought that even if things went well, the search might take a long time. Now." He paused, thinking. "Well, now I think that one more day will be enough. After that, we can wrap it up here."

"What about Topaz and Dawn?" asked Amethyst. "We can't leave without them."

"Of course not." Brewster was in too good a mood to cut her down as usual. "We'll have to wait for them. But after tomorrow we can take things easy. In fact, I have a great idea. We'll work tomorrow during the day, but tomorrow night we'll have a party. A celebration, with special food and drink. How does that sound?"

It sounded too bizarre for words, at least to Josh. Sol Brewster was the last man in the world you would want at a party—or expect to give one. But it was Amethyst who spoke.

"Topaz is our best cook, sir, and she's not here. Unless she gets back, no one else is nearly as good."

"That's where you're wrong." Brewster was grinning, for the first time since they had arrived. "You're forgetting me. You won't find a better cook this side of the Messina Dust Cloud. I'll do the cooking."

"And I'll make a special appetizer," added Winnie Carlson. Brewster frowned at her. Before he could object she went on,

"You'll love this, sir, I promise. I've made it a hundred times, and everyone says that my blini pancakes with synthe-caviar and sour onion cream are the best thing they've ever tasted."

Brewster was a greedy eater, and his expression showed that he was tempted. But still he hesitated, and Winnie hurried on, "I won't need the use of the kitchen, either. You will have that, and I'll make the blinis and onion cream using portable equipment."

"We-e-ll." Brewster stared at his assistant, seeking a reason to say no but not finding one. "Are you sure of that? You won't interfere with me?"

"Absolutely not, sir. And this won't interfere with my work day, either, because I'll do the preparation tonight. Just tell me what time you want it ready."

Brewster finally produced a grudging nod. "Very well. There will be more field work tomorrow, so we should plan to eat at sundown. Understood?"

There were nods all round, but Amethyst said, "Sir? I'm really glad we'll be having a party, and I'm looking forward to it. But can you tell us just what we found? I have no idea, and I don't think I'm the only one."

Brewster frowned again, but at last he shrugged. "I don't see why not. This information is Foodlines proprietary, but I don't see how you could give away any secrets on Solferino—particularly since Carlson assures me that our off-planet message capability is still crippled.

"A full analysis will have to be performed later with better equipment, but what was discovered today is a new variety of alkaloid. All alkaloids are crystalline solids, related to pyridine and found in a large number of plants on Earth. Some of them are poisonous, but they are often valuable. What was found on Solferino today is a whole new class of them. It's the first such discovery ever made on this planet. All right?"

"Yes, sir. Thank you, sir." But Amethyst didn't look enlightened—she seemed puzzled.

"Very good. Now I have my own work to do." Brewster glanced around, nodded to Winnie Carlson, and added, "And I'll need the use of the kitchen an hour from now, to get ready for tomorrow. Make sure that everyone has eaten by then, and the place is clean."

He swept out without waiting for her to agree. After a couple of minutes, Winnie followed. As she was leaving she said over her shoulder, almost as an afterthought, "Eat what you like, and be sure to clean up. I don't know when I'll be back."

The group of trainees was left to stare at each other. "I hate him," Ruby complained. "And I don't want to be at any party that he gives. What's happening?"

"The question of the hour," Sig said. "Would anybody like to answer it?"

"Curiouser and curiouser," said Amethyst. "Like Alice in Wonderland, only worse. I'm as puzzled as Ruby."

After another few seconds of uneasy standing, the seven of them settled down on the little chairs that folded out from the wall of the kitchen.

"We're all confused," Sig said at last. "But it sounds like it's over different things. Maybe we can find answers if we put our heads together. Who wants to ask their question first?"

Amethyst raised her hand. "I don't know about a question, but I'd like to make a statement. Sol Brewster said that alkaloids are crystalline solids—all of them. That's not true, some of them are liquids, or gums. And he said they are related to pyridine, when only some of them are."

"So what's your point, Amy?" asked Sig. "Or are you just showing off?"

"No. I'm telling you that either Brewster is lying to us on purpose, or else he doesn't know what he's talking about."

"You haven't proposed a question," Rick objected. "You've just made a statement."

Amethyst turned her nose up at him. "I'll bet you didn't understand it. So you give us a question, if you don't like what I say."

Rick nodded. "I will. Brewster is interested in plants, he says. So why when we left him was he digging in the *ground?*"

"And if it's plants he wants," Hag added, "why did he pick a place to explore where there's less plants than bare rock?"

That would have been Josh's question, too, but he had plenty of others. "I want to know," he said, "what's a Unimine ship doing close to Solferino? Why wasn't it on Cauldron, where it's supposed to be? I really did see a ship, you know, even though Brewster doesn't believe me. And Dawn saw one, too."

"We believe you," Sig said. "Sapphire? It's your turn. You don't have to say anything if you don't want to."

He spoke gently. Sapphire had been unusually silent, letting Amethyst speak on her behalf. Everyone knew that she had a bad case of the shakes. She had struggled to hide it in front of Sol Brewster and Winnie Carlson, but now, in front of friends, she was quietly unraveling. The long day outside must have been hell for her.

"I do have something." Sapphire spoke slowly, with her head bent forward. She would not meet anyone's eye. "What I'd like to know, right at this moment, is where Topaz and Dawn are. But I guess that's not the sort of question you mean. So I'm wondering, why does Brewster move us around so? He took us off to camp, then left us so he could fly back to the compound. Why did he do that? He said he'd had a message from the medical center, but when we returned to the compound the equipment to talk to the medical center wasn't working."

"And where *is* the medical center?" Amethyst added. "None of us ever heard of it in our briefings back on Earth."

"And we won't find out," Josh said, "as long as most of the data banks are out of action."

"Any more?" asked Sig. He looked around the group. "If not, I'd like to have my turn. I'll tell you what's been on my mind more than anything. Do you remember the first night, when we heard from Brewster that Solferino has all these miraculous powers to heal people? Allergies disappear, scars fade, teeth grow back."

The others nodded, and Sig crooked his forefinger into the left side of his mouth. He pulled sideways, to show a space in the top molars.

"I'm missing a tooth, right here. I got it knocked out when we were on the streets. No sign of *that* growing back. As for allergies disappearing, go and ask Winnie Carlson. She's sneezing and sniffling all the time. And scars. Hag, show us your calf."

Hag, reluctantly at first, bent down and rolled up his left pants leg. A long scar ran up the outside from ankle to knee.

"Street fight, too, months ago," Sig said. "Do you see any sign of it fading?"

Hag shook his head, and ran his finger lovingly along the white line of the scar. "Not a bit. As beautiful as ever."

"Yeah. Some people would be proud if they had their brain knocked out." Sig turned to the others. "So we're seeing no sign of anything magic on Solferino, to cure anything. I really didn't believe it when I heard it, so I don't feel I lost much."

"But maybe *Brewster* believes it," Amethyst said, "even if you don't."

"Quite true. Which finally gets me to my own question. Brewster told us, on our first night here, that there might be something on Solferino to let us live forever. Let's accept that Brewster believes it, exactly as he stated. Then *he* must be a candidate to live forever, too, because he has spent a lot of time on Solferino. So why isn't that the most important thing in the world to him?" Sig surveyed the little group, person by person. "So why, after that first night, has he never mentioned it to any of us ever again?"

CHAPTER SEVENTEEN

MORNING brought a dull, oppressive heat unlike anything since the trainees' first arrival on Solferino. It had rained again in the night, and a veil of steam and yellow smoke stood above the Avernus Fissure. Josh dreaded the thought of going near it. Even within the camp, air drifting from the fissure was like a breath from the mouth of a furnace. The sound of dripping water meeting red-hot rock could be heard hundreds of yards away.

In spite of the weather, Sol Brewster remained in an unusually good mood. The sight of a weary and hunched Winnie Carlson only seemed to add to his satisfaction. She was the last to rise, trailing miserably into the dining area yawning and rubbing her eyes as though it were the middle of the night.

"Rise and shine, Carlson." Brewster clapped his hands together. "Breakfast has to be over and done with in five minutes, because you have a full day ahead. Unless you propose to renege on last night's promise?"

"No, sir." Winnie made an effort and stood up straight, but she stared at the breakfast trays as if she never intended to eat again. "I did a lot of preparation last night. I'll have the appetizers ready by sundown, provided the day's work doesn't run too late."

"I don't see why it should. Yesterday we were engaged in a general search. Today we can be far more specific." Brewster moved over to the wall, where an image of the Avernus Fissure was divided into sections and marked with multicolored arrows radiating out from a central point. "I have noted the location of our first discovery. Now I want to explore around it, and determine the extent of the find. Each of you will be assigned your own test sector."

The trainees exchanged glances. It was going to be yesterday all over again, with heat enough to stifle, and without the excitement of a possible new discovery. One question remained: Which unlucky person would be given the test area closest to the Avernus hellhole?

"Let me end the whining before it begins." Brewster had been watching their reaction. "No one will be assigned the quadrant closest to the fissure. The heat there today will be extreme. *However*"—he cut through the murmurs of relief—"that area must be tested. So each of you will spend one hour at that site. I will define the rotation of duties. I will also be spending more time there, myself, than any one of you."

"But there are no plants in that sector," Amethyst objected. "It's too close to the fissure and too hot for anything to grow."

"Quite true, but not relevant." Brewster gestured to one of

the tables, where a number of items of new equipment had been laid out. "Today you will not be testing plants. You will be testing *soils*. Let me show you how these instruments work."

As they crowded closer to the table, it occurred to Josh that Rick and Hag's questions of the previous night had just been answered. Soil tests were an important part of plant biology. That was why they had seen Brewster digging the ground in the place where Josh had made his discovery.

On the other hand, Brewster's explanation was no explanation at all. It made sense to test soils, if you wanted to determine how well plants of a certain type might grow in them; but if you *knew* that nothing could grow close to the smoldering heat of the Avernus Fissure, why go to the trouble of testing soil there?

Josh pondered that question again later in the day, when his turn came to work close to the fissure. By noon, Solferino's sun had burned off the morning steam and fog. Grisel shone blazing hot on his back as he knelt to lift a soil sample and place it in his new test kit. This time there was no chance of a startling find. The instrument did not display its results, it merely stored them internally for later integration into a computer database. You might be dropping gold dust in there, but you would never know it.

The soil analysis of each specimen took longer than a plant bioanalysis. Josh had to remain crouched in one place for more than two minutes in every test, until the unit finally informed him that he was free to move on. The air around him shimmered. Sweat dripped steadily from his chin and ran down his forehead into his eyes, and he could feel heat from the reddish soil burning through the padded knee-cloth of his trousers and warming the soles of his shoes.

It was probably only one hour, but it felt like three before Sig Lasker finally arrived to relieve him.

"Any sign of Topaz and Dawn?" Josh had to ask the important question quickly. Brewster might be watching, and he came down hard on anybody who stopped work to chat.

"Not a sign, but I'm going to tell you what I told Saph: Topaz is smart, and they'll both be fine. If you can't do anything about a thing, stop worrying." Sig took Josh's test kit and pretended to be studying it. "*Schütz*, it's hot down here."

"Wait half an hour, then you'll know what hot is. Anything else happening?"

"Rick and Hag aren't feeling good. They had to go back to camp. Brewster insisted at first that they were all right, just faking it. But they weren't."

"He made them keep on working?"

"Not after Rick threw up all over Brewster's boots. Then even Brewster had to admit there was something wrong."

"How sick are they?"

"Those two morons?" If Sig felt any sympathy for his brothers, he didn't show it. "Not as sick as they deserve to be. Put their brains together, you'd be lucky to get a half-wit. I've seen 'em do it before, but they never learn. They had another eating contest at breakfast today. *Anybody* would be sick, gobbling until there's no room for one more bite, then coming out into this heat. I'm not worried about them. But Brewster seems to be. I told him they'd be all right, and still he seemed totally bent out of shape."

"Maybe he feels bad about the way he's been treating us."

"Brewster? Yeah, sure. And maybe I'll grow wings and fly across the fissure. Get real, Josh."

"So what's *your* explanation?"

"I don't have one. I'm just reporting what happened." Sig knelt down and pushed the little spoon-shaped sampler into the hard soil. He lifted it and dropped a few grams of red dirt into his test kit, then reached down and touched the ground with his bare hand. "It's even hotter when you get down to ground level. Why are you hanging around, when you could be somewhere cooler?"

"I'm not. I'm on my way."

Josh trudged up the hill. He could feel the temperature drop with every step. By the time he was back to his original station, halfway to the camp, the soles of his feet had stopped burning. He didn't try to fool himself, though; the air was still too warm for comfort. He squinted up at the sun. Grisel was high in the sky. About four more hours before the signal came to quit for the day. What were the chances that Brewster would accept another trainee reporting sick?

Not good, unless you were able to throw up on his boots. And if you did, there would surely be reprisals later. Rick and Hag Lasker weren't going to enjoy tomorrow.

Josh sighed, and stooped to test another sample.

Days had enough discomforts of their own to discourage thinking. Only when night approached did Josh begin to worry seriously about Dawn and Topaz.

Tonight, fortunately, there were distractions. It was strange, but the very word "party" produced a lift in everyone's spirits. Even if it were Sol Brewster's party, with the man himself presiding; even if half the group was not there (Rick and Hag had yet to put in an appearance; Sig reported that they were almost back to normal, except that any mention of food made them feel ill all over again); even if the food itself was a major question mark, because no one had any experience of Sol Brewster's or Winnie Carlson's cooking. In spite of all those things, Josh could feel his mood becoming more cheerful, and he knew from the rising noise level that others felt the same.

Certainly the two cooks seemed to be taking their jobs seriously. They were at opposite ends of the crowded dining room. Brewster had a gigantic pot bubbling on a heating element, and next to it a container of rice enough to feed twice their number. Keeping one eye on the pot, he was carefully pouring pale yellow liquid into disposable glasses from a large iced flagon.

Winnie Carlson, no less intent, hovered over two pans of her own and the portable autochef. She had made a great secret of its programming, refusing to allow anyone near while she was doing it.

Brewster called Sig over to him. "Where are those two good-for-nothing brothers of yours?"

"They don't feel like eating tonight, sir."

Brewster didn't seem surprised. He nodded as though he had expected that answer, glared down at his newly washed boots, and said, "Very well. Go and tell Hagen and Alberich that they can be excused from dinner, but only if they come here now. They must take part in a celebratory toast to the success of our efforts at the Avernus Fissure."

His last words were almost drowned by a crash of falling pans at the other end of the room.

"Sorry, sir." It was Winnie Carlson, rising flustered from beside the autochef. "They were empty, I knocked them over by accident. But everything is ready. Would you do me the honor of taking the first bite?"

Brewster was clearly more interested in making sure that Sig returned with his brothers. He was glancing frequently at the door, and at the same time lining up half-filled glasses in preparation for the toast. He frowned at Winnie as she approached carrying a small tray.

"First, the blini and caviar by itself, sir, to establish the flavor." She stood in front of him and held out the tray. "Then, we add the sour cream."

Brewster gave a curt nod. He sat down and helped himself to a small, flat blini pancake about the size of a half-dollar. The caviar formed a small, dark heap at the center. He nibbled the edge, just enough to sample the caviar, and his eyebrows rose.

"Why, this is *excellent.*" He put the rest of the blini into his mouth and chewed vigorously.

"I told you that it would be, sir. The blinis just melt in your mouth. And you'll find they're even better once I add the rest." Winnie took a spoon and dropped a great dollop of smooth yellow cream on top of another blini and caviar. She lifted the whole thing onto the spoon and held it out. "Here you are, sir. Open wide."

Brewster didn't need urging. He put his head back and allowed Winnie to slide the pancake off the spoon and into his open mouth. He started to chew with a look of total bliss on his face.

The enjoyment lasted until the mouthful was completely swallowed. And then, slowly, his expression changed.

First the dark eyes began to fill with tears. Brewster's face darkened and his mouth opened. He put his hands to his throat and made a horrible gargling sound.

"He's choking!" Sapphire cried. "Give him something to drink."

Amethyst reached out to put one of the glasses readied for the toast to Brewster's mouth. He knocked it away and rose to his feet, watering eyes bulging out of his head. He turned on Winnie Carlson.

"Aah-ll-hh . . . Aah-ll-hh." He panted like a dog, and tried again. "The cream. Aah-ll-hh—"

He advanced on Winnie Carlson, towering over her. She stood her ground and looked up at him. "Mr. Brewster, I'll put up with most things. But if there is one thing I won't stand, it's somebody criticizing my blinis with caviar and sour cream. I expect an apology from you, right now."

"A-a-apology!" He was drooling so much he could hardly speak, and at the same time panting desperately. His face had turned fiery red. "Aah-hhh, aah, you—"

"An apology," Winnie said firmly. "But since you clearly refuse to give one . . ."

She put down the tray, lifted the bowl of yellow cream, and pushed it into Brewster's face.

He gave a great roar of rage, and rushed at Winnie. He was on her before anyone else had time to move.

One twist from those great hands would be enough to break her neck. But at the last moment Winnie somehow swayed her head and upper body to the left, just a few inches, while her hips remained in the same position. As Brewster's momentum carried him up to her, she gripped him by the left arm and the right side of his shirt. She seemed to fall backward and he followed. But instead of landing smack on top of her he left the ground completely, turning in midair to fall headfirst onto the hard dining-room floor.

He was still conscious and cursing loudly, but before he could move again Winnie was on her feet and crouched behind him. Her fingers grabbed his thick neck and probed. For a few seconds he continued to try to stand up. He managed to reach his hands and knees, still straining upward, then toppled forward again onto his face. This time he did not move.

Winnie didn't give him another glance—not even to confirm that he was unconscious. She looked at the startled trainees and spoke in a commanding voice nothing like her own. "Don't drink from those glasses! Not one drop. Don't even touch them."

She jumped to her feet to make sure everyone was obeying. As she did so, Sig Lasker entered the dining room with his two brothers.

"Shit on skates." Sig's mouth opened as wide as Sol Brewster's. "What's the hell's going on here?"

"No need for cussing," Winnie said curtly. "Or if there is, I'm the one should be doing it. Lock that door behind you." She was moving around the room, gathering each glass and making sure that it had not been drunk from. "I'm pretty sure the excitement's over for the moment. I have one or two more things to do, then we can all relax. Don't touch that, either!" Amethyst had been reaching out an experimental fingertip to the fallen bowl of sour cream. "It won't kill you—not like the toast—but it will make your mouth and skin burn for days. I used the hottest spices in the known universe. Sol Brewster isn't going to enjoy the feeling when he wakes up, but I guess soreness will be the least of his worries."

"Kill us?" Sapphire had latched onto that one word. "Are you saying that if we'd drunk his toast, we would have died?"

"I'm saying exactly that. Of course, I'll have to test it and make sure. But I believe that Brewster was planning to poison the lot of us tonight. He had found what he wanted, and we were no more use to him."

"But what *did* he want?" Josh asked, as Sig, Rick, and Hag gathered round the fallen Brewster. Hag said in awed tones, "Did you all gang up on him?"

"No." Sapphire pointed at Winnie Carlson. "She did it—all by herself." Then Saph asked the question everybody wanted to ask: *"What's going on around here?"*

"Too many things." Winnie bent over to take another look at Sol Brewster, and apparently didn't like what she saw. "Give me a minute to take care of this. Then I'll explain all I know."

"Are you going to make him wake up?" Amethyst asked.

"Definitely not." Winnie was over at the cabinet containing medical supplies. "I'm going to make sure that he doesn't."

She applied an injection spray to the side of Brewster's neck, raised one of his eyelids, and checked his pulse. "Good enough. He'll be out for the rest of the night."

She gestured to them all to sit down. "You want to know what's going on here? That's a fair question. I'll tell you, but I'm not sure where to begin. I realized what was going on bit by bit, but it's too confusing if I tell it that way. There are an awful lot of pieces. Let me start the way I started, with questions, things that worried me and maybe you, too. Number one: Where are the other people, the forty-odd who ought to have been on Solferino when you arrived? I gather you never saw any of them."

"They're at the medical center," Rick said.

"I heard that, too. But did you notice, Brewster hardly mentioned it after I arrived? I thought that was significant. Question number two: Why did Sol Brewster drop everything, without warning, and take us all to the camp in the Barbican Hills, almost as soon as we had arrived on the planet? And the second part of that question, why did he then leave us there, and fly back to the compound and the main site of the settlement?"

"He said he'd had a message from the medical center," said Amethyst.

"So he did. The one and only message anyone has had since we've been here. Because after that the computer that services the communications center went down. We lost outside contact, and many of the databases. Question number three: How did the breakdown and loss of data happen?"

"I think we may have done it," Josh said. He looked defensively at Rick and Hag. "Well, we might have. It doesn't matter now."

"You didn't," Winnie said. "You smashed one backup data unit, but that had nothing to do with the general failures. What *did* cause it? Let's go on. Question number four: What were Unimine ships doing near Solferino? You all saw one as you were first arriving. And Josh thinks he saw another one later."

"I did see it. Dawn saw it, too—and she drew it."

"I believe you. But what was it doing here? Unimine has mineral rights to Cauldron, but no rights at all on Solferino. Just a couple more questions, then we'll look at answers. Number five: What were you really looking for, when you were doing plant tests around the Avernus Fissure? I didn't accept for one minute that it was new alkaloids."

"Nor did I!" Amethyst said triumphantly. "I told everyone that Brewster was lying when he said that."

"Good for you. It wasn't alkaloids, but you spent a whole day doing plant tests. Then Josh made his discovery. And after that Brewster switched to *soil* tests. Question number six: Why the changeover? In particular, why test on the brink of the Avernus Fissure, where plants won't grow if you wait for a thousand years?"

"That was *my* question, last night," Hag said excitedly.

"So you've all been wondering about things." Winnie nodded. "I'm not surprised. You're a bright bunch, and Brewster was crazy to think he could fool you for long with explanations he was dreaming up on the spur of the moment. All right, here's the final question. What is it, number eight?"

"Seven," said Amethyst.

"Good enough. Number seven. Maybe it would have been question number one, but I only heard about it from you much later. When you arrived on Solferino, Brewster wasn't at the compound. He arrived later in the day, and he was very surprised to see you. Either Foodlines headquarters didn't inform him that you'd be here earlier than the original date, or he was too busy doing something else to check for messages. I think it was the second reason. So here is question number seven: What had Brewster been doing, that took him away from the compound at the time of your arrival?"

"He had an answer for that," Sig said. "He told us he had been with the other exploration team members to the medical center. We decided that sounded fishy. We agreed last night that not one of us ever heard about a Grisel system medical center in any briefing."

"For a good reason. There is no off-planet medical center in the Grisel system."

"So where *did* the exploration team go?" Sapphire asked. She put her arm around Ruby, as though she already had an idea what the answer might be.

"That was my number-one question. The answer also gives the answer to number seven: What was Brewster doing when you first arrived on Solferino? One thing's for sure, he wasn't off-planet, because when I arrived there were no vehicles *capable* of going off-planet. All you had was a cargo aircar, able to operate in Solferino's atmosphere but not outside it."

"That's what he arrived in," said Sig. "We saw it."

"Yes, but there was no way he could have used it to come in from space. So when you first got here, he had been somewhere *on*

Solferino. I hate to tell you what I think he had been doing, but I must. He had been disposing of the bodies of the Solferino exploration team. He killed all of them, maybe by poisoning them as I'm sure he was going to poison you."

Ruby gasped. She shrank back closer to Sapphire, who held her sister tight and said, "Where did he put them?"

"I can only guess, unless Brewster chooses to tell us. But over there"—Winnie gestured in the direction of the Avernus Fissure—"is an environment where a human body would be completely gone in a few days. He had already been exploring in this area, and he knew it well. You arrived while he was busy disposing of the evidence. He wasn't expecting you. He had to make up a story on the spot and get rid of Bothwell Gage as soon as possible, too. Gage is lucky. If he hadn't been as keen to leave as Brewster was to get rid of him, I don't think he would have survived his first night on Solferino. Gage wouldn't have swallowed for a moment the story that Brewster gave you, about the healing effects of this planet—any more than I did."

"We didn't buy it, either," Sig said. "Not completely. I guess we hoped it might be true. But *why* would he want to kill everybody?"

"I'll get to that in a moment. First, I want to answer question number two. Why did he take us to the camp in the Barbican Hills, leave us there, and fly straight back to the compound? The answer to that is simple. Something you had found around the compound made him afraid there might be other evidence left behind. I'm talking about things that the exploration team would never have forgotten, if they had been alive when they departed from the settlement."

"The bodger," Josh said softly. "Rick and Hag found the bodger. Topaz insisted that no one would go away and leave a pet tied up to starve."

Winnie nodded. "Topaz was right. And nobody did. But when it was discovered, Brewster got scared. He realized that he had to get all of us out of the way so he could do a thorough search of the compound, inside and outside, without interference."

Josh remembered how his personal belongings had been moved in the dormitory room, but he said nothing because Winnie was continuing: "Brewster also wiped out parts of the computer while we were away at the camp. Deliberately." She glanced at Josh and the Lasker twins. "Brewster did it, not you. That's the answer to my question number three. As to *why*, it was because some of the files held information that he dared not let us see. I spent a lot of time trying to find backup copies—I've not had a decent night's sleep since I got here, that's why I'm always yawning."

"So that's the two people I saw wandering around at night," Josh burst out. "It was you, trailing Brewster."

"Must have been—though I didn't realize we'd been seen. But no matter how I tried, I couldn't find out anything about the personnel assigned to Solferino, particularly their medical records. Brewster didn't want anyone finding out that people here were as sick as people anywhere else. There were other missing files, too, that I didn't think were significant at the time, but I do now. I couldn't find files for the Foodlines charter for the exploration of Solferino, and I couldn't find the interfaces for different groups working in the Grisel stellar system."

Winnie looked at Sig. "Now it's time to answer question number four: What was a Unimine ship doing buzzing around this planet, where it had no business to be? This will answer your question, too, Sig, as to why Brewster had to kill everyone on Solferino, including us. And it's a simple answer: Brewster did it because he wanted to become one of the richest men in the known universe. He was an employee of Foodlines, but he had discovered something that made Solferino unique. It also made the planet far more suited to Unimine than Foodlines activities. Unimine has mineral extraction technology, Foodlines doesn't. Have you heard of stable transuranic elements?"

"Bothwell Gage told us about them," Amethyst said, "when

we were coming through the Messina Dust Cloud on the way here. They are enormously valuable, he said."

"He was right. Enormously valuable, but also enormously difficult to collect from the extended pockets of gas where they are found in the Messina Dust Cloud. A deposit of *solid* stable transuranics is a prospector's dream. Brewster had found traces of such a thing, here on Solferino. That's what the kits you were using were designed to test for. I know, because I checked late last night. That story about alkaloids was pure nonsense. Brewster knew pretty much where the deposits were, around the Avernus Fissure, but the more details he had on location, the better the deal he could make with Unimine. And Josh hit the jackpot."

"But I was testing *plants,*" Josh protested. "Not for those stable transuranic things."

"I know. But there is a branch of science called *geobotany.* It is a way of looking for minerals by knowing that certain plants will only grow in their presence or absence, and sometimes by knowing that the plants themselves concentrate particular minerals in their leaves and stems. I will bet my next year's paycheck that Sol Brewster's technical field is geobotany. You were testing plants, but you were actually looking for selected *minerals.* Of course, once Brewster had a strong enough geobotanical signal, he could go to that point and use ordinary mineral exploration methods. That's why you started testing with plants, but switched to soil samples when the location was pinpointed accurately enough. And that's the answer to my questions five and six."

"But I still don't get it," Sig said. "He wanted to make a deal with Unimine. I understand that. But why did he have to kill us? Why did he have to murder everyone who was already on Solferino?"

Winnie was ready to answer, but Ruby had begun to cry. All the talk of death and murder was too much for her. Sapphire looked at Sig reproachfully.

"See what you've done?" She put her arms more tightly

around her sister. "Don't cry, Rube. We're all safe now. Aren't we, Winnie?"

"Perfectly safe." Winnie went across and put her own arms around Sapphire. "Brewster won't be waking up for a long time, and I'll make sure he's tied up nice and tight. There will be people coming here from Unimine at some point, and I'll have to work out a way to make sure they don't cause trouble—some of them probably realize what Brewster has been up to, and maybe they've even been helping him. But Unimine won't come here at night. Tonight you can all relax. There'll be no more surprises."

As she was saying the final word, a loud banging came on the outside of the locked dining-room door. Winnie started up and turned in that direction. No one had to ask if she was frightened or worried. Her tense body posture said it all.

There would be more shocks before the evening was over—and Winnie had no more idea than anyone else what they might be.

CHAPTER EIGHTEEN

THE trainees sat frozen as the banging came again on the closed door. Only Winnie Carlson had the nerve to stand up, walk over to it, and call "Who's there?"

"It's us," said an impatient voice from outside. "Come on! Why do you have the door locked?"

Everyone gasped in relief, and Winnie leaned forward and rested her head for a moment on the frame as if she were praying. "Just a second, Topaz. I'm doing it." She worked the lock with fingers that trembled a little, and opened the door. "Come on in, girl."

"We can't yet." Topaz had backed up until she was standing a few feet away. "You'll have to dim the lights first."

"Why?" But Winnie gestured to Josh, who went and reduced the room lighting to a lower level.

"That enough?" he said.

"A little bit more," Topaz said from outside. "Bright lights are bad. That should be enough, though, you can hold it there." She moved inside, turned, and stood waiting. She was filthy and her clothes were torn and ragged, but she had a smile on her face. "Come on," she said in a coaxing voice. "Come on in."

Two figures entered side by side. One of them was Dawn. Unlike Topaz, she seemed as fresh and clean as if she had just bathed and dressed. She was smiling, too. Under her left arm she carried a big sketch pad. Her right hand held the paw of an animal that stood on its hind legs and slowly walked with her into the dimly lit room.

A few feet inside the door, Dawn sat down cross-legged on the floor. The animal sank onto its haunches beside her.

"I *told* you that a rupert has eyes!" Ruby said. "Maybe now you'll believe me."

Everyone stared at the strange newcomer. Fully upright, it was maybe four feet tall. Most of that was body, because all four limbs were short and stubby. The gray, beadlike scales that covered the torso suggested a family relationship to both the bodger and the spangle. Like the bodger, the front of the rupert's face carried a long, flexible trunk. Each side of the sleek head sprouted great winglike ears of iridescent blue and white. Those organs were in constant motion, turning from side to side.

There were also major differences from both spangles and bodgers. The most noticeable one was the eyes, black and beady and somehow too small for the rest of the head. They appeared to be fixed in their field of view. Although the ears turned to face and examine different members of the group in the dining area—the rupert seemed as interested in the humans as they were in it—the little dark eyes moved only with the whole head.

Josh looked at the paw that Dawn was holding, and saw that it had three short fingers and no thumb. He also noticed, for the first time, a thin strap that ran around the rupert's middle and had hanging from it a bulging pouch about six inches square.

He stood up and pointed to it. "He's got a carrying bag! That's a sign of intelligence, if anything is. I *told* you ruperts weren't just animals."

"His 'carrying bag,' as you call it," Topaz said coldly, "happens to be *her purse*. Ruperts are like humans. The females are smarter than the males. And she's *really* shy, so keep your voice down."

Topaz probably had more to say, but as she was speaking she had moved closer to Josh and noticed for the first time Sol Brewster, lying unconscious and shielded by the table. Her mouth opened wide. She pointed without saying another word.

"I know, I know." Winnie sighed. "We have lots to tell you, and you must have at least as much to tell us. Why don't we prepare some food, and then we'll talk? I think this is going to be a long night."

"Why not eat that?" Topaz pointed to the still-simmering pot and the great heap of rice, both of which had been ignored for the past half hour. She looked again at Brewster's body, which was lying face down. "Is it the food? Did he get food poisoning?"

"No, it's not the food," Winnie said. "I did that to him. But we can't eat the food over there because it may be poisoned."

Topaz stared at her, wide-eyed, and sank onto a seat next to Josh. "I thought Dawn and I were the ones with a story to tell. I guess I was wrong."

"I believe we both do." Winnie turned to Rick. "Can you rustle something up quick? Nothing fancy, and while it's getting ready I'll try to explain things to Topaz and Dawn."

"Easy." But Rick looked doubtfully at Topaz. "Unless I have to feed him, too."

"*Her*," Topaz said emphatically. "But it's all right. Ruperts won't eat our food, any more than we'll eat theirs. She'll go outside and get something if she wants it. She has a name, by the way. Dawn?"

Dawn nodded and picked up the sketchpad. She drew on it a series of marks, like little kites and darts and dashes. The rupert studied what she was doing, and after a few seconds made a clicking, hissing sound, followed by a high-pitched whistle.

"There," Topaz said. "G-ss-ee. I can't really pronounce it, nor can Dawn. But we've been calling her Gussie, and she responds to that and doesn't seem to mind." She stood up, moved over to Brewster, and bent down to examine him more closely. "What's that on his face, and on the floor?"

"Sour cream," said Sapphire. She beamed at Topaz, and in her pleasure at her sister's return she seemed for the first time in days free of snap withdrawal symptoms.

"Sour cream." Topaz sank back onto a chair. "You knocked Brewster out with sour cream? And it was Winnie Carlson that did it to him, right? And before that, he was poisoning your food. Nothing we got up to competes with that. I have to know what's been happening here."

"It's messy," said Winnie. "And I don't just mean literally. The rest of you, be patient. Topaz and Dawn have to hear this from the beginning."

She started again with her explanations. Josh found himself dividing his attention between what Winnie was saying and the actions of Dawn and the rupert. The latter two were completely silent, but while Winnie talked they constantly exchanged drawings. The rupert held a pen clumsily between two of her short fingers. She seemed to draw quickly and skillfully, and she and Dawn were obviously communicating. But what were they saying to each other?

One of Winnie's statements suddenly caught Josh's attention. She was adding to the ideas and suspicions that she had presented to them before.

"Actually," Winnie was saying, "we were given a hint, very early, as to what Brewster might have found on Solferino. Do you remember when you were in the cargo aircar on the way to the Barbican Hills, and you heard an educational recording? It said that Solferino is only four-fifths the diameter of Earth, but that the surface gravity is almost exactly the same. And the recording went on to point out the reason, which is that the average density of Solferino is twenty-six percent higher than the density of Earth. What the recording *didn't* say is that Earth is itself an exceptionally dense planet. In fact, it's the densest world in the solar system. Earth's interior is mostly solid iron. So Sol Brewster probably asked himself, what is it that makes Solferino even denser than the Earth? Well, it could be normal heavy elements, like lead and uranium and thorium. But most of the heaviest elements are radioactive, and there were no reports of high radiation levels on Solferino. Another answer, though, and one that probably occurred to Brewster, is that there could be lots of *stable transuranics* here. They are super-heavy, heavier than any elements formed naturally, but because they are stable they are not radioactive. I think that's when he probably began to examine the geobotanical properties of the stable transuranics, and plan his search . . ."

Winnie went on talking, but Josh was suddenly distracted by Dawn's actions. She had looked up from the pad, where the rupert was busily drawing, and she was staring at him. When she saw that she had his attention, she nodded and beckoned. He stood up and went to kneel at her side.

"What?" He spoke in a whisper.

"G-ss-ee." Her pronunciation was much closer to the sound that the rupert had made than Topaz's effort. She took his hand and placed in it one of the rupert's paws. "Joshua."

He suddenly realized what she was doing. It was his formal

introduction, as a member of Dawn's family, to the rupert. He didn't smile—he couldn't even guess the rupert equivalent of a smile—but he did his best to say "G-ss-ee" just as Dawn had said it. The rough paw rubbed backward and forward on the palm of his hand. It was surprisingly warm. Ruperts were warm-blooded, and they must have a body temperature quite a bit above humans.

"Outside," Dawn said.

"Me?" Josh didn't really want to go outside. He wanted to hear anything new that Winnie might have to say, and he was also starving. Rick looked as though he almost had something ready to serve.

"G-ss-ee outside." Dawn stood up, and the rupert did the same. Fully upright, it was about his height kneeling.

"Wait a minute." Josh stood up, too, and turned to Winnie. He waited for her to finish her sentence—she was talking now about the way Brewster had destroyed computer data banks—and asked, "Is it all right for Dawn and the rupert to go outside?"

"I think so. Will they come back?"

"Dawn will, if we ask her to. I don't know about the rupert."

"We don't own her. Gussie can do whatever she wants to do." Winnie nodded. "All right, they can both go."

Dawn was already moving toward the door. The rupert followed, after a final sweeping survey of the group in the dining room. Topaz caught Josh's eye. She had an I-told-you-so look on her face. He wondered just what she and Dawn had been doing in the two days they had been gone, and how long it would be before he found out.

"Where was I?" Winnie asked. "Right, the computers. We lost the ability to communicate off-planet. That's when I really became worried about Brewster's plans. I knew I might have to do something, and without any outside assistance."

"That's the piece I still can't believe," said Topaz. She stared at Brewster's great length sprawled out along the floor. "He's at least two meters tall, and he has all the muscles. I guess I'll have to believe that you were able to fight him and knock him cold, because the others insist that they saw you do it. But I don't see *how.* That can't be any part of a Foodlines maintenance technician's training."

"You're probably right." Winnie looked sheepish. "Though I can't say for sure, because I'm not really a maintenance technician. I haven't been quite honest with you. I don't work for Foodlines, and they didn't send me here."

That was enough to get everyone's attention. There was a long, electric silence. Hag stopped looking longingly at the door through which Dawn and Gussie had left. Rick abandoned his cooking and came to join the rest of the group around the table.

"So who do you work for?" Sig asked at last.

"I am an agent for the SDSI—the Solar Department of Special Investigations."

"A secret agent!" Amethyst said. "Wow."

"It's not what you might think." Winnie smiled wearily. "Lots of nights with not enough sleep, and lots of being ordered around like dirt by crooks and creeps. I've been trained to look after myself, without needing weapons. Normally there is no need for them. Most cases involve some bending of a corporate franchise, and maybe a bit of illegal export. There's usually not much action in my job."

"Except tonight," Topaz said. "You had plenty of action tonight. But you're still not being honest with us."

"I'm doing my best."

"I don't see that. If you were sent here by SDSI, you must have known all about Sol Brewster and what he was doing, before you ever left Earth. Otherwise, why come in the first place?"

"I was sent because SDSI believed that something illegal was happening, here on Solferino. But it had nothing to do with Sol Brewster, and Unimine, and stable transuranics. When I came through the node network, Sol Brewster was just a name—the name of the person I was supposed to report to. And the message to him, saying that I was on the way, didn't come from Foodlines at all. It was a fake—like my credentials."

Josh was losing track. Too many things were happening at once. Was he the only slow one in the group? If so, might as well admit it.

"I don't understand this," he said, and he saw other heads nodding in agreement. "Could you give it to us again. You weren't sent here to investigate Brewster, or what Unimine might be doing on Solferino. And you weren't sent here by Foodlines, to maintain their equipment. So why were you sent here?"

"Because SDSI had suspicions that something might be happening on this planet. Something that Foodlines was doing. Something even worse than what Brewster has been doing."

"It couldn't be!" Sapphire protested. "You said he's a *murderer.*"

"He is. But that isn't the worst thing in the universe."

"There isn't anything worse."

"I wish you were right, Sapphire. But there is. It's something called genocide."

Sapphire sank back in her chair. It was Ruby, sitting huddled in the crook of her arm, who said, "What's *genocide?*"

"I'm not sure I want to tell you." Winnie shook her head sadly, but she went on. "I wish the word didn't even exist. Genocide means killing not just one person, or a few people, or even a lot of people, but a whole *race* of people. It would also apply to killing off an entire intelligent species."

"Gussie!" Amethyst shouted. "And the ruperts. Oh, no!"

"It's all right, Amy, it hasn't happened. And we'll make sure it doesn't." Winnie turned to address the whole group. "You may not have a very high opinion of the government of Earth. It certainly hasn't done much for you during your lives. But Earth has worried for centuries about the problem of meeting other intelligences in the universe. There are definite rules. The most important ones are, first, that no intelligent species can be exterminated, exploited, or reduced to slavery. And second, that the *home world* of any intelligent species belongs to that species. It cannot be exploited by any human group."

"Brewster told us that the ruperts aren't intelligent," said Rick.

"He did. But he wasn't making that up. He was quoting the official position adopted by Foodlines."

"But ruperts *are* intelligent," Topaz said. "You only have to spend five minutes with Gussie, and you'd know it."

"I agree. So why do you think that Foodlines takes the opposite position, in every official filing of information back in the solar system?"

There was a moment's silence, then Topaz said uneasily, "So they can keep Solferino?"

"Exactly. They suspect that there are terrific opportunities here for new biological products. If they ever hinted that ruperts might be intelligent, they'd be in danger of losing their exploration rights."

"But what can Foodlines do about the ruperts?" Hag asked. "I mean, they're here. People know they are here."

"True. But no one on Earth *knows that they are intelligent.* Foodlines will insist that they are just animals, and ignore them. The ruperts are very shy, and they come out mainly at night. Unless you happen to be someone like Dawn, with great empathy for other species, you would never meet one. Foodlines can act as if ruperts don't exist."

"Act as if they don't exist for long enough," said Sig. "And eventually . . ."

"You are too old for your years, Sig Lasker." Winnie frowned, but it was obvious that although she was angry it was not with Sig. "Quite right. Eventually, they will not exist. Not if you destroy their habitats, and deprive them of their natural food supplies, and maybe shoot any that you happen to see. Then the problem is solved. I hate to say this, but the people at Foodlines who made the decision to keep quiet about the ruperts learned that lesson on Earth. Humans have made thousands of Earth species extinct, in just that way, right back to the beginning of history."

"I don't get it." Topaz was pushing right up against Josh. The group had been gathering closer and closer, as if they could not face alone the ideas that they were hearing. "I thought *Unimine* were the bad guys in all this. Now you seem to be saying the villain is *Foodlines*. And I don't understand why, if Foodlines kept quiet about the ruperts, the government back on Earth sent you out here to find out what was going on."

"It's both of them, sweetie." Winnie was sitting in the middle, with everyone crowded around her. "It's Unimine *and* Foodlines, though of course I didn't know that before I came out here. People in solar system government noticed that the first reports from Solferino said ruperts were the most intelligent life form on the planet, and fairly smart animals. Then later reports didn't say *anything* about ruperts. Not one word. That's when somebody in SDSI thought it might be worth taking a look. But a *quiet* look, so no one would become suspicious and start to destroy evidence or change behavior patterns. That's why I was sent under cover, as a maintenance technician. As for your other question, don't think of what's going on here in terms of Sol Brewster and ruperts and the death of a particular exploration team. Think of huge, powerful, rich conglomerates, run by people who will never get within light-years of Solferino. There's an old saying, but it's as true today as when it was first stated: *Power corrupts; and absolute power corrupts absolutely.* The people at the top of Foodlines and Unimine have immense power. What they care about isn't you and me, or individual rights, or even species rights. What they think about are company interests and corporate advantage. Foodlines wants control of Solferino, and for that control the conglomerate will gladly sacrifice the ruperts. Unimine doesn't care about ruperts, either, any more than Foodlines does. Unimine wants to take over Solferino to get at the stable transuranics, but can't do that as long as there are Foodlines representatives here. Only if every human on Solferino dies, or leaves, can Unimine move in and file for development rights. Now you see the plan. The original exploration team dies, officially of unknown causes. Then *we* die—Brewster picked you out, you know, as kids whose disappearance wasn't likely to create a lot of screaming from their heartbroken parents."

The trainees exchanged unhappy looks, but no one tried to argue with Winnie.

"Finally, when we are safely dead and disappeared, Brewster leaves," she went on. "And Unimine has a clear road to occupy Solferino. They can apply for mineral development rights, because no one else is on the planet, and Foodlines's license depends on maintaining a presence. So what if they have to strip-mine a whole planet to get at the transuranics? So what if you have something at the end that's a dark, lifeless world? All you had here, according to the official record, were low-level native life forms. Wipe them out, they only get in the way. Reduce the surface of Solferino to raw magma. And then show real nerve: Try for a terraforming contract from solar government, to make this world habitable again by humans."

It had been a long speech, delivered with great intensity and few interruptions. Everyone sat spellbound, until Topaz said, "But now they're going to be found out, aren't they? They won't get away with it. What will happen to them?"

"I can make a guess, but you won't want to hear this. Brewster will be charged with murder. Unimine will deny that they ever had anything to do with him. Foodlines will say that he certainly wasn't working for *them* in what he did on Solferino—which in a sense is quite true—and they'll drop him like a hot rock. So Brewster will have no one protecting him. He will be punished. But the real villains are the people right at the top of the conglomerates, the heads of Foodlines and Unimine. They allow this sort of thing to happen, and they even encourage it. And they'll escape without a slap on the wrist. At the very worst, there might be a small fine for concealing information. Even there, I'm not sure. They will act innocent, and say, well, nothing happened, did it? The ruperts are alive and well. So what are you charging us with?"

The silence that followed was long and unhappy. Saph looked at Sig and shook her head. It was Winnie herself who finally sat up, sniffed, and said, "What's that?"

"Oh, no." Rick had been part of the group, as mesmerized as anyone. Now he jumped to his feet. "The food!"

He ran over to the oven. "It's cinders. It's all ruined."

"Then don't worry about it." Winnie stood up and stretched her back as though it hurt. "We're not fated to eat hot food tonight, I can tell. Put out anything that's cold and quick, Rick; and you, Josh, go bring Dawn in. I don't want to lose her again. Then we'll hear from Topaz, if she feels up to talking. And *then*"—she yawned hugely—"then I don't know about you people, but I'm ready for a bit of sleep."

CHAPTER NINETEEN

JOSH didn't sleep well. Two things that he had heard, late the previous night, mingled and burned inside his brain. Winnie Carlson's words merged with Topaz's first-hand description of her adventures with Dawn, to produce a strange dream in which Josh was in two places at once. Sometimes he was inside Topaz's head as well as his own.

Brewster was glaring down at him: We'll strip-mine this whole planet to get at the transuranics. Don't think you can stop us, Kerrigan. We're going to reduce the surface of Solferino to raw magma.

But in the same moment he was with Topaz and Dawn, creeping away from the camp in Solferino's predawn stillness. They were heading for higher ground. They looked back, and in his dream Josh looked back with them. No one at the camp had noticed them leaving. Josh could see through the walls. There he was, sound asleep in Topaz's bunk.

It was important to be far away from the Avernus Fissure before stopping to rest. Dawn had said it, in her own economical way: "Day sleep, night wake." They and the phantom Josh walked at least five miles before wrapping themselves in blankets and lying down. When they fell asleep it was in the purple shade of a gigantic plant, a daisy with petals twenty feet long.

They awoke to find Grisel already low in the sky. While Topaz prepared a cold meal, Dawn removed her shoes and shinned barefoot and monkey-easy up the plant's smooth trunk. She spent ten minutes at the top, thirty feet from the ground, examining the terrain in all directions. Josh hovered unsupported at her side, staring back toward the Avernus Fissure. He could see it clearly, despite the hills in between. It was glowing brighter red, and it was steadily widening.

Dawn offered not a word when she came down, until Topaz asked, "Which way, Dawn?" Topaz had decided before they left: Dawn was the expert on finding ruperts, therefore she would dictate their movements.

Dawn did not speak, but pointed north, at right angles to their first line of travel.

"And we'll stay there tonight?"

Dawn picked up her food box and began to examine the contents. She paid no attention to anyone. Topaz glanced again at the sun. They had maybe two more hours before dark, and they knew from the previous night that finding a way through a forest, even a moonlit one, was tricky. Daylight would be a lot easier. And those looked like rain clouds on the eastern horizon.

"Any sign of people coming after us, when you were up there?"

Dawn calmly went on eating. She did not look in Topaz's direction.

"All right." Topaz packed away her own food box. "I guess that's an answer. As soon as you've finished, let's go."

She was finding it easier to interpret Dawn, feeling her way slowly into the strangeness of an autistic's universe. For Dawn, the words "Yes" and "No" did not exist. If you steered clear of them, and the concepts that went with them, you had a far better chance of understanding what went on behind that rounded, unlined forehead. You learned not to ask questions calling for an abstract reply. Questions with a thing *as an answer, or an* action, *had a much greater chance of success. In Dawn's world, actions were significant; words were either meaningless or of marginal interest.*

Topaz stood up. An action. *"Let's go. I'm ready when you are. You go in front."*

Dawn tucked away her food box, lifted her pack, and led the way.

They walked nonstop until dusk, to a place where the continuous forest ended and was replaced by great islands of low and wiry ground cover, surrounded by straggling thickets of woody chest-high scrubs. Dawn walked to the middle of one of the flat islands, halted, and sat down.

Topaz followed and stared around her with no enthusiasm.

"Dawn, if we spend the night here we'll be visible from every direction. There's no place to hide within fifty yards. This is right out in the open."

"This is right," Dawn said in firm tones. "Out in the open."

If Dawn was in charge of rupert-finding, then you either had to do what she said, or you might as well go back to the camp. Topaz sighed, and sat down.

The invisible Josh settled by her side. A few drops of rain were already falling. Had they left the cover of the giant daisy plant's leaves so they could spend a long night being rained on? Apparently. He turned his eyes back to the direction of the camp. He couldn't make out what he and the others were doing there, but even from this distance he could feel the heat from the orange-red lava. It had begun, the reduction of the surface of Solferino to molten magma.

There was nothing to do but make the best of it. Topaz arranged blankets so that they could sit on one, and put one each around their heads. It was the only way to remain reasonably dry, but Dawn would not go along with it. She pushed her blanket off her head and shoulders and dropped it in a wet heap. As the rain strengthened, she insisted on sitting fully out in the open, letting the raindrops fall onto her unprotected head.

A total retard. Except that on Solferino the roles seemed to be reversed. Topaz was the retarded one, while Dawn appeared to know exactly what she was doing. She must want *to be visible. After a few minutes, Topaz put aside her own shielding blanket. She sat like Dawn, head bare, and felt the rain gradually soaking every part of her.*

At least it wasn't cold. Dawn showed no interest in talking about what they were doing, or in answering questions. After an hour or so of damp silence, and in spite of her intention to remain fully awake, Topaz felt her eyes start to close.

She opened them again after a few moments. It was amazing to be able to sleep at all, when you were sitting upright in the middle of nowhere, soaking wet, on an alien planet. And maybe it had been more than a few moments. Her back was aching, and she had a stuffy nose. Her head felt too heavy for her neck. She needed some real sleep.

And then, suddenly, Topaz was wide awake. Although she was still soaked, the rain had ended. There was a glimmer of moonlight across the broad clearing; Dawn no longer sat at her side.

Until this moment, she hadn't realized how much reassurance she felt because of Dawn's calm presence. Topaz stood up with an effort—she had been sitting cross-legged, and felt frozen into one position—and stared around her. The darkness at first seemed absolute.

"Dawn!" she spoke the word softly yet urgently, as she began to make out the first hint of a moonlit horizon separating earth and sky.

"Ssh!" The reply was equally soft. It sounded like Dawn, but it was echoed many times and by many voices. "Ssh—ssh—ssh—ssh—ssh." They all spoke at once, from a point to Topaz's left.

She peered in that direction. She had the conviction that she was being watched, by many eyes, and yet she could not see a thing. It took all her nerve to walk slowly and steadily in that direction. The night was quiet, the squelching of her shoes on the soaked vegetation the only sound.

"Dawn?" she said again, in hardly more than a whisper. She

walked even slower. When they had settled down to sit in the drenching darkness, she knew there had been nothing between them and the scrubby thickets, forty to fifty yards away. That had been one of her objections to the place, the lack of possible hiding places. Now, only a few yards in front of her, she sensed a clump of indistinct objects.

Decreased distance, and a tiny increase in light from the cloud-shrouded moon, made all the difference. Suddenly, the amorphous, soft-edged view ahead became a clear and surprising tableau. Dawn was sitting on the ground, facing Topaz. In front of her, bodies turned so that the heads were also pointing toward Topaz, sat a dozen animals. Even without being able to make out eyes in the sleek heads, Topaz was sure from their size and posture that they were ruperts.

The hardest thing was to keep quiet, suppressing even the urge to gasp. Topaz forced herself to walk forward, very slowly and calmly, and sit down without a word at Dawn's side. She did not move, even when the whole group rose up onto their hind legs and came to surround her. If she was interested in them, they surely felt the same about her. Even so, it took every ounce of self-control not to flinch or cry out, when a rough-furred paw reached out and lifted a lock of her rain-soaked hair.

Don't make any sudden moves. But let them know that you are interested, too. *Topaz saw that one of them was wearing a kind of shoulder satchel, supported by broad straps. Very gently and slowly, she lifted her hand and touched it. The rupert reached down, did something invisible with stubby fingers, and held out to her the open satchel. Presumably she was supposed to be able to see what was inside, but it was too dark. If they were nocturnal they must have excellent night vision, supplemented by the sort of batlike echolocation made possible by those wide-spreading ears. But she had neither. Topaz put one hand carefully inside the satchel, and felt a sharp and hard-edged object.*

She drew it out. It was a knife. So far as she was concerned, here in her fist sat the final proof of intelligence. The ruperts were tool-makers and tool-users. But Brewster, and almost all humans, still insisted that the ruperts were no more than animals. *That meant that they had no more rights than animals.*

"Dawn." She knew the danger of making a noise—if they were too shy and nervous they would surely flee—but she had to speak, and she had to make herself understood. "We must find a way to take a rupert with us to the camp. We must make them understand how important it is for all of them, that one of them go with us. This planet belongs to the ruperts, not to us, and we have to make people realize that."

Dawn said nothing. There was an almost irresistible urge to speak again, to repeat the same urging on the assumption that Dawn had not grasped its meaning the first time. Topaz fought against it. She said to herself, over and over, Dawn is smart, Dawn is smart, she knows what you are saying, *and she managed to sit silent and motionless. After a while she realized that she was still holding the rupert's knife. She reached out, and gently returned it to the pouch.*

"This planet belongs to the ruperts, not to us," *Dawn suddenly repeated. At those words, Topaz felt excitement and a tremendous relief. Dawn had* understood. *Now, if only she could do what Topaz suspected that she herself could never do, and find a way of communicating their message to the ruperts. . . . One of them sat very close to Dawn, and she was holding its paw as though they were old friends.*

This planet belongs to the ruperts, not to us. *But this time Topaz breathed it herself. She repeated it a hundred times in the next twenty-four hours. She said it to herself. She said it to Dawn, while the latter was busy exchanging incomprehensible drawings with half a dozen of the ruperts. And finally, she would say it to Josh and the rest of the trainees, when she returned travel-stained and weary to the camp with a fresh-as-ever Dawn—and with Gussie.*

This planet belongs to the ruperts, not to us.

Unfortunately, no one took any notice. It was too late, and all mineral rights had been assigned to Unimine. The strip-mining of Solferino, ripping off the upper layers of the planet to get at the stable transuranics below, was under way. The Avernus Fissure provided a starting point for those monstrous world-mining automata. The smallest of them, two kilometers long, began to widen and deepen the great crack in the planetary surface. It tore away forests, plains, and streams, to leave behind the smoking, red-hot underlayers.

As habitats vanished, the ruperts retreated. Josh and Topaz ran with them under cold Solferino moonlight, toward highlands where rupert survival was marginally possible. Higher and higher, into more and more difficult and inhospitable badlands. The air grew hotter, sulfurous and steamy. Black-and-red fuming magma rolled across the landscape, pursuing them as they fled. The retreat went on, day after day and mile after mile, until finally, one evening, Josh saw the deadly red glow ahead as well as behind. He watched the surface around them vanish, engulfed by mile-high maws. With the last of the ruperts, he stood at bay on a final small island of untouched surface.

The mining machine reared far above, blocking out the fading red light of Grisel. It threw a dark shadow across Josh and his companions. There was no place to run. Josh watched helplessly as the great black jaws opened, moved forward, and began to close.

It was the end. He put his arms around Topaz. As he did so, something lifted and shook him . . .

Josh awoke, sweating and gasping, and found himself staring up into Winnie Carlson's face. She had him by the shoulders, and she was shaking him.

"Josh. Wake up. I need you."

He looked at her, dazed. "The rupert—Gussie. And Topaz. Are they all right?"

"Perfectly fine. The rupert is with Dawn. Topaz is dressing. I need both of you for something. Get your clothes on, quick, and come outside."

Josh sat up. The vision of doomed ruperts and a Solferino turned to hell was slowly fading. "What do you need me for?" he asked, as Winnie hurried out of the door.

"As a witness," she said over her shoulder.

Which told him absolutely nothing. Witness to *what?*

He dressed in seconds, and hurried outside. Winnie had van-

ished, but Sig, Sapphire, and Topaz stood waiting. He stared at
Topaz. His dream had been so real, he expected her to say something about the destruction of Solferino and the death of all the ruperts. Instead Topaz said, "What *is* this? Winnie wouldn't tell me
why she needs me."

"She needs witnesses," said Sapphire. "But we're really too
young, all of us, so I don't see how it helps legally, no matter how
many of us there are."

"What are we going to witness?" Josh noticed that Sapphire
didn't look so shattered, though she was pale and blinking in the
light of a clear Grisel morning. It was Sig who seemed oddly uneasy and fidgety.

"Brewster," Saph said. "Winnie is going to question him.
She'll make a recording of everything, but she wants live witnesses,
too."

"Live witnesses, but mostly silent ones," said Winnie. She
had reappeared from the next building, which was Brewster's own
dormitory. "It's important that you observe everything, but once
we're inside I don't want you to say one word unless I ask you a direct question. No matter if it seems to make no sense, you all keep
quiet—except Sig, who will ask one question and make one statement that he and I have already discussed. Can you do that?"

The other three stared at Sig. He shrugged, but his face gave
nothing away.

"All right," Sapphire said at last, and the others nodded.

"But I have a question *before* we go in," Topaz said. "Was the
drink that he was going to give us poisoned?"

"It was."

"Then why do you need to question Brewster? I don't see
him confessing to anything. And you've got enough evidence already, haven't you?"

Winnie nodded. "More than enough, if all we needed to do
was prove that Brewster was guilty of attempted murder, and

maybe of actual murder—though that will be harder to prove. But I want more. I want to use him to snare Unimine."

"How?" Topaz asked. "I thought you said they're really cunning types, who'll vanish at the first sign of trouble. I can't see them trying to save Brewster."

"They won't. Not in a million years."

"So how can you use him to catch them?"

"You'll see in just a few minutes." Winnie glanced at her watch. "All right, he's been awake and alone in there for over half an hour. He's had time to think about things. Let's go."

Josh couldn't speak for the others, but his stomach was tight with tension as they went inside. Sol Brewster might not scare Winnie Carlson, but he still scared Josh.

The man was sitting in the biggest chair in the room. Broad gray restraining straps held him at forearms, wrists, waist, ankles, and knees. It was difficult to read his facial expression, because his mouth, chin, and cheeks were daubed with an orange ointment. He gave the trainees one glance of loathing, then looked away.

"Are you ready to cooperate yet?" Winnie asked. "I've told you what I want. You didn't set all this up by yourself. Unimine is in it, too. I need the details of that. And I'd like some practical help, too."

Brewster said nothing. He did not even look at her.

"You know, you ought to be a bit more appreciative," she went on. "I didn't have to wipe those spices off your face, and wash them out of your mouth. I could have let you sit there all night, and this morning you wouldn't have been able to speak even if you wanted to."

That persuaded him to look at her—not in appreciation, but with a glare of hatred and anger. Josh noticed something odd. Brewster seemed to have *shrunk* since the previous day; and Winnie seemed to have *grown*. She had become the dominant one, clearly in charge.

"You probably think you know exactly where you stand," Winnie said. "I told you who I am, and why I am on Solferino. I had to. My job requires that as a representative of SDSI I state my true identity when making an arrest. And I'm sure you know all your rights. I've accused you of certain things, including multiple murder, but you don't have to defend yourself to me. In fact, you don't have to say one word, until we're back Sol-side and you have your own legal counsel. You probably figure that you're better off sitting tight. We can accuse you of all sorts of things, you feel, but we can't *prove* them."

Brewster did not smile, but his head nodded a fraction of an inch and he gave her a sneer of contempt.

"And if I were the only person on Solferino," Winnie went on, "you'd be quite right in all your assumptions. But I'm not. The trainees are here, too." She pointed at Josh and the other three, standing in a silent row facing Brewster. "They are under-age, all of them. It would be quite irresponsible for me to leave them alone on Solferino, while I was taking you back through the node to a Sol-side arraignment and trial. So I have a problem, don't I? I have to be in two places at once. I asked these four—the oldest of the trainees, as you know—if they had any suggestions as to how to solve my problem."

For the first time, Brewster seemed puzzled and faintly alarmed.

"Nothing bad, of course," said Winnie. "I have explained to them that although you are legally a prisoner, you cannot be mis-treated in any way. Even if they felt that you deserved to have the shit kicked out of you—which they do—I cannot allow it."

"Damn right." Brewster relaxed again. "I know my rights."

"I'm sure you do. Very well." Winnie turned to Sig. "Why don't you ask Mr. Brewster your question?"

Sig walked to stand directly in front of Brewster. "Agent Carlson insists that you made a deal with the Unimine conglomerate, to get rid of us and leave them free to take over Solferino and obtain mineral development rights here. Is that true?"

Brewster shook his head. "It's total bullshit. She doesn't know what she's talking about. I work for Foodlines, and only Foodlines. I have no deal with Unimine, and I never had one." He gave Winnie Carlson a confident glare. "Try to prove anything different, and you'll make a fool of yourself."

"I hear you," said Winnie. "All right, Sig. Now make your suggestion."

"Even if you are innocent of every charge, Mr. Brewster, according to Agent Carlson you must return at once through the node network to Earth, where you will be formally tried. However, it is not necessary that Agent Carlson accompany you. She must reach Earth in time for your trial, but she does not have to leave here at once. We trainees would like Agent Carlson to remain with us, until someone else can be sent out to continue our training. So the question becomes, who could accompany you to Earth, and be responsible for your safekeeping? We suggest that the job be given to Unimine. They are already present in the Grisel system, working on Cauldron. If we send them a message, they can pick you up from here and have their next ship take you to Earth. Please think about this possibility. If you agree, Agent Carlson will make the request of them at once."

Brewster thought—but not for long. He lowered his head to his chest, then a second later raised it to glare at Winnie. "Damn you, Carlson. This wasn't *their* idea—it's yours."

"I will deny any such suggestion, Mr. Brewster. It sounds like an excellent idea, although as I say it had not occurred to me. Unless you have something more to tell me, I will go now. I will use our crippled message equipment to send a request for assistance to the Unimine work force on Cauldron."

"You can't do that!" Brewster fought against the straps, his face turning red with effort. After a few seconds of useless struggle, he slumped back in the chair.

"All right, Carlson." He croaked the words like an old man. "You win, damn you. I'll talk."

"And will you cooperate, in any way that I request?"

"I'll cooperate. Just get me a drink of water." He raised himself a little in the chair. "And get rid of those damned—those—"

" 'Trainees' is the word you are looking for." Winnie nodded to Josh and the others. "All right, you can go. You do not need to be here for this. In fact, it is better if you are not."

They trooped out, into a Solferino morning so bright that they all had to shield their eyes. Grisel, high in the sky, seemed almost golden.

"What was going on in there?" Topaz turned to Sig. "All right, admit it. You knew what was happening, didn't you?"

"I didn't. But I do now." Sig led the way toward the camp kitchen. Josh suddenly realized that he was starving, after a makeshift dinner last night and nothing this morning. They walked together into the empty kitchen, and Topaz began to pull out the makings of a quick meal.

"I've decided something," Sig went on, as they sat down. "I'm never, ever, going to do anything to get on the wrong side of Winnie Carlson. She's worse than sneaky. When she told me what she wanted me to say, I had no idea why."

"It's because of what Winnie Carlson can do," said Sapphire. "But mostly what she *can't* do. Am I right, Sig?"

"You've got it. Winnie can accuse Brewster, and arrest him, and even ask him to cooperate with her. But she can't force him, or hurt him. She certainly can't kill him. But she *can* trap him, and she did. Once he said that he didn't have any deal with Unimine, and never had, Winnie had every legal right to say that she could then trust Unimine to be responsible for transporting Brewster back to Earth for trial. But in fact she knew, and he knew, that there *was* a deal, and it had involved murder. The only person who might talk about that deal, other than the Uniminers who were involved in it, was Brewster. The Unimine people are not bound by

SDSI rules. They *can* kill people. They have done it on Solferino, and they'd do it again to protect themselves. Put Brewster into Unimine hands, and he would never live to be charged on Earth. There would be an unfortunate 'accident,' somewhere between here and the node, that killed him.

"Brewster is a swine, and a murderer, but he's not an idiot. Winnie was telling him, plain as day, that if he wanted to live to see his next birthday, he'd better tell her anything she wanted to know." Sig glanced back toward the building where they had left Sol Brewster and Winnie Carlson. "I wish I was a fly on the wall over there. I'd like to know what's being said."

"No." Sapphire took his hand in hers. "That's the way you feel at the moment, Sig. But if you think about it a bit more, you'll decide that you don't really want to know."

CHAPTER TWENTY

SIG had warned them—never get on the wrong side of Winnie Carlson. Less than twelve hours later, Josh did. He felt like he was leading a mutiny.

"I know we have to return to the compound." He was standing by the aircar steps. "And I told Dawn to get on board. She won't."

"She refuses?" Winnie said.

"That's the wrong word for it. She takes no notice of me, or of Topaz. She just sits there, holding Gussie's paw and staring at the fissure. And I won't leave without her."

"Does Topaz know what the problem is?" Winnie, like Josh, had come to accept that Topaz was the best hope for dealing with Dawn, just as Dawn was the best—maybe the only—way to communicate with the rupert.

"Sure," Josh said. "It's all because of Gussie. She won't go near the aircar, and Dawn won't leave her."

"Do you realize that at some point we may have to take Gussie, or some other rupert, back to Earth to prove how smart they are? Oh, never mind. That's a problem for the future. Let me think." Winnie was sitting on the aircar steps. The camp had been dismantled and was already loaded in the cargo hold. Everyone except Dawn, Josh, Gussie, and Winnie was already aboard. Sol Brewster, sitting in the rear, had his hands and feet taped, but Josh didn't think it was necessary. Since yesterday, Brewster had had a dead, defeated look to him, as though he had already been tried and sent to prison. Whatever Winnie Carlson had said to him in private had certainly worked.

"Looked at from one point of view," Winnie went on, "I'd rather you *all* stayed in the camp until Unimine has been taken care of. You'd be safer here than back at the compound." She sat with her chin on her hands, more debating with herself than talking to Josh. "On the other hand, I'll really need some help. But I won't need *everybody* with me." She looked up at Josh, who moved back to make the point again that he was not about to enter the aircar. "Do you really have to stay with Dawn, *yourself*? Or would you trust someone else to be here with her?"

"Who?"

"Sig, and Topaz. No, better still, let's say that everyone stays here, except you, me, Brewster, and Sapphire. And we'd be back in a day."

It seemed an odd grouping of people, but Josh had a suspicion as to how Winnie was thinking. He decided to say something—he had mutinied, he might as well go all the way.

"I don't think that's a good choice. Sig's bigger and stronger than Saph. If there's any sort of trouble he'd be better. It would make more sense to take Sig and me with you, and leave Saph in charge here. But you don't trust her, do you? Not after what happened at the other camp, with Ruby."

"Maybe not."

"She's been fine ever since."

"I know. You've all helped her." Winnie stood up. "But I can't risk it. Trust isn't something that's *given*, it's something that's *earned*. For the moment I want Saph with me, where I can keep a close eye on her. And Sig will stay in charge here. All right?"

Josh nodded—reluctantly. He knew that Sapphire would understand the reason for Carlson's decision, and be unhappy with it.

He was right. She avoided his eye as the others piled out of the cargo aircar. Winnie and Josh ascended the steps. When the car rose into the calm morning air Sapphire stared out of the window at the group waving good-bye. Her profile could have served as the model for one of his mother's standard acting expressions: remorse and misery.

As the car carried them east, Winnie gave both Saph and Josh something else to think about. She came and sat between them, allowing the car to pilot itself.

"I want to go over what will happen when we arrive," she said, "and I want to do it *in detail.* Move by move, second by second, so there's no possible doubt about what each of us will do. Brewster already sent the signal we wanted. He had a small transmitter hidden away, and he told the crew of the Unimine ship that everything went according to plan, the trainees were disposed of, and it was safe for a Unimine lander to come down to the main compound. What's wrong, Josh?" She had seen him frown.

"Suppose there was a code in the signal, telling people on the ship that something had gone wrong? Then they might not arrive at all—or they might show up ready to shoot."

Winnie Carlson did not seem to take his worries seriously. "Brewster is cracked and broken," she said, "but he's still smart enough to evaluate comparative risks. If he helps us, he knows he'll live, even if it's only in jail. But if he crosses us, and things go wrong, I've assured him that I'll tell the Unimine group he was in this from the beginning and part of our plan to capture them."

"But that's not true!"

"Of course it's not. That isn't the point. If the Unimine group had the slightest suspicion that Brewster worked against them, that would be the end of him. 'Innocent until proven guilty' isn't the operating philosophy of the conglomerates. 'Anyone who isn't a friend is an enemy' is more their line."

Sapphire hadn't said one word, but Josh was pleased to see that she was listening closely. "What do you want us to do?" she said. "So far you haven't mentioned why we're here."

"I'll get to that. Yesterday the two of you were just witnesses. This time, you have a more active role—only don't overdo it. I want you to stay hidden in this aircar until I give you a signal. Then I want you to stand up, so that your heads are visible through the car windows. That's all. Don't move around after that. Don't come out until I tell you. All right?"

They nodded, and Winnie went on, "Then here's the sequence of events. We land. Brewster and I get out. You stay here, heads down—out of sight of anyone on the ground. Brewster and I go to the compound communications center. And we all *wait*. You may find that's the hardest part. Don't worry, it will be for me, too. We wait, until the Unimine ship lands and the crew comes out. According to Brewster, there should be two of them.

"At that point, Brewster will come out of the building and wave to the ship. He won't go over to it, though; he will beckon them to come to the building. I'll be at an observing position in the next building over, out of sight. When Brewster beckons them I'll let you know. Then you can take a peek. As they approach him, I will leave my observer position and step out of my building. I will tell the Unimine lander crew that I am SDSI, that they are on the scene of a crime, and I am arresting them for questioning. I'll tell them to keep their hands away from their bodies and hold them high in the air. You'll hear all this, because I'll pipe their conversation and my comments through to this car's audio system. Then I'm going to point to this aircar and add, 'Don't get any ideas about resisting. We have you covered.' I don't want you to wait for that, though, before you move. When you hear the words, 'under arrest for questioning,' you stand up so they can see your heads. I want them to know you're there as soon as they turn to look your way."

"Suppose they don't believe we have weapons?" asked Sapphire.

"Because we *don't*," Josh added.

"Then we would all be in trouble." Winnie was reassuringly casual and certain. "But actually, we will be all right. You have to understand the way their minds operate. *They* would have weapons if they had the drop on us, so it will be beyond their belief that we might act differently. They won't fight back, because they don't know how much firepower we have. In a similar situation, they'd bring enough to vaporize us, and our ship, too.

"Once they have their hands raised, I'll disarm them. I assume they'll be carrying weapons from habit, even if they never expected to need them. While I'm doing that, don't under any circumstances come outside. I don't want them to know that the 'SDSI agents' on this aircar are two kids. Once I have their weapons, I'll tie them up the way Brewster was tied last night. It will all be over except for the questioning and the trial. Clear to you? Can you think of anything I've missed?"

Sapphire shook her head, but Josh said, "It *sounds* great. But suppose things *don't* go the way you say they will?"

"Good." Winnie nodded approvingly. "You're thinking the right way. You must *always* allow for surprises. It's impossible to allow for them really, because if you can they're not surprises. Here's what we will do, just in case. I will leave this aircar on full emergency standby. You, Sapphire, will sit at the controls. If any-

thing looks, sounds, or feels wrong, you don't wait around to discuss it with me. You hit full power, and you head off in any direction you like. Be ready for a big starting kick if you have to do that. You'll accelerate out of here like a streak, three Gs plus."

"Where should we go?" Sapphire asked.

"Back to the camp. But don't head in that direction to start with. You don't want to give anybody watching you clues as to where you're going. Any more questions? All right, you sit here and relax. I'll go chat with friend Brewster."

Sit and *relax*. Sapphire and Josh stared at each other. "What does she mean, look, sound, or feel *wrong?*" Sapphire said, when Winnie had gone aft.

"I don't know. I think Winnie is saying she doesn't know, either. You'll only realize something's wrong when you see it."

The aircar was descending smoothly to the clearing within the compound fence. It rolled to a halt, and Winnie and Brewster stepped down. Josh marveled. She was walking *in front* of her captive. If he had the nerve, he could knock her down and run away.

But run to where, and away from whom? At this point it wasn't Winnie and SDSI who had Brewster worried. It was Unimine, who might believe him to be an SDSI accomplice.

Brewster went into the communications center. Winnie entered the kitchen in the next building. The two doors closed. The wait began.

Three hours later, when Josh was convinced that something had already gone wrong with Winnie Carlson's plan, the familiar whine of lander engines sounded inside the aircar. Josh felt his heart beat faster, and he and Sapphire looked at each other.

"Take a peek?" he said. It was a question, not a statement, and it was answered not by Sapphire but by Winnie, whose voice sounded in their audio sets. "Here they come. Heads down until they land and are out of the ship. I'll tell you when Brewster comes out of the com center and beckons them to him. Then I'll make my own move and leave this building."

It was the most difficult time of all. Josh was itching to *see*, and it had to be just as hard for Sapphire. She was sitting with head bowed, her fingers tense on the pad entries that would hurtle the aircar away at maximum acceleration.

After a minute that felt like an hour, Winnie's voice came again. "All right. They're out of the lander, two of them, and Brewster's waving them over. You can take a look now. You won't hear from me again until I'm outside."

Cautiously, Josh lifted his head until he could peer over the control panel of the aircar. Brewster had moved four or five steps beyond the door of the communications building and was standing waiting. Two gray-uniformed men, their backs to the cargo aircar where Sapphire and Josh sat, were walking casually toward Brewster.

"Went all right, then?" said the smaller of the two.

"Like a charm." Brewster's voice was forced and ragged. "Don't worry about them. Dumped into the Avernus Fissure, every one."

"Good, good," the taller man said. "Nice to have them out of the way, and a clean planet to work with. That ends one phase of the operation. Now for the next one." Without another word he took something from his pocket, aimed it at Brewster, and fired. There was a dull, ploppy sound, like a ripe melon dropped on a hard floor. Brewster's head vanished in a mist of gray and red. His body toppled backward to the ground.

Josh couldn't believe his eyes. It was Sapphire who gasped, "Winnie can't see that—she doesn't know. She'll come outside any second."

Josh opened his mouth to cry out and distract the lander crew. Before he could shout he was thrown far back in his seat. An invisible hand held him there. The aircar was suddenly racing toward the communications building.

It traveled low, just a foot from the ground, gaining speed so fast that everything became a blur. Josh saw two pale faces turn in

their direction. The tall man's hand came up, and the windshield of the car disintegrated in a shower of sparks. Josh felt intense pain as hot shards of the lasered windshield burned his face.

A scream of agony from Sapphire made him turn his head in her direction. Her hair was smoking, and she had both hands up covering her eyes. The car was still accelerating, out of control.

He made a great effort and lunged sideways. He could not reach the wheel or pedals, but he turned off the main power just as the metal prow of the car smashed into the two men in front of it. The taller man was thrown off to one side, the other clear over the top. And then the car, no longer accelerating but still moving at high speed, hit the wall of the communications building.

There was a scream of breaking metal. The car spun completely around. Josh was not strapped in. He jerked forward, sideways, backward again. His head hit the side window, then the padded door column.

He did not pass out, not quite, but everything became slow and dreamy. Someone was groaning, and after a little while someone else was talking. That went on for an annoyingly long time. He could not understand the words, because a red tide was sweeping over him and lifting him on its flood. He decided he would have to swim. That was a real pain, because he didn't like swimming, not even at the best of times. He started a dolphin kick and flailed with his arms.

"Josh! Josh!" The irritating voice was back, and suddenly he could understand it. "Stop fighting me. Do you hear? Relax!"

It was Winnie, dragging him toward his right. She had him by the arm, and it *hurt*. He wanted to protest, to tell her to leave him alone, but he couldn't find the words. Something banged him hard on the head. He blinked the red tide away from his eyes.

He was halfway out of the aircar, and the blow on the head had come from the molding at the top of the car door. Instead of resisting, he allowed Winnie to pull him the rest of the way. He felt himself dragged across a hard, smooth floor, and then suddenly he was on a dense carpet of purple plants. He sagged to his hands and knees and stayed there.

"Damn, damn, damn, *damn.*" Winnie sounded furious, but not with Josh. "I'm an idiot, a total idiot. Can you stand up?"

Now she *was* talking to him. Stand up. Could he? He didn't know. He lifted his head.

He was just outside the building. A gray-suited figure lay crumpled a few feet in front of him. The arms and legs were twisted into strange positions, and the man was not moving. Blood dripped from his nose and open mouth. Josh fought back nausea and looked farther. Sapphire, her singed hair in a wild tangle over her forehead, sat leaning against the building wall. Bright red burn marks on her forehead and cheeks stood out against the pallor of her face, and she cradled her left arm in her right. Beyond her was Brewster's headless body. To his left lay a second contorted and broken doll figure.

Winnie stood by the aircar. It had smashed into the wall of the building, spun around, and finished halfway inside. The tail section had been sheared off and lay on the floor of the ruined communications center.

"Not a chance." Winnie came to where Josh still rested on hands and knees. "It will never fly again. We'll have to take their lander. Can you stand up?"

She had asked him that before. He still didn't know the answer. He reached for her outstretched hand, made a great effort, and with her assistance lifted himself to his feet. He stood teetering, fighting for balance.

"Good," Winnie said brusquely. "Can you walk?"

He wasn't sure he could even remain standing if she let go. Josh did not speak, but began to weave his way toward Sapphire, one arm held out toward the building wall in case he needed it.

"Don't touch her," Winnie said. "You're more likely to fall over Saph than help her. Go to the Unimine lander. I'll bring her."

"Don't need to." Sapphire spoke through clenched teeth. She was standing up, very slowly and carefully. "I can make it. But I think it's broken."

"It sure is." Winnie hovered near in case Sapphire needed help. "I took a look when I was getting you out of the car. You have a fractured humerus. Luckily it's a clean break, and not compound."

"It hurts like hell. Worse than the burns."

"You bet it does. Wait there for a minute, and we can do something about that. You're a brave girl."

Winnie disappeared into the kitchen, leaving Josh and Sapphire wavering on their feet and gazing at each other.

"They're all dead," Josh said.

"I know." Sapphire nodded slowly, and winced as the movement ran down to her arm. "But we're not. And Winnie isn't."

"They would have killed her, wouldn't they? If we hadn't run the aircar into them."

"Her. And then us. I didn't mean to kill them. But I couldn't see anything after the windshield burned out."

"It was their own fault." Josh didn't want to think about the question of just who had killed the two men. He felt confident enough of his balance to move away from the wall of the building, as he went on, "But how did they *know?* What told them it was a trap? Did we do something to tip them off?"

"Not that at all." Winnie had reappeared. "I ought to be locked up for terminal stupidity. Hold still, Saph. This is a painkiller. You'll stop hurting in a minute or two, but after that you're going to feel dopey. I want us all in the lander before then." She applied the spray to Saph's neck, and went on, "You didn't tip them off, nor did I. They didn't know it was a trap. But I was a fool, and Sol Brewster an even bigger one. How are you doing?"

Her question was to Sapphire, who nodded and took a tentative step forward. "It's not too bad now. Won't I need a splint?"

"You will. First things first. I want to get into the lander and out of here. The splint can wait until we're back at the camp with the others."

"What do you mean, you were a fool?" Josh hurt, too, but he wasn't about to admit it when Saph had a broken arm and didn't complain.

"I'm right out of my depth on this case." Winnie sounded angry and depressed at the same time. "The situations I've had to handle in the past were minor-league stuff, smuggling and embezzlement and sometimes encroaching on claims. SDSI didn't expect to find multiple murders here, or they'd never have sent someone as junior as me. But Unimine operates on a different scale from anything I've seen before, and they are completely ruthless. I had it wrong when I said their philosophy was 'Anyone who isn't a friend is an enemy.' It's more like, 'Dead men tell no tales.' "

They had reached the lander, and Winnie was opening the door and examining the interior. "Look at things from the Unimine point of view. They were an accomplice to the murder of everyone in the original settlement group on Solferino, and also the new trainees. Their claim will be that those people died from unknown but natural causes, that Unimine found the planet empty of humans, and that they are laying claim to it. The only person who can say anything different is Sol Brewster. Not only that, he is expecting a huge reward for all his work in discovering the stable transuranics, and then for disposing of the Foodlines employees on Solferino."

Sapphire and Josh were occupying separate rows in the rear of the lander, where they could lie down if they wanted to. Winnie had been studying the control panel, and was preparing for takeoff. "The people from Unimine had their plan made before they came here," she said. "Brewster was out of his depth, too. He had outlived his usefulness, and he could be a nuisance. So he had to be killed. But he didn't realize that—and I'm ashamed to say that I didn't, either."

"But what will happen now?" Sapphire was sprawling full length across her seat, and her speech was slower and slurring. "Won't they try to kill us?"

"No." Winnie lifted the lander smoothly off the ground and set a heading for the Avernus Fissure. "I shouldn't sound so confident when I was so wrong before, but I believe we're safe. I'm going to use the lander's own communicator to send a message. It will say that Solferino is under SDSI quarantine, and no one except SDSI ships will be admitted. Unimine won't have any idea what's been happening here, but they know two of their people didn't return. The last thing they'll do is come to find out why. They'll stick their heads in the sand and if anyone asks they'll say, 'Solferino? Never heard of it. We're doing mining work on Cauldron.' "

"But this is their lander," said Josh. "Won't they ask for it back?"

"They might—they have that much gall. But they won't ask *us* for it. They'll have their lawyers make the claim, back Sol-side. And you know what? The terrible thing is, they'll probably win the case." Winnie set the lander to fly on autopilot, and turned in her seat. "All right back there?"

"I'm all right, but I think Saph has gone to sleep."

"Best thing that could happen. She won't want to be awake when we set that arm."

"She saved your life, didn't she? My life, too."

"All our lives, Sig and Ruby and everyone else. If Unimine had killed Brewster and the three of us, they'd have realized that he hadn't done the job he said he'd do. They'd have been forced to hunt down and dispose of everyone. Sapphire showed a lot better instincts than I did, and after she was burned you took over like a trained professional. I'm going to make sure you two get full credit in my report. You were supersmart, and superquick to do the right thing."

"Will Solferino really be put under SDSI quarantine?" As always, praise embarrassed Josh.

"It will. Even without Unimine, the probable existence of an intelligent alien species would ensure that."

"It's not *probable*—it's definite."

"Definite for us. It still has to be proved to everyone else. This is going to be an interesting few months. Unimine may not say a word, but Foodlines is sure to scream. They'll insist that ruperts are animals, and Foodlines' development rights have been taken away. They're as bad in their way as Unimine, you know. They would have been quite happy to wipe out the whole rupert species. It will be our job to prove that Gussie and her relatives are too smart to be thought of as animals."

"And what about us—me and Topaz and the other trainees?"

"You can go home. You've earned it, every one of you. It won't happen at once—I have to be sure it's safe—but as soon as we have SDSI ships here to navigate the node network, you'll be able to go home to your families. Doesn't that sound great?"

"Yes." Josh leaned back in his seat and closed his eyes. *Go home.* To where? To a mother who didn't want him? To an aunt who couldn't wait to send him and her "retarded" stepdaughter as far away from Earth as possible? And what about Sig and his brothers, or Sapphire and her sisters? Their parents had been as bad, or worse.

"That's good." Winnie misinterpreted Josh's action. "You take it easy, have a nap if you can. You've had more than enough shocks for one day."

Josh opened his eyes. "Suppose I don't want to go?"

"What?"

"Suppose some of us want to stay on Solferino."

"Well, that's more complicated." Winnie blinked. "You couldn't remain as Foodlines trainees, because once the ruperts are established as intelligent, the Foodlines development franchise will be scrapped. On the other hand, you seem to be the only communication link with the ruperts. That may make you eligible to work with Earth's government. I certainly think you ought to have a say in where you go, and what you do—but I'm afraid I'm not in charge."

She turned back to the controls, as Josh's eyes once more closed. "It will also depend on what the other trainees say. We can't decide anything now, but you'll have to stay here anyway until I've been Sol-side and explained what happened. Why don't you talk to each other after I'm gone, and see what you all want?"

It was not much of an answer; but Josh suspected that it was the best one that he was going to get.

CHAPTER TWENTY-ONE

IG emerged from the lander as Grisel was going down in a red blaze of glory.

"Two more days," he announced, "and Winnie says she'll be here with a team of observers. She says everything went great Sol-side, and she gave Sapphire and Josh the credit for saving everyone. Now it's up to us to decide what we want."

The whole group had congregated outside. The evenings were growing cool, but no one was willing to miss the daily appearance of the ruperts. Gussie and family slept during the day, and were not about to change that. Sunset was the best time for meetings.

The ruperts had also made it clear to Dawn that they would not travel by lander. As a result, the camp had become the base of operations. At first there had been some misgivings. It took the colder evenings to make the warmth of the Avernus Fissure more of a blessing than a threat.

Tonight, however, as though to make the point that Solferino's weather could be every bit as fickle as Earth's, the air was balmy and pleasant and gave no hint of approaching winter. Everyone was sitting in a circle, with Sapphire holding court in the middle. In the three weeks since Brewster's death the small burns inflicted on her face and hands by the disintegrating windshield had disappeared, but she still had a cast on her arm. She was forced to rely on others to help her. It gave secret and special satisfaction to Topaz and her sisters to know that for the first time ever, Big Sister depended on *them* to look after *her.*

Sig walked across to sit at Sapphire's side. "So what do we tell Winnie when she gets here? It's going to be our call."

He was talking to everyone, but nobody answered. Although Sapphire was at the center, the people around her had split into separate groups. Rick and Hag were sitting on the ground and devising their latest masterpiece, a meal made entirely from ingredients collected on Solferino. Amy and Ruby had volunteered to be taste testers, and were looking on dubiously at the preparation process. Ruby finally said, "Look, if it's gross, I won't do it. You can eat it yourselves."

"If it's gross," Hag said. "I won't want it."

"Rick and Amy will. They'll eat anything."

Amethyst swiped at her sister. Rick scowled, but he didn't deny it.

On the opposite side of the circle, Topaz was talking to Dawn while Josh watched and worried. Suppose the other Karpov sisters decided to go back to Earth? Then Topaz would surely leave, too; but Dawn wanted to stay with Gussie; and Topaz was far better than Josh or anyone else at talking to Dawn. And Josh had to stay with his cousin. But he wanted to be with Topaz, too.

Dawn suddenly turned away from Topaz. "G-ss-ee coming," she said, with no doubt in her voice.

Everyone stopped what they were doing. Josh looked around, and saw nothing. "Where?"

But Dawn was again taking no notice of anything. She was carefully inscribing something in a bare patch of red soil. When she was finished, she picked up a handful of the powdery grit that she had scraped away and examined it closely.

"Earth," she said. "Right?"

"That's earth all right," said Topaz. "In your hand. And it's *red*. You know that word, too."

Dawn gave her a puzzled look. "*Earth!*" she said again, with great emphasis. She pointed down.

Topaz gasped. "Look, Josh. Everybody!"

In the dirt, Dawn had carefully written five letters: E—A—R—T—H.

"She's writing, and *spelling*." Topaz looked around in triumph. "I told you she would, if we only gave her a decent chance! Dawn, you're wonderful."

But Dawn still looked puzzled. "Earth?" she said again. Now she lifted her hand, and allowed the dusty red soil to trickle out onto the ground.

Sig and Sapphire looked not at Dawn, but at each other. "I think she's right," Sapphire said.

"So I guess that settles it." Sig surveyed the scene around them, from the purple sward at their feet to the distant hills that caught the last gleam of sunlight. "We stay."

A hundred yards away, over the brow of the hill, Gussie and three of her family were slowly approaching. They had an addition, a tiny baby rupert still too small to walk. Gussie waved a greeting. Ruby, Rick and Hag waved back.

"You're quite right, Dawn," Topaz said softly. She bent down and picked up a handful of red dirt. She took Josh's hand, held it, and allowed the soil to sift into his open palm. "This is Earth."